ARTHUR C. CLARKE'S VENUS PRIME™

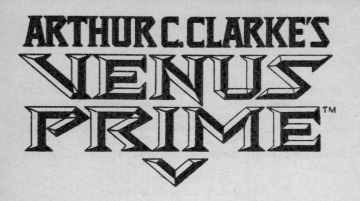

ARTHUR C. CLARKE'S VENUS PRIME™

VOLUME 4

THE MEDUSA ENCOUNTER

PAUL PREUSS

A BYRON PREISS BOOK

AVON BOOKS ◆ NEW YORK

ARTHUR C. CLARKE'S VENUS PRIME, VOLUME 4: THE
MEDUSA ENCOUNTER is an original publication of Avon Books.
This work has never before appeared in book form. This work is a
novel. Any similarity to actual persons or events is purely coincidental.

Special thanks to John Douglas, Russell Galen, Alan Lynch, and Mary
Higgins.

AVON BOOKS
A division of
The Hearst Corporation
105 Madison Avenue
New York, New York 10016

First Avon Books Printing: March 1990

Stephana McClaran kindly shared journals and photographs of her travels in Nepal and India, for which I thank her.

PROLOGUE

She lay exposed on the operating table. Men and women sheathed in sterile plastic film leaned over her, wielding black instruments. The rank smell of onions threatened to suffocate her. Her mind's eye involuntarily displayed complex sulfur compounds as the circle of lights above her began to swirl in a golden spiral.

William, she's a child

As the darkness closed in, she clutched harder at the hand she held, trying to keep from falling.

To resist us is to resist the Knowledge

She was sliding away. She was tilting up into the spiral. The hand to which she clung slid from her grasp. Around her, shapes swarmed in the maelstrom. The shapes were signs. The signs had meaning.

The meaning engulfed her. She tried to call out, to shout a warning. But when the blackness closed over her, only one image remained, an image of swirling clouds, red and yellow and white, boiling in an immense whirlpool, big enough to swallow a planet. She left herself then, and fell endlessly into them. . . .

Blake couldn't see what was going on; they'd put up a curtain of opaque fabric to screen his view of Ellen's body. He was frightened. When she'd let go

1

of his hand, her own hand falling limp on the sheets, he'd thought for a moment that she was dead.

But the blue vein in her throat still pulsed; her chest still rose and fell beneath the rough gown; the surgeon and his assistants went on with their work as if nothing unusual had happened. "She's under," one of them said.

Blake fought back dizziness when he saw the clamps and tongs, saw the scalpel and scissors go down gleaming and reappear above the curtain streaked with blood. The surgeon moved with swift precision, doing whatever he was doing to the middle of Ellen. Suddenly he stopped.

"What the *hell* is this stuff?" he said angrily, his voice muffled inside his clear film mask. Blake saw an assistant's nervous glance in his direction. The young surgeon turned to stare at Blake—they hadn't wanted him here, but Ellen had refused to let them begin without him at her side. With his tongs the surgeon lifted a bit of something slippery and fishlike and slapped it on a tray. "Biopsy. I want to know what it is before we close."

The technician hurried away. Meanwhile the surgeon bent and pulled up more of the stuff and threw it on a larger tray held by his assistant. Blake peered at it in fascination, the silvery tissue lying in sheets like a beached jellyfish, trembling and iridescent.

The surgeon was still working to clean the last of it out of Ellen when the technician handed him the analysis. On the pages Blake glimpsed graphs, lists of ratios and molecular weights, false-color stereo images.

"All right, we'd better close," the surgeon said. "I want this woman under intensive surveillance until we hear what the research committee makes of this."

* * *

Blake stood looking out upon the glowing glass city and the Noctis Labyrinthus beyond, a maze of rock pinnacles and deep-cut ravines, midnight blue under the unblinking stars.

Ellen lay deeply sleeping under a coarse sheet, her short blond hair framing her unlined face. Her full lips were slightly parted, as if she were tasting the air. No tubes or wires intruded upon her slim flesh; the monitoring probes hovered without touching her delicate skull and slight breasts and slender abdomen. The silent graphics above the bed displayed reassuringly normal functions. The room was quiet and warm, almost peaceful.

The silhouette of a tall man appeared in the doorway, blocking the light from the hall. Blake saw the reflection in the glass wall and turned, expecting to see one of the doctors.

"You!"

"She needs to get out here. Her life could depend on it." The man who stood in the darkness had blue eyes that glittered in his dark face. His iron gray hair was cut to within a few millimeters of his scalp, and he wore the dress-blue uniform of a full commander of the Board of Space Patrol.

"No."

"I'm going to take the time to reason with you, Blake . . ."

"What a favor," Blake said hotly.

". . . for two or three minutes. Did you see what they pulled out of her?"

"I . . . I saw something, I don't know what."

"You know she's not like other people."

"It doesn't matter. What *she* needs is time to get well."

"She's vulnerable here. We're moving her off Mars. The records are going to show that Inspector Troy had a routine appendectomy, spent the usual eight-hour recovery period in hospital, and walked happily away. That's what the doctors are going to say, too."

Blake's face darkened. "You've got argument down to a fine science, Commander—do it your way or else."

"I've given you choices before. Think you made a mistake to trust me?"

Blake hesitated. "Maybe not in Paris."

"I promised I'd get you to her and I did. A lot of lives were saved because of it. Trust me again, Blake."

"What do you care?" Blake shrugged in frustration. "We both know I can't stop you. But I'm staying with her."

They got her out of town in a sealed van, taking a route that the tourists in Labyrinth City never saw, through the utility tunnel to the shuttleport. They made a quick, silent transfer to the cabin of a sleek spaceplane. In deference to Ellen, the trajectory was low and slow, with minimal gees applied over a long boost out of the thin atmosphere, finally achieving the orbit of Mars Station.

But the plane didn't dock with the station. A gleaming white cutter with the blue band and gold star of the Board of Space Control rode "at anchor" half a kilometer from the giant space station's starside docking bay. As the spaceplane sidled up to it on maneuvering jets, a pressure tube snaked out from the cutter's main hatch and slammed tight over the spaceplane's airlock.

Ellen and Blake and the commander were the only people who went through the tube. The cutter's crew made them secure; countdown took half an hour. Ellen slept through it all.

Just before the cutter lifted from orbit, Blake overcame his resentment enough to ask the commander a question. "Where are we going?"

"Earth," he said.

"Where on Earth?"

"For reasons you'll soon figure out, I'm not telling you."

PART
1

THE WRECK
OF A QUEEN

1

They stood on a precipice of dark rock above a wide river. The air was cold and the sky was clear, washed blue. The light was the color of October.

Her hair was the color of straw, and it glowed in the October light; her high-collared black wool coat reached from her short hair to her high boots, hiding the rest of her and absorbing all the other light that fell upon her. The blackness was relieved only by a scarf tied loosely around her throat, dark blue raw silk woven with fine stripes of red and yellow thread; her small strong hands clutched at its knotted and tasseled ends.

She looked at the men who stood close to her with a smile so tentative and hopeful that his heart swelled and hurt him.

"Will you be with me always?" Sparta whispered.

"Always," Blake said. The breeze caught his stiff auburn hair and a swatch of it fell across his forehead, shadowing his face with cool shadow, but his green eyes gleamed with warmth. "As long as you want me."

"I do," she said. "I will."

Across the wide waters a shimmer of sunlight danced. If light had sound, they would have heard glass wind bells. Sparta took Blake's hand and tugged. He walked beside her along the wall, holding her hand lightly, glancing back up the hill toward the big house.

The steel king's mansion crowned a tor above the Hudson, a chimneyed pile of basalt decorated with exotic granites and limestones from Vermont and Indiana, roofed with slate, pierced with stained-glass windows. The old freebooter who'd had the place built had made his loot in a different age; he would have been startled but not necessarily disapproving of the uses to which his estate had been put in the two centuries since.

Clipped green lawns, damp in the October sunshine, sloped away from the house, ending at cliff's edge and the neat border of the woods. In front, a long gravel drive meandered through the trees and looped around before the main entrance.

Behind the stone wall that surrounded the place, hidden among the thickly clustered tree trunks and autumn foliage, were lasers, covered trenches, antiaircraft railguns. . . .

The gray robot limousine moved slowly up the drive, the crunch of its tires in the gravel louder than the whisper of its turbines. As it stopped, the mansion's big doors swung open and the commander came out. When he saw the much smaller man who got out of the back seat of the car, his face wrinkled into a smile, thin but warm. "Jozsef!" He strode down the steps, hand outstretched.

Jozsef met him halfway up the steps. "How very good to see you." Their handshake was prelude to a quick, firm embrace.

The two men were the same age but in every other way different. Jozsef's tweedy suit was elbow-patched and baggy at the knees; it and his middle-European accent suggested that he was a displaced intellectual, an academic, a denizen of the classroom and the library stacks. The commander wore a plaid shirt and faded jeans that said he was most comfortable out of doors.

"Surprised to see you in person," said the commander. He had a faint Canadian accent, and his voice had the texture of beach stones rattling in receding surf. "But damn glad."

"After I analyzed the material you sent, I thought it would be good to share some of my thoughts with you personally. And I . . . I've brought a new drug."

"Come in."

"Is she inside?"

"No, they're both on the grounds. You want to see her?"

"I . . . not yet. It would be best if she did not see the car," Jozsef added.

The commander spoke gruffly into his wrist unit and the robot limousine rolled off toward the garage. The men walked up the steps into the house.

They walked down an echoing paneled hall toward the library. White-uniformed staff people nodded deferentially and moved out of their way.

"Already three weeks since you rescued her from Mars," said Jozsef. "Astonishing how time slips past us."

"Rescued?" The commander smiled. "Kidnapped is a better word. And 'persuaded' Redfield to come along."

"You didn't bother persuading her physicians," Jozsef remarked.

"I didn't much like the chief surgeon."

"Yes, well . . . however arrogant, he seems to have done a good job on her," said Jozsef. "She seems well."

"In her body."

"Her dreams are not symptoms of illness. They are the key to all that confronts us."

"So you've explained."

"Once we understand what she knows—but does not know she knows—we will triumph at last."

"Then maybe you'll let her know about you," the commander suggested.

"I look forward to that day."

"You know I'm with you, Jozsef." The commander fixed the older man with a cold blue stare. "Whatever the cost."

Beyond the wall overlooking the river the trees grew to the cliff top. Unseen, screened by the woods below, a magneplane whistled past on the riverside track. A falcon settled in the top of a ruddy oak, carefully folding its angled wings, oblivious to the man and woman who walked a few meters away, at eye level.

"What did you say when he asked you to join the force?"

"What I told you. I said no."

"You could never resist explanations."

"Oh, I made explanations." He smiled. "I was born rich, I said, and it ruined me. I told him I was insubordinate by nature and disinclined to accept arbitrary discipline from a bunch of . . . from people not self-evidently more intelligent or more experienced or otherwise more deserving of respect than I. That I already knew all I wanted to know about combat and disguise and sabotage and a few other black arts, and that if he wanted to hire me he could hire me as a consultant anytime, but that I had no interest whatever in going through basic training—again—and putting on a funny blue suit and being paid dirt wages just to get in on his fun."

"That must have impressed him," she said dryly.

"It made my point." He said it without bravado. "That I'm no soldier, that I'm not interested in dying or killing."

"My hero," she said, pulling him closer to her side with a tug of her hand, meshing her fingers in his. "What are you interested in?"

"You know. Old books."

"Besides old books?"

He grinned. "A little noise and smoke can be fun."

"Besides making things go bang?"

"I'm interested in keeping us alive," he said.

She glanced toward the thick copse of elms and oaks that intruded into the lawn. "Come in here with me," she whispered, smiling. "I have an urge to live a little. . . ."

The library's tall windows overlooked the morning lawn. "What will we do about him?" Jozsef turned away; he'd been watching the two young people by the wall.

"Give him one more chance. After this morning, let him go," the commander said. He stood at the fieldstone fireplace, warming himself at the crackling oakwood fire.

"You said you could recruit him. . . ."

"I've tried. Mr. Redfield is his own man." His smile was thin. "He was taught well."

"Is it safe to let him go?"

"Her welfare is important to him. Of the greatest importance."

"He is in love with her, you mean." Jozsef's expression was invisible against the glare of the high window. "Does he have any idea of how she can be hurt?"

"Do any of us?" It wasn't cold in the high-ceilinged room, but the commander kept chafing his hands at the fire.

"Yes, well . . ." Jozsef pulled at the flesh under his chin and cleared his throat. "If we let him go, he must be isolated."

"I'll arrange it." The commander's voice was a bare whisper past the gravel in his throat.

"Can you guarantee it?"

"Not absolutely." The commander turned hard blue eyes on his companion. "We've got limited choices, old friend. We can explain things to him, ask him to come along. . . ."

"We can't tell him more than he knows already. Not even *she* must know."

"She will take the case, I think. He may not want her to."

"If he refuses, you know what we must . . ."

"I *hate* these drugs of ours," the commander said vehemently. "*Hate* using them. They go against the principles you taught me yourself."

"Kip, we are in a struggle that . . ."

"A man's own memory . . . a woman's . . . *lying*. It's worse than no memories at all."

For several seconds Jozsef watched the weather-beaten man who stood by a blazing fire but could not seem to warm himself. What winter was he reliving in memory?

"Okay," the commander said. "If he won't join us on this . . . this Falcon business, I'll isolate him."

Jozsef nodded and turned back to the window. The couple who'd been standing at the wall had disappeared into the trees.

They tumbled in the autumn leaves, gasping and giggling like children. The smell of mold was as rich as a winery cave, the very smell of it intoxicating, filling her with the joy of life. Their breath steamed in the sharp air. The moment arrived, like the edge of the first rapid, when the emotion they were riding tipped into the current of their blood, and they felt not at all like children. Her dancer's finely muscled body was pale white against the black of her coat, spread open on the leaves.

There were microscopic cameras and microphones in the little copse, as there were everywhere on the grounds. Sparta knew they were there, although she thought Blake did not. Her eye sought one out where it glistened like a carbon crystal against the gray trunk of a tree. She stared at it over his shoulder.

She exposed herself to those who watched and listened partly to defy them, but mostly because

she loved Blake and would have him this way if
they would not let her have him any other.

Later he lay touching her, close against her, flank
to flank. His skin tingled and his face was flush
with a happiness he had often imagined but now
knew for the first time. Her head was on his arm;
his other arm hovered over her skin, close enough
to feel its radiant warmth. He trailed his middle
finger down the faint pink line of the scar that ran
from her sternum to her navel.

"It's almost gone," he said. "In another
week . . ."

"I'll pass for a human being again," she said.
Her voice was flat. Her eyes stared past him, up at
the colorful leaves overhead, and through them to
the dark sky-vault beyond. "And then we'll leave
this place."

"Ellen . . . do you understand what's happening?" With practice it got easier to call her Ellen,
although he would always think of her as Linda,
the name she was born with.

Only Sparta thought of herself as Sparta. No one
else knew her secret name, any more than a human knows the secret name of an animal. "I think
the commander's keeping his word. This is the
R & R he's been promising me for so long."

"R & R." He smiled. "Very restful." He leaned
over her and kissed the corner of her swollen, perpetually parted lips. "Very recuperative. But why
won't he tell us where we are?"

"We both know where we are—the Hendrik
Hudson nature preserve. We could pinpoint the coordinates on any map."

"Yes, but why won't he name the place? And
why not let us come and go? The night we arrived
here, after you were asleep, he told me I could leave
whenever I wanted, but if I did I couldn't come
back. Why the mystery? We're on his side."

''You're sure of that,'' she said—not quite a question.

But he took it as a question, and it surprised him. ''It was you. . . .''

''I'm sure of one thing''—she pulled him down to cover her, to feel his warm weight hiding her from the sky—''that I love you.''

2

"The man who proposed *Kon-Tiki* is Howard Falcon," said the commander. "He will personally pilot the Jupiter probe."

It was the same bright morning, but no one could have known it from the surroundings—a dim, quiet basement briefing room, its walls and ceiling carpeted with the same brown wool as its floor, its only illumination leaking from brass-shaded lamps on low tables beside the leather armchairs where Sparta, Blake, and the commander nestled.

"How did one man get that kind of power?" Blake asked.

"Falcon is . . . an unusual specimen. This will explain." The commander's raw voice was without resonance in the slowly vanishing room . . . in the darkest center of which an image had begun to form, filling space with the moving landscape of Arizona's high sagebrush plains, seen from a great altitude. "What we've pieced together here happened eight years ago."

The *Queen Elizabeth* was over five kilometers above the Grand Canyon, dawdling along at a comfortable 300 kilometers per hour, when from the liner's bridge Howard Falcon spotted the camera platform closing in from the right. He had been expecting it—nothing else was cleared to fly at this altitude—but he was not too happy to have company. Although he welcomed any signs of public interest, he also wanted as much empty sky as he could get. After all, he was the first man in history to navigate a ship half a kilometer long.

So far this first test flight had gone perfectly. Ironically enough, the only problem had been the fifty-year-old aircraft carrier *Chairman Mao*, borrowed from the San Diego Naval Museum for support operations. Only one of *Mao*'s four nuclear reactors was still operable, and the old battlewagon's top speed was barely thirty knots. Luckily, wind speed at sea level had been less than half this, so it had not been too difficult to maintain still air on the flight deck. Though there had been a few anxious moments during gusts, when the mooring lines had been dropped the great dirigible had risen smoothly, straight up into the sky as if on an invisible elevator. If all went well, *Queen Elizabeth IV* would not meet *Chairman Mao* again for another week.

Everything was under control; all test instruments gave normal readings. Commander Falcon decided to go upstairs and watch the rendezvous. He handed over to his second officer and walked out into the transparent tubeway that led through the heart of the ship. There, as always, he was overwhelmed by the spectacle of the largest space yet enclosed by humans on Earth.

The ten spherical gas cells, each more than thirty meters across, were ranged one behind the other like a line of gigantic soap bubbles. The tough plastic was so clear that he could see through the whole length of the array and make out details of the elevator mechanism at the other end, half a kilometer from his vantage point. All around him, like a three-dimensional maze, was the structural framework of the ship—the great longitudinal girders running from nose to tail, the fifteen hoops that were the circular ribs of this sky-borne colossus, whose varying sizes defined its graceful, stream-lined profile.

At this comparatively low speed there was little sound—merely the soft rush of wind over the envelope and an occasional creak from the joints of the ribs and stringers of titanium and carbon-carbon compound, flexing as the pattern of stresses changed. The shadowless light from the rows of lamps far overhead gave the whole scene a curiously submarine quality—

—and to Falcon this was enhanced by the spectacle of the translucent gas bags. Once while diving he had encountered a squadron of large but harmless jellyfish, pulsing their mindless way above a shallow tropical reef, and the plastic bubbles that gave *Queen Elizabeth* its lift often reminded him of these—especially when changing pressures made them crinkle and scatter new patterns of reflected light.

He walked down the axis of the ship until he came to the forward elevator, between gas cells one and two. Riding up to the observation deck, he noticed it was uncomfortably hot.

The *Queen* obtained almost a quarter of its buoyancy from the unlimited amounts of waste heat produced by its miniature "cold" fusion power plant. Indeed, on this lightly loaded test flight, only six of the ten gas cells contained helium, an increasingly rare and expensive gas; the remaining cells were full of plain hot air. Yet the ship still carried 200 tonnes of water as ballast.

Running the gas cells in hot-air mode created technical problems in refrigerating the access ways; obviously a little more work would have to be done there. Falcon dictated a brief memo to himself on his microcorder.

A refreshing rush of cooler air hit him in the face when he stepped out onto the big observation deck, into the dazzling sunlight that streamed through the clear acrylic roof. He was confronted with a scene of controlled chaos. Half a dozen workers and an equal number of superchimp assistants were busily laying the partly completed dance floor, while others were installing electrical wiring, arranging furniture, and fiddling with the elaborate louvers of the transparent roof. Falcon found it hard to believe that everything would be ready for the maiden voyage, only four weeks ahead.

Well, that was not *his* problem, thank goodness. He was merely the captain, not the cruise director.

The human workers waved to him, and the "simps" flashed toothy smiles. They all looked quite spiffy in the blue and white coveralls of the *Queen*'s corporate sponsors. He walked among them, through the orderly confusion, and mounted the short spiral stairs to the already finished Skylounge. This was his favorite place in the whole ship, but he knew that once the *Queen* was in service he would never again have the lounge all to himself. He would allow himself just five minutes of private enjoyment.

He keyed his commlink and spoke to the bridge, confirming that everything was still in order. Then he relaxed into one of the comfortable swivel chairs.

Below, in a curve that delighted the eye, was the unbroken silver sweep of the ship's envelope. He was perched at the highest point forward, surveying the immensity of the largest vehicle ever built to contend with gravity near a planet's surface. The only larger craft in the solar system were the space freighters that plied the trajectories among the space stations of Venus, Earth, Mars, the moons, and the Mainbelt; in the absence of weight, size was a secondary concern.

And when Falcon had tired of admiring the *Queen*, he could turn and look almost all the way to the horizon of that fantastic wilderness carved by the Colorado River in half a billion years time.

Apart from the remotely operated camera platform, which had now fallen back and was recording the spectacle from amidships, Falcon had the sky to himself. It was blue and empty up here, although the horizon was opaque with the purple-brown stain that had become the permanent color of Earth's lower atmosphere. Far to the south and north he could see the icy trails of ascending and descending intercontinental space planes, specifically prohibited from the corridor across the desert skies that today had been reserved for the *Queen*.

Someday, cheap fusion plants would supplant the fossil fuels upon which so much of the Earth still depended for economic sustenance, and ships like the *Queen* would ply the atmosphere gently and cleanly, carrying cargo and passengers. Then the sky would belong only to the birds and the clouds and the great dirigibles. But that day was still decades in the future.

It was true, as the old pioneers had said at the beginning of the 20th century: this was the only way to travel—in silence and luxury, breathing the air around you and not cut off from it, near enough to the surface to watch the everchanging beauty of land and sea. The subsonic jets of the past century's final quarter had been hardly better than cattle cars, packed with hundreds of passengers seated up to ten abreast. Now, a hundred years later, a great many more passengers would soon be able to travel in greater comfort, at comparable speed, and with less real expense.

Not that any of them would be traveling on the *Queen;* the *Queen* and her projected sister ships were not a mass-transit proposition. Only a few of the world's billions would ever enjoy gliding silently through the sky in highest luxury, champagne in hand, the symphonic strains of a live orchestra drifting from the stage of the observation deck below. . . . But a secure and prosperous global society could afford such follies and indeed needed them for their novelty and entertainment, as a useful distraction from the kind of aggressive interplanetary business affairs that too often threatened to erupt into a brushfire wars. And there were at least a million people on Earth whose discretionary income exceeded a thousand "new dollars" a year—that is, a million of the ordinary dollars everybody else was used to having deducted from their credit chips at every transaction. So the *Queen* would not lack for passengers.

Falcon's commlink beeped, interrupting his reverie. The copilot was calling from the bridge.

"Okay for rendezvous, Captain? We've got all the data we need from this run, and the viddie people are getting impatient."

Falcon glanced at the camera platform, now matching his speed and altitude a quarter of a kilometer away. "Okay, proceed as arranged. I'll watch from here."

He went down the spiral stairs from the Skylounge and walked back through the busy chaos of the observation deck, intending to get a better view amidships. As he walked he could feel a change of vibration underfoot; the silent turbines were powering down, and the *Queen* was coming to rest. By the time he reached the rear of the deck, the ship was hanging motionless in the sky.

Using his master key, Falcon let himself out onto the small external platform flaring from the end of the deck; half a dozen people could stand here, with only low guardrails separating them from the vast sweep of the envelope—and from the ground, thousands of meters below the envelope's sharply sloping artificial horizon. It was an exciting place to be, and perfectly safe even when the ship was traveling at speed, for it was sheltered in the dead air behind the huge dorsal blister of the observation deck. Nevertheless, it was not intended that the passengers would have access to it; the view was a little too vertiginous.

The covers of the forward cargo hatch had already opened like giant trap doors, and the camera platform was hovering above them, preparing to descend. Along this route in years to come would travel thousands of passengers and tonnes of supplies. Only on rare occasions would the *Queen* have to drop down to sea level to dock with her floating base.

A sudden gust of cross wind slapped Falcon's cheek, and he tightened his grip on the guardrail. The Grand Canyon could be a bad place for turbulence, although he did not expect much at this altitude. Without anxiety he focused his attention on the descending platform, now some fifty meters above the ship; the crewman who was piloting the robot platform from the *Queen*'s bridge was a highly skilled operator who had performed this simple maneuver a dozen times on this flight already. It was inconceivable that he would have any difficulties.

Yet he seemed to be reacting rather sluggishly. That last gust had drifted the camera platform almost to the edge of the open hatchway.

Surely the pilot could have corrected before this. . . .

Did he have a control problem? Unlikely. These remotes had multiple-redundancy, fail-safe takeovers—any number of backup systems. Accidents were unheard of.

But there he went again, off to the left. Could the pilot be *drunk?* Improbable though that seemed . . .

Falcon keyed his commlink. ''Bridge, put me in . . .''

Without warning he was slapped violently in the face by a gust of freezing wind. That was not what had interrupted his orders to the bridge. He hardly felt the wind, for he had been checked by the horror of what was happening to the camera platform. The operator was fighting for control, trying to balance the craft on its jets, but he was only making matters worse. The oscillations had increased—twenty degrees, forty degrees, sixty degrees.

Falcon found his voice. "Switch to automatic, you fool!" he shouted at the commlink. "Your manual control's not working!"

The platform flipped over on its back. The jets no longer supported it, but drove it swiftly downward, sudden allies with the gravity they had fought until this moment.

Falcon never heard the crash. He felt it, though, as he raced across the observation deck toward the elevator that would take him down to the bridge. Workers shouted at him anxiously, wanting to know what happened.

It would be many months before he knew the answer to that question.

Just as he was about to step into the elevator shaft, he changed his mind. What if there was a power failure? Better be on the safe side, even if it took a few seconds longer. Even if time was the essence.

He ran down the spiral stairway that enclosed the elevator shaft. Halfway down he paused to check the ship for damage. He had a perfect view, and what he saw froze his heart. That damned platform had gone straight through the ship, top to bottom, rupturing two of the gas cells as it did so. They were collapsing slowly even now, in great falling veils of plastic.

Falcon wasn't worried about lift—the ballast could easily take care of that, with eight cells still intact. Far more serious was the structural damage. Already he could hear the latticework of carbon-carbon and titanium all around him, groaning in protest under sudden abnormal, excessive loads. Strong and flexible as the metal and carbon-fiber members were, they were no stronger than their sundered joints.

Lift alone wasn't enough. Unless it was properly distributed, the ship's back would break.

Falcon ran again. He'd gotten a few steps down the stairs when a superchimp, one of the workers' assistants from the observation deck, came racing down the elevator shaft, shrieking with fright—moving with incredible speed, hand over hand, along the *outside* of the elevator's latticework. In its terror the poor beast had torn off its company uniform, perhaps in an unconscious attempt to regain the freedom of its recent ancestors.

Falcon, still descending as swiftly as he could, watched the creature's approach with some alarm. A distraught simp was a powerful and possibly dangerous animal, especially if fear overcame its conditioning against striking out at humans.

As it overtook him, it started to call out a string of words, but they were all jumbled together, and the only one he could recognize was a plaintive, frequently repeated "boss." Even now, Falcon realized, it looked toward humans for guidance. He felt sorry for the creature, involved in a human disaster beyond its comprehension, for which it bore no responsibility.

It stopped exactly opposite him, on the other side of the lattice. There was nothing to prevent it from coming through the opening framework if it wished. And then it moved toward him, its wide thin lips hovering over yellow fangs, bared in terror.

Now its face was only inches from his, and he was looking straight into its terrified eyes. Never before had Falcon been so close to a simp, able to study its features in such detail. He felt that strange mingling of kinship and discomfort that all humans experience when they gaze thus into the mirror of time.

Falcon's presence seemed to have calmed the animal; its lips closed over its fangs. Falcon pointed up the shaft, back toward the observation deck. He said, very clearly and precisely, "Boss. Boss. *Go.*"

To his relief, the simp understood. It gave him a

grimace that might have been a smile and at once raced back the way it had come. Falcon had given it the best advice he could. If any safety remained aboard the *Queen*, it lay in that direction, upward.

His duty lay in the other direction.

He had almost reached the bottom of the spiral stairs when the lights went out. With a sound of rending polymer, the vessel pitched nose down. He could still see quite well, for a shaft of sunlight streamed through the open hatch and the huge tear in the envelope. Many years ago Falcon had stood in a great cathedral nave watching the light pour through the stained-glass windows, forming pools of multicolored radiance on the ancient flagstones. The dazzling shaft of sunlight through the ruined fabric high above compulsively reminded him of that moment.

He was in a cathedral of metal and polymer, falling down the sky.

When he reached the bridge and was able for the first time to look outside, he was horrified to see how close the ship was to the ground. Only a thousand meters below were the beautiful and deadly pinnacles of rock and the red river of mud, carving its way down into the past. There was no level area anywhere in sight where a ship as large as the *Queen* could come to rest on an even keel.

A glance at the display board told him all the ballast had gone. However, rate of descent had been reduced to a few meters a second; they still had a fighting chance.

Without a word, Falcon eased himself into the pilot's seat and took over such control as remained. The instrument board showed him everything he wished to know; speech was superfluous.

In the background, he could hear the communications officer giving a running report over the radiolink. By this time all the news channels of Earth and the inhabited worlds would have been preempted—and he could imagine the frustration of the program managers: one of the most spectacular wrecks in history was occurring without a single live camera to transmit it! Someday the last moments of the *Queen* might fill millions with awe and terror, as had those of the *Hindenburg* a century and a half before, but not in real time.

Now the ground was only about four hundred meters away, still coming up slowly. Though he had full thrust, he had not dared use it lest the weakened structure collapse. Now he realized he had no choice. The wind was taking them toward a fork in the canyon where the river was split by a wedge of rock like the prow of some gigantic, fossilized ship of stone. If the *Queen* continued on its present course it would straddle that triangular plateau and come to rest with at least a third of its length jutting out over nothingness; it would snap like a rotten stick.

Far away, above the groans of the straining structure and the hiss of escaping gas, came the familiar whistle of the turbines as Falcon opened up the lateral thrusters. The ship staggered, and began to slew to port.

The shriek of tearing metal was now almost continuous—and the rate of descent had increased ominously. A glance at the damage-control board showed that cell number five had just gone.

The ground was only meters away. Even now Falcon could not tell whether his maneuver would succeed or fail. He switched the thrust vectors to vertical, giving maximum lift to reduce the force of impact.

The crash seemed to last forever. It was not violent, merely prolonged and irresistible. It seemed that the whole universe was falling about them.

The sound of crunching laminate and metal came rapidly nearer, as if some great beast were eating its way through the dying ship.

Then the floor and ceiling closed upon Falcon like a vise.

* * *

The holographic image vanished from the briefing room. Sparta and Blake and the commander sat quietly in the dark for a moment.

Finally Sparta said, ''A very convincing reconstruction.''

''Yeah.'' Blake stirred in his armchair. ''I remember seeing the videos when I was a kid. They weren't like this, though. It's like being inside the guy's head.''

''We had good coverage from the flight recorders, a lot of it classified information,'' the commander said. ''And you're right, we also had access to Falcon's experience.''

''From deep-probe debriefing of the survivors?'' Sparta asked.

''That's right,'' the commander replied. In the gloom, his pale eyes were reflected points of light.

Sparta locked gazes with him in the dark. His face enlarged itself a dozen times under her telescopic inspection; the little jumps of his cold eyes betrayed him. Even the sudden sharp smell of him betrayed him. She knew the commander and his colleagues were using the same deep molecular-probe techniques on her, tapping her nightly dreams, recording her nightmares for later reconstruction—reconstructions that might easily be as terrifying as this ''documentary.''

His eyes shifted ever so slightly in the direction of Blake, before coming back to her almost instantly. He was acknowledging her suspicions, and at the same time silently telling her this was information they could not afford to share with Blake.

Sparta said, ''Run the incident with the simp again, please.''

The commander complied, keying the holo controls. Almost instantly they were back inside the *Queen*, that slowly collapsing cathedral of plastic and metal. . . .

Falcon, descending the stairs beside the elevator as swiftly

*as he could, watched the simp's approach with some
alarm. A distraught simp was a powerful and possibly
dangerous animal, especially if fear overcame its conditioning.*

*As it overtook him, it started to call out a string of words,
but they were all jumbled together, and the only one he
could recognize was a plaintive, frequently repeated
"boss".* . . .

"Stop there," Sparta commanded.

The hologram froze.

"You've analyzed the animal's speech?" she
demanded.

"The crash investigators tried. Falcon's recollec-
tion wasn't that precise. Not good enough to
recover the words."

"All right, go on."

*Even now, Falcon realized, the simp looked toward hu-
mans for guidance. He felt sorry for the creature, involved
in a human disaster beyond its comprehension, for which
it bore no responsibility.* . . .

*It moved toward him, its wide thin lips hovering over
yellow fangs, bared in terror.*

*Now its face was only inches from his. Falcon felt a
strange mingling of kinship and discomfort.* . . .

Falcon pointed up the elevator shaft. "Boss. Boss. Go."

*The simp gave him a grimace that might have been a
smile and raced back the way it had come.*

"That's enough," Sparta said. "You can cut it
off."

"Poor animals," said Blake.

"What analogy are you drawing here, Commander?" Sparta's tone edged on mockery. "Could
it have something to do with the fact that there
wasn't nearly as much of Falcon left as there was
of me, each time they tried to kill me?"

"What *are* you talking about?" Blake asked her,
exasperated.

The commander evaded her question. "The next
scene we've reconstructed is much more recent, recorded two years ago in the Earth Central offices of

the Board of Space Control. The subjects weren't aware"—he coughed—"that I had access to the chip."

"Why do you want to go to Jupiter?"

"As Springer said when he lifted for Pluto, 'because it's there.' "

"Thanks, I'm sure. And now that we've got *that* out of the way . . . what's the real reason?"

Howard Falcon smiled at his interrogator—though only those who knew Falcon very well could have interpreted his slight, leathery grimace as a smile.

Brandt Webster was one of the few who could. He was the Board of Space Control's Deputy Chief of Staff for Plans. For twenty years he and Falcon had shared triumphs and disasters, not excluding the greatest disaster of them all, the wreck of the *Queen.*

Falcon said, "Springer's cliche . . ."

"I think somebody said it before Springer," Webster put in.

". . . is still valid, at any rate. We've landed on all the terrestrial planets and a lot of the small bodies—explored them, built cities and orbital stations. But the gas giants are still pristine. They're the only real challenges left in the solar system."

"An expensive challenge. I assume you've worked out the costs."

"As well as anyone could. You've got the estimates there on your flatscreen."

"Mmm." Webster consulted his screen.

Falcon adjusted himself backward. "Keep in mind, my friend, that this is no one-shot deal. It's a reusable transportation system—once it's been proved out it can be used again and again. It will open up not merely Jupiter, but *all* the giants."

"Yes, yes, Howard . . ." Webster peered at the figures and whistled. It was not a happy whistle. "Why not start with an easier planet—Uranus, for example? Half the gravity, and less than half the escape velocity. Quieter weather, too, if quieter is the right word for it.''

Webster had done his homework. It wasn't the first time Plans had thought about the giants.

''There's very little saving,'' Falcon replied, ''once you've factored in the extra distance and the logistics problems. Beyond Saturn, we'd have to establish new supply bases. On Jupiter, we can use the facilities on Ganymede.''

''If we can work a deal with the Indo-Asians.''

''This is a Council of Worlds expedition, not a consortium venture. There's no commercial threat. The Space Board will simply rent the Indo-Asian facilities on Ganymede we need.''

''I'm just saying you'd better start now to recruit top-notch Asians for your team. Our prickly friends aren't going to be happy if they see a lot of European faces peering into their backyard—which is how they think of the Jovian moons.''

''Some of us European faces *are* Asians, Web. New Delhi is still my official address. I don't see it becoming a problem.''

''No, I suppose it won't.'' Webster studied Falcon, and his thoughts were transparent. Falcon's argument for Jupiter sounded logical, but there was more to it. Jupiter was lord of the solar system; Falcon was fired by no lesser challenge.

''Besides,'' Falcon continued, ''Jupiter is a major scientific scandal. It's been more than a century since its radio storms were discovered, but we still don't know what causes them. And the Great Red Spot is as big a mystery as ever, unless you're one of those who believes that chaos theory is the answer to every unanswerable question. That's why I think the Indo-Asians will be delighted to support us. Do you know how many probes they've dropped into that atmosphere?''

''A couple of hundred, I believe.''

''That's just in the last fifty years. If you count

back to Galileo, *three* hundred and twenty-six probes have penetrated Jupiter—about a quarter of them total failures. We've learned a hell of a lot, but we've barely scratched the planet. Do you realize how *big* it is, Web?''

''More than ten times the size of Earth.''

''Yes, yes—but do you know what that really means?''

Webster smiled. ''Why don't you tell me, Howard?''

Four planetary globes stood against the wall of Webster's office, representing the settled terrestrial planets and Earth's moon. Falcon pointed to the globe of Earth.

''Look at India—how small it seems. Well, if you skinned Earth and spread it out on the surface of Jupiter, oceans and all, it would look about as big as India does here.''

There was a long silence while Webster contemplated the equation: Jupiter is to Earth as Earth is to India. He stood up and went to the globe of Earth. ''You deliberately chose the best possible example, didn't you, Howard?''

Falcon moved to face him. ''Hardly seems like nine years ago, does it, Web? But it is. We did those initial tests three years before the *Queen*'s first and last flight.''

''You were still a lieutenant.''

''That I was.''

''And you wanted to let me preview the grand experiment—a three day drift across the northern plains of India. Great view of the Himalayas, you said. Perfectly safe, you promised. Said it would get me out of the office and teach me what the whole thing was all about.''

''Were you disappointed?''

''You know the answer to that.'' Webster's grin split his round, freckled face. ''Next to my first trip to the moon, it was the most memorable experience of my life. And you were right—perfectly safe. Quite uneventful.''

Falcon's mask seemed to soften with the memory. ''I planned it to be beautiful, Web. The lift off from Srinagar just before dawn, because I always loved the way that big silver bubble would suddenly brighten with the first light of the sun. . . .''

''Total silence,'' Webster said. ''That's what made the first impression on me. None of this blowtorch roar from the burners, like those ancient propane-fueled hot-air balloons. It was impressive enough that you'd managed to package a fusion reactor in a hundred-kilogram bottle, Howard, but that it was silent as well—hanging there right over our heads in the mouth of the envelope, zapping away ten times a second—you must know what a miracle-in-action that seemed.''

''When I think about flying over India I still remember the village sounds,'' Falcon said. ''The dogs barking, the people shouting and looking up at us, the bells ringing. You could always hear it, even as you climbed, even when that whole sunbaked landscape expanded around you and you got up to where it was nice and cool—five kilometers or so—and you needed the oxygen masks, but otherwise all you had to do was lean back and admire the scenery. Of course the onboard computer was doing all the work.''

''And meanwhile sucking up all the data it needed to design the big one. The *Queen*.''

''We hadn't named her yet.''

''No,'' Webster concurred, a bit sadly. ''That was such a perfect day, Howard. Not a cloud in the sky.''

''The monsoon wasn't due for a month.''

''Time sort of stopped.''

''For me, too, even though supposedly I was used to it. I got irritated when the hourly radio reports broke into my daydreams.''

''I tell you, I still dream of that . . .'' He searched

for the word. ''. . . infinite, ancient landscape, that patchwork—villages, fields, temples, lakes, irrigation canals—that earth drenched in history, stretching to the horizon, stretching beyond. . . .'' Webster moved away from the globe, breaking the hypnotic spell. ''Well, Howard, you certainly converted me to lighter-than-air flight. And I also got a sense of the enormous size of India. One loses sight of that, thinking in terms of low-orbit satellites that go around the Earth in ninety minutes.''

Falcon's face stretched into its minimal smile. ''Yet India is to Earth . . .''

''As Earth is to Jupiter, yes, yes.'' Webster returned to his desk and was silent a moment, fiddling with the flatscreen that displayed Falcon's estimates of the Jupiter mission parameters. Then he looked up at Falcon. ''Granted your argument—and supposing funds and cooperation are available—there's another question you have to answer.''

''Which is?''

''Why should you do better than the—what it is?—three hundred and twenty-six probes that have already made the trip?''

''Because I'm better qualified,'' Falcon said gruffly. ''Better qualified as an observer and as a pilot. *Especially* as a pilot. I've got more experience with lighter-than-atmosphere flight than anyone in the solar system.''

''You could serve as a controller, sit safely on Ganymede.''

''*That's just the point!*'' Fire blazed in Falcon's unblinking eyes. ''Don't you remember what killed the *Queen?*''

Webster knew perfectly well. He merely answered, ''Go on.''

''*Time lag—time lag!* That poor sap controlling the camera platform thought he was on a direct beam. But somehow he'd gotten his control circuit switched through a satellite relay. Maybe it wasn't his fault, Web, but he should have known, he should have confirmed and reconfirmed. Switched through a comsat! That's a half-second time lag for the round trip. Even then it wouldn't have mattered if we'd been flying in calm air, but we were over the Canyon, with all that turbulence. When the platform tipped, the guy corrected instantly—but by the time the platform's onboard instrumentation got the message, the thing had already tipped the other way. Ever tried to drive a car over a bumpy road with a half-second delay in the steering?"

"Unlike you, Howard, I don't drive at all, much less over bumpy roads. But I take your meaning."

"Do you? Ganymede is a million kilometers from Jupiter—a round-trip signal delay of *six* seconds. A remote controller won't do, Web. You need someone on the spot, to handle emergencies *as* they emerge—in real time." Falcon adjusted himself stiffly. "Let me show you something . . . mind if I use this?"

"Go ahead."

Falcon picked up a postcard lying on Webster's desk; postcards were almost obsolete on Earth, but Webster seemed to have a fondness for things obsolete. This one showed a 3–D view of a Martian landscape; its verso was decorated with exotic and very expensive Martian stamps.

Falcon held the card so that it dangled vertically. "This is an old trick, but it helps to make my point. Put your thumb and finger on either side, like you're about to pinch it, but not quite touching."

Webster reached across his desk and put out his hand, almost but not quite gripping the card.

"That's right," said Falcon. "And now . . ." Falcon waited a few seconds, then said, "Catch it."

A second later, without warning, he let go of the card. Webster's thumb and finger closed on empty air.

Falcon leaned over and retrieved the fallen card.

"I'll do it once again," he said, "just to show there's no deception. Okay?"

He held out the card. Webster positioned his fingers, almost brushing the card's surface.

Once again the falling card slipped through Webster's fingers.

"Now you try it on me."

Webster came out from behind his desk and stood in front of Falcon. He held the card a moment, then dropped it without warning.

It had scarcely moved before Falcon caught it. So swift was his reaction it almost seemed there was an audible "click."

"When they put me together again," Falcon remarked in an expressionless voice, "the surgeons made some improvements. This is one of them"—Falcon placed the card on Webster's desk—"and there are others. I want to make the most of them. Jupiter is the place where I can do it."

Webster stared for long seconds at the postcard, which portrayed the improbable reds and purples of the Trivium Charontis Escarpment. Then he said quietly, "I understand. How long do you think it will take?"

"With the Space Board's help and the cooperation of the Indo-Asians, plus all the private foundation money we can drag in—two years. Maybe less."

"That's very, very fast."

"I've done lots of the preliminary work. In detail." Falcon's gaze flicked to the flatscreen display.

"All right, Howard, I'm with you. I hope you get your luck; you've earned it. But there's one thing I won't do."

"What's that?"

"Next time you go ballooning, don't expect *me* as a passenger."

The commander touched the button; the hologram collapsed into a dark point and vanished.

''I don't know about Ellen, but I'm hungry,'' Blake said. ''I don't want to talk about this on an empty stomach.''

''You're right. Past time for lunch.''

3

"I don't get it."

"The Free Spirit *made* Falcon,"
Sparta said. "Remade him, I should
say. For the same reason they remade
me. Close your mouth, dear—"
Blake's mouth had opened in disbelief—"your arugula is showing."

The commander's stone face almost softened into
a grin, but with effort, by shoveling a forkful of
crumpled lettuce into his mouth, he kept his dig-
nity.

"You were the first to tell me what they were
after, remember?" she said to Blake. "The Em-
peror of the Last Days."

Sparta picked at her excellent food, of which
there was as usual four or five times too much. Today, the printed menu cards announced, it was a
choice of salads, to be followed by a tomato bisque
en croute, then a selection of individual quiches and
finger-sized *croque-monsieurs*, and finally orange sor-
bet with vanilla cookies—all accompanied by several wines which Blake and Sparta and the
commander would as usual ignore.

The people who served this opulent fare (and
lunch was nothing compared to dinner) were
young and scrubbed and cheerful, uniformed in
white, enthusiastically talkative when company

was wanted but always remarkably discreet. Today they were staying almost invisible.

Sparta and Blake had been living as the commander's guests in this strange "safe house," as he called it, for a week now, often dining alone together beneath the heraldic banners that hung from the high walls of the gothic main hall. On sunny days like this one, dramatic shafts of golden light poured through the stained glass clerestories, windows that depicted dragons and loosely draped maidens and knights in armor. The man who'd built the mansion was evidently a fan of Sir Walter Scott's, or had had dreams of Camelot.

"We think they had Falcon targeted before the wreck," said the commander, setting down his plate.

"*Targeted* him?" Blake had gotten his greens down without choking, but he was still incredulous—not least because this Space Board officer, this old guy whom at first he'd taken for nothing more than Ellen's fellow employee, was making sounds like he knew as much about the Free Spirit as Blake himself knew, information that Blake had risked his life to get.

"The best balloon pilot in the world," Sparta said, as if it were self-evident. "Someone realized— even before Falcon did—that to live in the clouds of Jupiter, you need a balloon."

"What's Jupiter got to do with it?" Blake demanded.

"I don't know," said Sparta. "But it's Jupiter that I keep going to in my dreams. . . ."

"Ellen." The commander tried to warn her off the subject.

"Falling into the clouds. The wings overhead. The voices of the deep."

Blake eyed the commander. "Her dreams?"

"We're working from the evidence," the commander said. "Consider that even for the Board of Space Control it's almost impossible to mount an operation of this technical and logistical and political complexity in two years. We think Webster must have known Falcon wanted to go to Jupiter before Falcon told him.''

''Exactly, Blake. Before he knew it himself,'' Sparta said. She turned to the commander. ''They sabotaged the *Queen*.''

His voice got gruff. ''You were always quick to reach conclusions . . .''

''Nobody's ever put a remote link through a satellite by accident, before or since.''

''That's crazy,'' said Blake. ''How did they know Falcon would survive the crash?''

''They have a habit of taking long chances.''

The commander said, ''The camera platform started having trouble as soon as he was topside. Not until then.''

She nodded. ''It should have been the safest place, if you were calculating the odds. Falcon himself thought so.''

''Then they really screwed up,'' Blake protested. ''He was back down at the controls before the *Queen* hit. He almost saved the ship.''

''The crash worked for them anyway,'' Sparta said. ''Maybe better than they hoped.''

''Unlike you,'' the commander said, ''with him there wasn't much of a thinking human being left to get in their way later.''

Blake, agitated, thrust back his chair and stood up. ''All right, I asked this before. *You*—sitting there—you personally represent the high and mighty Space Board Investigations Branch? What do you want from Ellen? What can she do that the Board hasn't already done?''

Before he answered Blake, the commander signaled the stewards to clear the table and bring the next course. ''There are some things that the Space Board doesn't do well,'' he said. ''Investigating itself is one of them.''

''Are you saying what I think you're saying?''

"Don't assume anything," the commander said. "And don't miss the tomato bisque."

He hesitated, then abruptly sat down. "If you want my cooperation, *sir*"—the resort to sarcasm was childish, a measure of Blake's complete frustration with the course of events—"I need to know that whatever you're planning, you're not going to expose her to any more danger than she's in already."

"Before we men make any deals for her, Blake, perhaps Ellen will tell us her own thinking."

"I'm certainly curious. I'd like to find out more about Howard Falcon and the *Kon-Tiki* mission," she said.

"Then you're still on the team."

"No, I don't think so," she said thoughtfully. "I don't think this is a team sport."

Blake spent the afternoon trying to talk her out of her curiosity about Falcon, which to him seemed founded upon the flimsiest of circumstantial evidence. Oh, he admitted that he'd been a great conspiracy theorist in his day, but for his own part, he had come to the conclusion that the Free Spirit— the *prophetae*, the Athanasians, whatever you wanted to call them—while admittedly a bunch of dangerous nuts, had made so many mistakes they were on the verge of putting themselves out of business. Now that the Board of Space Control obviously knew all about them, why should Ellen continue to risk her life?

She humored him, agreed with him, did everything except promise to do what he asked—resign from the Board of Space Control. On the other hand, she didn't say she wouldn't. Her love and affection for him seemed steady. But for all his passion and argument, some cold part in the center of her was untouchable to his reasoning.

That night they stopped outside her bedroom door and Blake moved impetuously to kiss her. She responded, pressing her taut dancer's body to his hard frame, but broke off when he tried to go farther and push past her into the room.

"I've told you, there are cameras and microphones in there," she said. "In your room, too."

"I almost don't care."

"I do." She said, "Until tomorrow, darling," then closed the door firmly and locked it behind her.

In the cold dark room she stripped and went naked to bed. In this century and culture, modesty hardly noticed nakedness—and certainly her body had often been rendered transparent, inside and out, to anyone who might be peering at her now. It was not because of Blake that she cared about the watchers; it was because of what they watched while she slept.

She did not want him to share her visions—her nightmares—as she knew *they* did.

With the aid of a private mantra, what some might call a prayer, she forced herself to fall asleep.

Blake shoved the narrow casement open just enough to let night air enter. He hung his clothes carefully in the walk-in closet; he was a bit of a dandy, some said, and it was true that he liked to look his best, whatever part he was playing. And with the cameras watching, he liked to keep everything neat.

He hopped naked into the bed and stretched out under the cool sheets. He lay there bursting with hope and fear and love—*she loves me!*—and stiff with renewed, frustrated lust.

A long time ago they had been children together in the same school, a special school for ordinary kids who were being taught to be something more than ordinary. The SPARTA project, it was called—SPARTA stood for SPecified Aptitude Resource Training and Assessment—and it had been created by Linda's parents . . . Ellen's parents, that is . . .

to demonstrate that every human is possessed of multiple intelligences, and that each of these intelligences may be developed to a high degree by stimulation and guidance. SPARTA vigorously contested the prejudice that intelligence was one thing, some mysterious ectoplasm called ''I. Q.,'' or that I. Q. was fixed, immutable, or in any meaningful sense real.

Not all the children in SPARTA were equally capable in every area—people are rather less like each other than are pea plants—but every child blossomed. All became competent athletes, musicians, mathematicians, logicians, writers, artists, social and political beings. In one or more of these fields, each excelled.

But for Linda and Blake, growing up, this extraordinary education was just school, the school they went to whether they wanted to or not, and to each other they were nothing more than schoolmates. Later, when it came to sex, the experience should have made them treat each other as casually as siblings.

Not in their case. She'd been slower to realize it— or more reluctant to admit it—but they were in love with each other. And, evidently, very much in the physical way.

It occurred to him that there is something about making love to the person you love that cannot be mimicked by any other experience in life; no amount of intelligence, no amount of sexual inventiveness, no amount of friendly feeling, not all the goodwill in the world, will lift you to that plane where all seems good and all good things seem possible, without love.

So he lay there between his fresh cotton sheets, grinning inanely at the stars visible through the narrow slit in the stone wall that was his window, dreaming of Linda . . . of Ellen. And renewing his determination to take her away from all this. He never noticed the moment when his daydreams turned to night dreams.

An hour later, when the house was dark and her body was immobile and her mind was sunk deep in its own undreaming depths, the locked door to Sparta's room silently opened.

The commander entered the room and shone the beam of a tiny bright flashlight into the corners, then gestured to the door. A technician came into the room and, while the commander held the spot of light steady on the side of Sparta's neck, pressed an injector pistol against her skin. There was no sound of protest, no evidence of sensation as the drug entered her bloodstream.

Her nightmares resumed not long after.

4

The moon was a fat caïque riding on cold, billowing seas of October cloud. Something was chasing the moon. He heard it coming long before he saw it, a black winged thing whose wings beat the night. . . .

This was no dream. Blake opened an eye and saw a black silhouette slipping silently down the sky, past his window.

He tore aside the covers and rolled out of the bed, sprawling flat on the floor. He didn't know how long he'd been asleep—the pattern of moonlight on the carpet suggested that it was already after midnight—but he knew what the thing outside was—

—a Snark, an assault helicopter, its blades and turbines tuned to whisper mode, settling gently onto the wide lawn below his window.

One of ours or one of theirs? But who were they? Who were *we?*

Whose side was Blake on anyway? He kept low and rolled across the moon-dappled carpet into the cover of his closet. Inside, he dressed as quickly as he could, slipping into dark polycanvas pants and a black wool pullover, snugging black sneakers onto his feet and pulling a roomy, many-pocketed black canvas windbreaker around his shoulders.

After the escape from Mars, when Blake had been shown to his room here, he'd found all his things already neatly cleaned, pressed, and hung up or put away in drawers. Thoughtful of the troops. Only his toys had been missing, his wire-working tools, his oddments of integrated circuitry, his scrounged bits of *plastique*.

He didn't blame them; that stuff was dangerous. And anyway, in the days since he'd arrived he'd managed to replace most of it. Remarkable, the amount of deadly and destructive chemicals required to maintain even the average studio apartment—not to mention the average estate. That thick green lawn upon which the Snark had just come to rest, for example: that kind of lush plant growth doesn't come without generous applications of nitrogen and phosphorus. Out in the gardener's shed, high explosives were there for the taking. Fusing and timing circuitry were here and there for the taking, too, hidden in odd corners of the estate, in rarely used alarm and surveillance mechanisms.

Blake knew where the cameras were. He knew where they were placed in his room, and in Ellen's, even where they were scattered among the trees in the woods. Ellen wanted to pretend she didn't know about some of those; fine with him. Meanwhile, he cannibalized whatever he thought the cameras couldn't see him cannibalizing; he stole what his hosts wouldn't miss and put it where he hoped they couldn't find it.

From behind loose strips of molding, from the undersides of shelves, he retrieved the fruits of his explorations and borrowings. He spent a long minute assembling disparate parts before shoving them into his pockets. Finally he took a roll of adhesive tape from the tie-rack where it hung beneath a handful of knit ties; he circled both his palms with tape, ripping it off the roll.

He stood at the closet door and listened. He could barely hear the twin rotors of the Snark whispering on the lawn below. He opened the closet door and walked straight to the window, knowing that the cameras would be on him by now, even if earlier he'd managed to elude them. He peered around the stone jamb.

Three floors below, meshing rotors were whistling in close harmony at the edge of audibility, not free-wheeling; the Snark's engines weren't shut down, which meant it was prepared to take off instantly.

A metallic scrape and click at the door of his room. . . .

Blake jumped onto the sill. He squeezed through sideways and hung by his fingers until the toes of his rubberized shoes found a deep seam in the rustic masonry. With his right hand he reached into his pocket and brought out a small package, which he left beneath the casement frame, before he transferred his grip sideways and began to move in a deliberate traverse along the face of the mansion.

The moonlight was mottled and constantly shifting, a drifting cuckaloris pattern on the irregular wall that could not have been better designed to hide him from ordinary visual surveillance.

Ellen's room was a long way off, but he'd studied the route for days. It had occurred to him even before they arrived at this place that he and she might be wanting to leave it on short notice, and not through the front gate.

He made it around the corner bastion of the house before the inevitable white flash and bang split the night. Somebody had shoved at his casement window to look out.

Phosphorus makes a bright light. Simultaneously he heard the man's scream. There hadn't been enough charge to maim, but the stuff did burn fiercely, and Blake wouldn't be surprised if whoever had tripped the booby trap was in for a bit of skin grafting. He felt only a twinge of guilt. They should have known better than to walk into his room in the middle of the night without knocking.

Lights went on all over the perimeter; the moonlight was washed away in a glare a hundred times brighter. The house was crossed by searchlight beams like the night sky over London in the blitz. Blake braced himself for the ack-ack.

But it seemed he still had a few spare seconds. He moved his taped hands and sneakered feet one at a time, as rapidly as he could, until he found the bay window of Ellen's room. It was locked.

No time for subtlety. He had his left hand and both sets of toes firmly lodged in the crevices of the masonry; with his right hand he punched the pane of glass through its leading, taking a nasty scrape across the back of his fist, above the tape.

As he cranked open the slat, it occurred to him for the first time that something fishy was going on. Extra fishy.

No alarms. No sirens or bells. All the outside lights were on, but the klaxons hadn't sounded. Even the window wire hadn't tripped.

"Ellen—it's me," he said, loud enough to rouse her from sleep. "Don't do anything drastic." He pulled himself through the window, a little wider than the one in his room, and landed in a crouch on the floor.

No bells, no sirens, and the helicopter hadn't lifted from the lawn. A Snark was smart enough all by itself to find a guy climbing on a wall and shoot him off it. They weren't out to kill him, then. Maybe they were hoping Ellen wouldn't wake up.

Too late for that. By the stark white light that poured in through the windows, it was plain that her bed was empty.

Warm, with the sheets in a nest where she'd been sleeping until minutes ago, but empty.

Her door was ajar. Had they gotten her first, or had she heard them—he knew she could hear things no one else could—and made her escape? Gone to rescue *him?*

He crouched and stuck his head out the door.

A loose pattern of rubber bullets from a silenced weapon whacked the floor and doorjamb, hard enough to dent the wood. He rolled back into Ellen's room, scrabbled in his pocket—

"Come out of there, Mr. Redfield, we aren't going to hurt you."

—he tossed another little package into the hall.

This time the flash and bang were instantaneous, and he was through the door almost as quick as the flash. No way they were going to trap him inside the room.

He rolled across the burning rug and leaned up and over the stair rail in a low vault, ignoring the residual flaming matter that stuck to the back of his jacket. He dropped half a floor to the landing below, rolling again as he hit, rolling right on down the stairs in a tight tuck, shedding the burning stuff as he rolled.

He hit the corridor and bounded to his feet, a little dizzy but unhurt.

No pursuit. Teach *them* to take that superior tone. *Mister* Redfield, his ass.

He had an inspiration. Maybe the Snark was still out there on the lawn; maybe it hadn't moved since it had landed. Maybe there was nobody in it. Maybe they were all inside chasing him and Ellen, because maybe they'd thought this was going to be easy.

Maybe he'd show them how wrong they were.

He sprinted down the hall and kicked his way through a door into a corner room, a sort of pantry to one of the mansion's big reception halls. He knew that everywhere he went the cameras could follow him, so he wasted no time hiding. He punched his already-skinned fist through the face of a knight in shining armor—shining from the light of exterior floodlights—and punched again and again, using his forearm to tear away the leading, until he'd made a big hole in the stained-glass window, big enough to climb through.

He was close enough to the ground to risk jumping. He flexed his knees and ankles to absorb the shock. He let himself fall from the stone sill.

He hit the lawn and rolled and bounced to his feet, none the worse for the five-meter drop. The Snark was just sitting there, twenty meters away, its rotors still whispering. When he had that formidable machine in his control, he'd be able to stand off an army. Then he'd find Ellen quick enough, and they'd be out of here. . . .

He ran, not bothering to conceal himself. They weren't going to shoot him; they'd had their chance, and they'd used rubber bullets. If somebody came into the chopper's open door right this minute, Blake would decide what he had to do. Rush? Run? Raise his hands in surrender?

He ducked under the drooping blades.

A white face appeared, framed in the darkness of the open door. Ellen. She beckoned sharply.

His heart leaped. "You did it!" She'd already captured the machine! As he ran forward she extended her hand to him. Her hand, slender and strong and white . . . her face, a pale white oval framed in short blond hair . . . the rest of her was armored in black canvas, nearly invisible in the darkness; all he saw of her was a disembodied hand and face.

He took the hand as he stepped on the chopper's skid, feeling her firm, familiar grip through the tape. She pulled him into the open doorway—

—but as she did so she twisted and he staggered, off-balance, and almost before he knew it he was lying on his back on the metal floor. A man leaned out of the darkness behind her. Blake tried to sit up, but in Ellen's other hand, hidden until now, she held a hypodermic pistol. She'd already shot its paralyzing charge into the base of his skull.

"Ellen . . ." His mouth lost its ability to form words. His vision seemed to narrow on her face, her moving lips.

Her face held no sympathy, no love, only a stark

white smile in which her teeth gleamed like fangs and her tongue was as wet and red as fresh liver. "You're starting to get in the way, Blake. We won't be seeing you for a while."

She straightened. The man behind her came forward and tugged Blake upright, hefting him into a canvas sling seat against the bulkhead, strapping him firmly into place. Blake could feel nothing except the cold in his fingers and toes. He could do nothing to prevent the man's expert fingers from searching all his pockets, his other hiding places, finding everything he'd had time to conceal.

Ellen hadn't even stayed to watch. His last glimpse of her was of her shadowy form jumping lithely out the door.

5

In places where the day approximated twenty-four hours, Sparta habitually rose a quarter hour before the sun; in other places she had trouble sleeping at all.

Blake, on the other hand, sometimes managed to sleep until midmorning, a trick Sparta envied but could not comprehend. But she had been around him long enough by now to get used to it, so she didn't think it odd when he failed to appear at the breakfast table.

She thought it distinctly odd when he didn't show up for lunch. His appetite had never, in her experience, allowed him to skip two meals in a row.

No one else showed up for lunch, either. The young blond steward had no idea where Mr. Redfield was—done with that salad, Inspector? The young blond stewardess couldn't say why, but she was certain the commander would be returning soon—sure you won't try the wine, miss?

The rules here were unspoken, but clear enough: this was a place where guests minded their own business. And everybody else minded Sparta's.

When, at the end of another shamefully opulent meal, the perfectly brewed dark-roast *arabica* coffee arrived, she sipped it without enthusiasm.

After lunch she went upstairs to Blake's room. Outside his door, she *listened*.

In the walls of Blake's room she could hear the gurgle of ancient pipes, the clatter of pots and pans in the ground-floor kitchen and the voices of the kitchen workers; they were talking about nothing of consequence.

The narrow leaded windows of his room had been pushed open; she could hear the curtains stirring in the fitful draft. She could hear birds outside in the autumn trees, only a few sparrows that were late for the southward migration. Overhead she could hear the rattle of a crumb of slate roof-tile— weathered for centuries, warmed by the sun, and expanding until, just at this moment, its last attached grains were stressed beyond crystalline integrity—splitting from its parent and rolling down the steep roof into the copper gutter above Blake's open window, where it landed with a tiny "ping."

She could not hear Blake, however. He was not in his room, not sleeping or rooting around in his closet or in the bathroom shaving or cleaning his teeth. He was not there.

This was very curious. Sparta bent swiftly until her face was level with the latch, not to peek through the old-fashioned keyhole—as it no doubt appeared to those who watched—but to taste the air near the doorknob. She sensed the spicy flavor of Blake's characteristic skin oils and acids, freshly overlying a couple of centuries' worth of brass polish.

Something else. She remembered the old riddle, "Twenty brothers in the same house. Scratch their heads and they will die." Matches. A whiff of phosphorus, very faint.

She stood up. Since she knew they were watching she decided not to enter his room.

The situation wasn't necessarily bad. Blake had disappeared before. After the *Star Queen* incident, for example, when she'd stayed behind on Port

Hesperus and he'd gone back to Earth and she hadn't heard a word from him for months and hadn't seen him until he'd shown up walking toward her across the surface of the moon. On Mars, when he'd insisted on working underground and they'd both almost gotten themselves killed. But he'd always had a good reason for his vanishing acts.

Something else odd—she wondered if there was a connection. When she'd gotten out of bed that morning, she'd noticed a smell of fresh putty. One of the panes in her own window had been replaced during the night.

Sparta spent the next hour wandering the house and grounds, determined to seem unworried. Blake was not in the library or the game room or the screening room; he was not in the basement firing range or the gym or the squash courts or the indoor pool. He wasn't in the conservatory. He wasn't playing a solitary game of horseshoes or croquet. He wasn't lawn bowling or shooting skeet or practicing his fly-casting. He hadn't taken any of the horses out for a midday canter. In the garage next to the stables, all the estate's usual cars were in their usual spaces.

But a big window on the first floor had also broken since yesterday; glaziers were at work replacing a piece of the pearly stained glass.

At midmorning Sparta stood on the wide back porch, leaning on the rustic railings of peeled and varnished pine, watching the woods. Nothing moved besides the occasional squirrel or field mouse or little gray bird. And the falling leaves. She watched them fall. By *listening* she could hear each leafy collision with the leaf-covered ground.

Blake was gone.

The commander found her there.

"Where is he?" she asked quietly.

"I told him he could go when he wanted to." His voice was a rattle of stones, but there was something hollow in it. This morning he wasn't wearing his country clothes, he was wearing his crisp blue uniform, with the few imposing ribbons over the breast. "This morning, early. We took him out by chopper."

She turned away from the railing and fixed him with her dark blue eyes. "No."

"You were asleep. You couldn't hear . . ."

"I couldn't have heard the chopper, I was too full of your drugs. But he didn't want to go."

His blue eyes were lighter than hers, knobs of turquoise. "I can't change your opinion."

"I'm glad you know that. If you want this conversation to continue, Commander, stop lying."

His mouth twitched, an aborted smile. He'd used that line himself, a time or two.

"By now you know quite a lot about me," she said, "so you may suspect that if I get it into my head, I could bring this house to the ground and bury everybody in it." Her pale skin was red with anger.

"But you wouldn't. You're not like that."

"If you've hurt Blake and I find out about it I will do my best to kill you. I'm not a pacifist on principle."

He watched the slight, fragile, immensely dangerous young woman for a moment. Then his shoulders relaxed a millimeter or two and he seemed to lean away from her. "We took Blake out of here at four this morning under heavy sedation. He'll wake up in his place in London with a false memory of a quarrel with you—he'll have the notion that you told him you were engaged in a project too sensitive and too dangerous for him to get involved, and that for your sake as well as his own you insisted that he leave."

"I won't accept that"—because she knew he was still lying—"I'm leaving here now."

"Your choice, Inspector Troy. But you know as well as I do, it's the truth."

"I never said that or anything like it . . ."

"You should have." For a split second his anger flared to match hers.

". . . whatever memory you planted in him, it was not that." She walked away.

"Do you want to know what really happened"—the catch and tension in his voice gave him away; he was playing his last card—"to your parents?"

She stopped but did not turn. "They died in a car accident."

"Let's drop that pretense. You were told they died in a helicopter crash."

Now she turned, poised and dangerous. "Do you know something different, Commander?"

"What I know I can't prove," he said.

In his rasping voice she heard something else, not exactly a lie. "Oh, but you want me to think you could—and just won't." Is that what he really wanted? "Do you know my name too, Commander?—*don't* say it."

"I won't say your name. Your number was L. N. 30851005."

She nodded. "What do you know about my parents?"

"What I've read in the files, Miss L. N. And what I've learned from the *prophetae*."

"Which is?"

"That's not for free." His face had hardened again; this time the simple truth. "Are you on the team or aren't you?"

And that's why the uniform. R & R was over, the whistle had blown, back to the game. She sighed tiredly. "Send me in. . . . Coach."

PART 2

THE SIGN OF THE OF THE SALAMANDER

6

Blake woke up in his London flat feeling as clear-eyed and peppy as he had for months—since before he went underground in Paris, since before he chased Ellen to the moon, since before he went to Mars. Since before the last time he'd slept in this, his own bed, in fact. Which did not necessarily mean he was in good health. Somebody had shot him full of anti-hangover serum.

He jumped out of bed—he was wearing *pajamas,* for Pete's sake; he never wore pajamas, although his mother kept giving them to him for Christmas —and went into his bathroom.

Hmm, only a day's growth of beard. Odd. The back of his hand—he must have scraped it somehow—was shiny with new skin. Had the same Somebody used Healfast on him?

He ran his chemosonic shaver quickly over his cheeks and chin and throat and splashed his face with lime-scented aftershave; he probed his teeth with his ultrasound brush and ran his tongue over their polished surfaces, then slid a comb through his thick, straight hair and grimaced at his freckled face in the mirror.

For the first time on months Blake experienced the pleasure of having a full wardrobe open before him. He pulled on snug flexible cords and chose a loose black softshirt from his dresser. His watch and commlink and I.D. sliver were neatly laid out on the dresser top—even his black throwing knife. What must they have thought of that, whoever they were?

He slipped his bare feet into rope-soled navy blue Basque slippers. He didn't plan to go anywhere for an hour or two—not until he'd reacquainted himself with his home, not until he'd let the memories filter back. That was one of the little problems with anti-drunk drugs—they tended to block recent memories, at least until they wore off.

His sunny little kitchen was spotless, dustless, everything put away. Somebody had been over the place and wiped it clean—not his charlady; he didn't have one—and there was more food in his refrigerator than he could recall leaving there. Fresh, too.

He was hungry but not famished. On the gleaming gas range he made a two-egg omelet with herb cheese and ate it at the beechwood table overlooking his tiny brick-walled garden and those of his neighbors. The eggs disappeared fast; he followed them with a glass of orange juice he'd squeezed himself and a cup of French-roast coffee. His home was London, but he was still an American; no beans on toast for *his* breakfast, and he wanted something stronger than black tea to start his day.

The phonelink chortled, but he heard the click as he picked up the kitchen extension. Wrong number? Or Them, checking.

He took a second cup of coffee into the living room and sat contemplating the clear autumn sky through the branches of the big elm outside his window. The leaves were falling and the branches glistened in the low sun; sunlight brought out the rich blues and burgundies of the kilim on the floor and illuminated his floor-to-ceiling bookshelves, filled with rare printed books. The bold black Picasso minotaur in the alcove, the warm Arcadian

Poussin watercolor over the desk, reassured him that he was home.

Another sip of coffee. A tiny headache had started throbbing in his right temple. Memory was creeping back.

Night. An ivy-covered granite wall, lit by brilliant spotlights. Was he climbing on it? Yes, he was inching across its face toward . . . Ellen's window . . .

Window glass splintered and sprayed across the kilim. But this was real time! Blake reacted to the crash before he knew what it was, diving and rolling through the door into the hall.

A dragon's exhalation of flame spurted through the doorway behind him, searing the painted wooden frame into blisters and charring the papered wall opposite; he'd rolled just half a meter past the plume of fire, and he kept going on knees and elbows, into the kitchen.

He knew the smell of phosphorus and jellied gasoline intimately, thus knew that his books and paintings were already gone, that in minutes the whole apartment, the whole building would be going. Already the air under the ceiling was seething with black smoke.

Keeping to the cooler air near the floor, he went on through into his back porch workshop and kicked through the locked back door.

His flat was on the second floor. He leaped from the backstairs landing and crashed into the roof of a potting shed, taking the impact with flexed knees. On the rebound he jumped, landing in a myrtle tree in the garden.

He extricated himself from the branches. He didn't dare linger in the open. The attacker probably didn't have a gun, or maybe didn't know how to use one, for Blake had been literally a sitting target. But his assailant must be close, probably on an adjacent roof.

"Fire! Fire! Everybody out!" Blake yelled as he smashed his way through the garden gate and ran on through the narrow basement passageway to the street. "Fire!"

He came through the front to find people from across the street already pouring out of their doors. A big red-faced bobby was pelting toward him down the walk, jabbering into his comm unit as he ran. Blake looked up at the side of his flat.

A sucking gout of oily flame was rushing out of his shattered windows, blackening into a rising column of foul-smelling smoke. The old elm that had shaded his living room—it was in his neighbor's garden—was on fire. The roof of the building was beginning to shed scales of gray-brown smoke.

Old Mr. Hicke, his downstairs neighbor, stumbled out onto the porch, wearing flannel pajamas and a threadbare robe. "Mister Redfield! You've returned! Oh my—are you aware that your face is scratched?"

"This way, Mr. Hicke, away from the building. That's better. I'm afraid there's been a rather serious mishap."

Blake was about to plunge back through the front door when Miss Stilt and her mother, the only other residents of the building, emerged in wraps, bothered by the commotion and blinking at the light.

"That's all right, sir, if you'll just give us a bit of room here . . ." The bobby moved in to escort the ladies to safety; other police had arrived to hold back the quickly gathering crowd. Blake retreated with the crowd to the opposite side of the street.

He stood watching the graceful old building dissolve in flames. It was well on its way to becoming a gutted ruin before the first trucks arrived minutes later.

Whoever had thrown or launched the bomb must be long gone, unless that person was a committed firebug or for some other reason lacked a sense of self-preservation. Blake doubted it. Blake had been the specific target of the attack, and there was a message in the medium.

Blake himself had a weakness for blowing things up. Whoever had tried to kill him knew that.

He reviewed the morning's events and simultaneously realized that his memories of the night before—it must have been two nights before, allowing for the change in time zones—were almost fully restored. Along with a full-blown headache.

He remembered trying to rescue Ellen. He remembered her betrayal. He couldn't believe it.

Maybe she'd cut a deal with the commander to get him out safely. The commander knew Blake didn't trust him, and Blake knew he wanted to get him out of the way. Had she seen to it that Blake was treated well, returned to his home? And had the commander then betrayed *her?*

Or was someone else after his well-crisped hide? There were certainly enough candidates.

He watched the building burn, taking with it the last of the things he cherished. If he was to survive long enough to revenge himself, he'd better not hang around here waiting for the authorities to begin their tedious inquiries.

The hypersonic aircraft outraced the sun across the sky. It was still early morning when Blake landed on Long Island, and only a little after 10:00 A. M. when he let himself into his parents' Manhattan penthouse.

"Blake! Where on Earth have you been?"

"Mom, you look terrific. As usual."

Emerald Lee Redfield was a tall woman whose pampered skin, careful makeup, and exquisite clothing—today she was wearing a gray wool suit and a blouse of blue watered silk—always made her look thirty years younger, at least in the eyes of her son.

For all her elegance she was not skittish. She hugged him with enthusiasm. Then, keeping her

grip on his shoulders, she studied him at arm's length. "I wish I could say the same for you, dear. Did you sleep in your clothes?"

He laughed and shrugged.

"Come." She took his hand and led him toward the sunny living room. Eighty-nine stories up, it had a 120-degree view of the towers of lower Manhattan and the surrounding shores. "What are you doing home? Why haven't you called? We were so worried! Your father contacted practically everyone he knew, but no one . . ."

"Oh no!"

"Discreetly, discreetly."

"I'll have to have a talk with Dad. When I'm on the trail of a rare acquisition, I sometimes have to sort of . . . go underground. I must have explained all this a dozen . . ."

"Blake, you know how he is."

Edward Redfield had endlessly criticized Blake's career choice—that of a consultant specialist in old books and manuscripts—and occasionally launched into angry tirades against the money Blake was "throwing away" (money Edward could not control, as its source was a trust left to Blake by his grandfather). For Edward was of that class of old-family Eastern Seaboarders who were not required to do anything to make a living except watch over their investments—not that that was an insignificant task.

But _noblesse oblige_, and the Redfields were busy in the administrative and cultural affairs of Manhattan—this model city, the center of the Middle-Atlantic Administrative District. Indeed, so active had generations of Redfields been in public life that the present organization of the continent of North America (which no longer included a United States, except as a geographical fiction) owed much to their efforts.

Emerald seated herself on an Empire chair upholstered in blue velvet and pressed a button on the table beside her. "And I really did emphasize that he should act with discretion."

Blake fell back into an overstuffed, brocade-upholstered armchair. "Well, anyway, here I am. And, as you see, in good heath."

"This quest of yours . . . did you succeed?"

"Perhaps I'll be able to tell you when the, uh, transaction is complete."

"I understand, dear." A maid had appeared in response to Emerald's signal. "Your father and I are having lunch in today. Will you join us?"

"Love to."

"Another setting for lunch, Rosaria." The woman nodded and left as silently as she'd come. His mother smiled brightly at him. "Now Blake, what *happened?*"

"I got home this morning to find that my flat—not just *my* flat, the whole building—had burned to the ground. Everything I owned."

"My poor boy . . . your furniture? Your clothes?" She peered at his soiled canvas slippers.

"Not to mention the books, the art."

"So depressing, dear. You must be in a *state*. But of course you're insured."

"Oh, yes. Insured."

"That's a comfort, then."

"Well—I'll tell you all about it at lunch. Will you excuse me long enough to change out of these sweaty clothes?"

"Blake . . . it's so good to have you home."

He headed for the room that was always there for him, furnished precisely as he'd left it when he'd graduated from college. Despite the slight air of distraction with which his mother navigated life, she spoke from the heart. Love between parents and children is more complicated than it should be, he thought, and more subtle than anyone he'd read had ever been able to express adequately, but despite all the emotional harmonics and bass rumbles that accompanied the love between him and his mom and dad, love was solidly there among them.

He emerged from his old room wearing a respectable suit and tie, dressed the way he knew his father would want to see him.

"So you lost all those books you'd spent a small fortune on." Redfield *pere* was taller than his son, with a square patrician face mounted upon a squarer, even more patrician jaw. His gingery hair and eyebrows and the sprinkle of freckles across his fine nose hinted at his Boston Irish origins, suggesting that the money in the family was perhaps only two centuries old, instead of the three or four centuries claimed by those with names such as Rockefeller and Vanderbilt.

"Yes."

Edward glared at his son in ill-disguised triumph. "I hope you learned a lesson."

"More than a lesson, Dad. I lost everything. I won't be collecting anything of so perishable a nature again."

The dining room was in the southeast corner of the penthouse, overlooking old New York harbor. In the weak sunlight of autumn, the algae farms that covered the wide waters from the Jersey shore to Brooklyn were a dull matte green, like pea soup; stainless steel harvesters grazed languorously on the stuff, converting it to food supplements for the masses.

The Redfields were not of the masses. Edward sliced through the medium-rare *magret de canard* and put a left-handed forkful into his mouth, European-fashion. "The insurance wasn't adequate?" he mumbled.

"Oh, the financial loss is covered. Not allowing for appreciation. But I realized how ephemeral those old books and paintings are." Can I really get away with this? Blake wondered—but people are desperate to believe what they want. "Perhaps I've finally grown up."

Edward kept chewing and mumbled again.

"I've been thinking I might look around a bit and see if I can apply myself to public service," Blake added. His father having written him off as a dilettante, nothing could be sweeter to Edward than to hear his son come around to his point of view.

"What a fine idea, dear," his mother said brightly. "I know our friends will be more than happy to help you find something suitable."

"Why government, Blake? Why not something with more potential?" By which Edward meant buying and selling.

"I'm not really a statistics kind of guy, Dad. The market never made sense to me." False, but it fit Edward's prejudices. "If I'd followed your advice I'd have gone to law school," Blake added, truistically, "but it's too late for that."

"Well, what *are* you good at?" A whiff of the old rancor. After all, sending Blake to SPARTA had not been an inexpensive proposition; sure, that enhanced-education project had had foundation support, but parents like Edward who *could* pay had paid plenty to get their kids enrolled.

"I'm a good investigator—anybody who's serious about scholarship has to be. I know my way around old libraries as well as I know my way through electronic files. I can be inconspicuous when necessary." All this was true, and not the half of it; his father would not have believed even the half of it. "I read and write a dozen languages, I'm fluent in almost that many, and I can pick up more when I need them." Blake added something musical in Mandarin for the benefit of his mother, meaning roughly, *I owe it all to you.*

His father, who didn't speak Mandarin, although he was fluent in German and Japanese and the other old languages of diplomacy, emitted another skeptical mumble. When he finally swallowed his mouthful of duck he asked, "What sort of job do you think all this qualifies you for?"

"I forgot to mention that I've become a fairly experienced space traveler in the last year."

"You mean that trip to Venus?"

"I've been to the moon, too. And Mars. I guess it's been a while since I phoned home."

Edward put down his fork and glared at his son. "So. You're a multilingual . . . *investigator* . . . who knows computers and doesn't get spacesick. Maybe you should be a . . . a consumer advocate or something."

Emerald's thin black eyebrows shot up and her delicate mouth curved into a happy smile. "What an excellent suggestion, dear! I'm sure Dexter and Arista would be delighted to have someone of Blake's talent and abilities on their staff."

"At Voxpop?" Redfield looked at his wife, angrily. He hadn't intended to be taken seriously. "Doing what?"

Dexter and Arista Plowman, although born to wealth, were a brother and sister team of professional reformers, the sort of ascetics whose roles in previous centuries had been played by such as Ralph Nader and Savonarola. What money the Plowmans had once had, and whatever came their way, they invested in their Vox Populi Institute.

Emerald said, "If Dexter Plowman or his charming sister . . ."

"Peculiar sister," Edward growled. Away from his clubs and boardrooms, Edward's confusion frequently expressed itself as temper.

". . . wish to employ Blake, they will certainly use his best talents."

"And he gets nothing in return. No way to get rich."

Blake said, "Dad . . ." He cut himself short. We're al*ready* rich was a reminder his father didn't need to hear.

''Let's think about this for a day or two,'' said Edward.

Blake could see the wheels turning in his father's head. The Plowmans were Currently Fashionable Persons in Manhattan, somewhat of the rank of crusading district attorneys, people whose good opinions Edward Redfield had courted and to whom he would be honored to loan the services of a son. No money in it, but . . . his prodigal son Blake, reformed, and now a well-known public servant . . . Edward allowed himself a thin smile.

Late that night Blake tiptoed into his father's den, feeling his way by the faint light reflected through the windows from the hazy sky outside. Years ago, as a child, he had learned the combination to his father's desk, and he used it now to open the upper drawer in which was secreted Edward's whisper-quiet, gas-cooled, micro-super computer.

It was a machine Blake had always regarded with awe and a tinge of jealousy, since his father used only a vanishingly small fraction of its power in his business dealings and did not appreciate what his money had bought. Blake hunched over it and went quietly to work; his project would test the machine's mettle.

What was really going on at that ''safe house'' on the Hudson?

Four hours later: for all Blake's skill, his search had so far gained him little but negative knowledge.

The steel king's mansion was where it was supposed to be, all right; nowadays it was called Granite Lodge, a good, gray, innocuous name, and was supposedly used as a place where North American Park Service employees and their families could vacation, where dignitaries could retreat, where managers could confer, and so on—the usual sort of cover one might expect for so opulent a safe house.

Except that this cover seemed airtight. Blake could discover no links whatever between the Park Service and the Space Board, much less the commander's investigative branch. On the other hand, there were plenty of documented instances of use by vacationing employees, conferring managers, and retreating dignitaries.

In state files Blake found floor plans and other documents describing the house and grounds, all accurate as far as his personal knowledge went, and the Park Service's budget for the place with lists of the staff and their salaries and so on—and it all seemed aggressively innocent.

With sour amusement Blake read a wholly "factual" account of what had been going on there recently, when he and Ellen had somehow had the impression that they were the only guests. Seems they had overlooked a convocation of Anglican bishops, not to mention a creative writing seminar and a study session of high-school curriculum developers; this week the lodge was hosting a gathering of Jungian analysts.

A few minutes of effort produced independent "confirmation" of these events on the open network: notices and bulletins from bishops, writers, curriculum developers, and Jungians, all impenetrably convincing. Off the public net, Blake confirmed the existence of these people and the apparent authenticity of their recent itineraries.

Perhaps if he had had Ellen's uncanny ability to sniff out and avoid the electronic trapdoors and blind drops and cut-outs, to slip through layers of electronic subterfuge, to uncover fake I. D.s and fake addresses and commlinks and life histories and travel vouchers and so on, he could have gotten what he wanted from the computer net. But Ellen's powers were beyond him.

What was left to him was his skill as a thief and

saboteur. He would have to break into Granite Lodge.

Blake was bold, even excitable, but he was not foolhardy, and he was not in the habit of undertaking unknown risks or risks where the odds were too great against him; he had a healthy respect for the defenses of Granite Lodge. But although he would have much preferred to have stayed way from it, that option was closed.

He went back to the computer. In the latter years of the 21st century, weather prediction was still an art rather than a science, but it had become a fine art. The fractal patterns of the Earth's atmospheric system spilled across the flatscreen, unfolding in vivid false color a probable series of meteorological events for the lower Hudson valley in the coming days. If he acted soon, the weather would be on his side.

7

A green-eyed, red-haired young woman stood in a narrow London street, watching a bulldozer root and wallow in a mudhole across the road. To the left of the construction site, over the brick wall of the neighboring garden, a man in a yellow slicker was perched on a ladder, sawing a burned limb off a huge elm. To the right, plastic sheeting covered a hole in the roof of a neighboring building.

Where the bulldozer was snorting like a boar, Blake Redfield's apartment building had disappeared.

Sparta belted her shabby raincoat more tightly around her waist and hoisted her umbrella against the wind. She hurried along the pavement, dodging the umbrellas of the bent-over pedestrians coming her way. Half the oncomers seemed to be tangled in the leashes of their dogs, who were more eager than their masters to be outside on the wet, cold afternoon.

She walked half a mile through streets of declining prosperity to reach the nearest red-enameled infobox, which stood on a busy commercial corner. She collapsed her umbrella and shook it, then squeezed the door closed behind her. The glass panes were steamy, running with rain; the traffic on the street outside was a colorless blur. She slipped off her thin woolen gloves and leaned over the machine. PIN spines extended from beneath her sensibly short nails and probed the machine's ports.

The tang of dataflow rose in Sparta's olfactory lobes. Within seconds she had bypassed a hierarchy of barriers and, like a salmon swimming upstream, followed the current of information upstream to its source, a confidential file in Scotland Yard's bureau of records. It told her that Blake's apartment had been firebombed two days after he'd disappeared from the castle on the Hudson. He'd escaped unharmed and gone to join his parents in Manhattan.

The file revealed that the authorities had been irritated with Mr. Redfield for leaving the vicinity without notice. But when they'd finally tracked him down, he'd been most cooperative—and ultimately persuasive. He really had no idea who might want to kill him. He'd been away from home—spending most of his time in France, he explained—in connection with his profession as a consultant in rare books and manuscripts. Scotland Yard had accepted his explanation that he'd fled because he feared for his safety and that of his acquaintances in London.

Nice going, Blake, she thought, withdrawing her spines from the machine. You're safe and out of my way, which is apparently what we both want—and what I came here to ensure. I don't need your help on this one. I will smoke out the *prophetae* without you.

She left the booth and walked the wet pavement toward the nearest underground entrance. Robotaxis and private hydros hissed along the busy road, spraying oil and water in an aerosol like a heavy ground fog, but she was a working girl who could not afford the dry luxury of a cab interior.

As she bundled herself into the smelly warmth of the crowded tube station, she thought of the files she'd seen back on the Hudson and experienced a moment of regret. She'd let the commander persuade her not to call Blake, not to explain anything, even though she believed he deserved to know what she knew of the truth. But Sparta understood even better than the commander that if Blake learned the truth now, he'd do something. Dear Blake, so eager to help . . . but what he usually did under stress was go out and blow something up.

It always seemed to him so logical and necessary at the time. And it always made the situation worse. In this investigation she couldn't afford to have Blake going out and blowing things up, complicating matters. She would have to let him believe that she'd fired him, that she'd told him to get lost and stay lost. Or that she'd betrayed him. What the commander said he "remembered."

She would have to hope that when it was all over, when she could tell him the whole truth, he could learn to remember something different. And that he'd still love her.

That had been her first, not her only, disagreement with the commander. After agreeing not to try to contact Blake, she'd refused to say another word of substance to her boss until he'd kept his own parole. He'd handed her a triplet of chips, grudgingly, she thought, and left her alone in the downstairs conference room of the safe house.

The first chip held files from the long-defunct Multiple Intelligence project. In them, guarded by the logo of the quick brown fox, were details of the courses to which she'd been subjected—everything from quantum chemistry to southeast Asian languages to flight training—and all the surgical procedures to which she'd subsequently been subjected: nanochips in half a dozen locations in her brain, polymer electrical cells under her diaphragm, the PIN spines spliced into her nervous system. . . . It was all here, laid out in depth and detail: the plans and specs for taking a female human adolescent and converting her into a species of wet war machine.

Detailed too was the depth of her parents' involvement. Far from innocent victims, they had been eager participants in the establishment of M. I. At least in the beginning. As long as they thought the subjects of M. I. were going to be other people's children. . . .

But the files covered only one side of the correspondence, the M. I. side. The North American government, represented by the man who then called himself William Laird, had asked Linda's parents to act as principal consultants to the project. They were to be well paid, but that was not the only inducement. Concerning human potential, Laird had a vision that they evidently shared.

To them, this Laird apparently seemed visionary and sensible at the same time; he was not a believer in such superstitious nonsense as "memes" (one of her father's pet peeves), supposed "units" of culture with no common definition, discernible only after the fact. Laird meant evolution at the level of the organism itself, the physical human being as well as, inevitably, the cultural human being—thus not a teleonomic process, having the mere appearance of purpose, but an actual progression toward a well-defined goal: teleology from within.

Linda's parents were central in establishing the educational and testing programs of the Multiple Intelligence project. Then, suddenly, the record of their involvement ceased—shortly before the date corresponding to Linda's admission to the program, as its first subject. And its first, most spectacular failure.

Her parents were not mentioned again in M. I. files. Years went by; suddenly, almost overnight, Laird and many of his top staffers fled and M. I.

itself was disbanded, under circumstances Sparta knew intimately, for she herself had precipitated them.

A second set of files consisted of interrogations of captured *prophetae*. Captured by whom? Where the commander had obtained these, Sparta did not know. They were encoded in the commonest commercial system, and all identifying marks had been removed.

These were hair-raising tales. Deep probes had reconstructed the subjects' living memories: of terrifying childhoods; of failure, homelessness, addiction, and despair before first contact with the *prophetae*; of blossoming hope after recruitment, of indoctrination and training in the tenets of the Free Spirit; of their missions. To plug into these files was to relive a hell of lost souls.

Those whose memories had been extracted for display here had been soldiers of the Free Spirit. Two had been there the night Linda's father had tried to rescue her, the night his bodyguards had been slaughtered and Linda had been shot and the rescuing Snark, acting on her orders, had carried her wounded father and her mother into the night sky. By the witness of these files, Sparta—living what they felt, feeling what drove them—confirmed what she had believed, that it was the duty of the *prophetae* to kill anyone who had successfully resisted indoctrination.

And from these soldiers she learned the story they all believed, the story that had been reported in all media, that a Snark had crashed that night on a military reservation in Maryland, killing its passengers, her parents—other details withheld "in the interests of administrative security."

The last set of files was a various batch, some of them from the North Continental Treaty Alliance, some from police records and other terrestrial authorities. The Snark in which Linda's parents had tried to rescue her had been stolen from the

NCTA—how had they accomplished that extraordinary feat?—and the testimony of Laird and others placed the machine in Maryland, where the rescue attempt, described by Laird as assault and attempted kidnap, had failed.

But Sparta knew she had sent it off with orders to take all necessary measures to protect its passengers. It had obeyed, and vanished. The files revealed that no trace of it was recorded on radar scopes. No transmissions from it were overheard. It was never seen again. There had been no helicopter crash. Her parents had simply disappeared.

"Seen enough?" the commander whispered from the darkness. He had returned while she was absorbed in the last of the files, but she had not failed to hear him coming, to identify him in the dark.

"You promised to tell me what really happened to my parents. This doesn't do that."

"I admitted I couldn't prove what I know. But they are alive."

"You can't know that from this."

"What I firmly believe, then."

He was still holding something back, but she would not get it out of him with argument. In truth, he had given her something of great value. Often she'd roamed secretly and at will through the files of the agencies that had reported the helicopter crash. She had never found anything but obvious fakes replacing stolen records—fakes, booby-trapped with sticky bits, so that unauthorized persons who lacked her expertise peeking into those records would be automatically tracked back to their own terminals.

The commander's files were the stolen originals. Where and how he had gotten them, she didn't know.

"What do you want from me?" she asked.

"We'll be running a team on *Kon-Tiki*, some of them undercover, some in the open. You'll be on the clandestine side."

"You didn't keep your promise, Commander—I'm rewriting our contract. I'll cooperate with you, but not on a team."

"You're too well known, Troy. As soon as you stick your head up, somebody's going to shoot it off."

"I'll keep my head down. I will report to you and you only."

He heatedly argued the need for constant communication—impossible if she worked alone—the need for surveillance teams to follow suspects one person could not follow undetected, the need for close coordination with intelligence support, logistical support, etc. . . . She was unmoved.

"Alone then, if you must," he said at last. "I've arranged clinic sessions beginning tomorrow afternoon, at Earth Central."

"What sessions?"

"You can't keep that mug, Troy. You're an interplanetary viddie star."

"No."

"Do you like your looks better than the ones you were born with?" He sounded genuinely astonished.

"No more surgery."

He grew very still. "All right, why don't you just tell me now: what orders *are* you willing to take?"

"No orders, Commander. I'm willing to hear your suggestions."

"You think you don't need us, is that it?"

For an instant her gaze slid away, evading his.

"You're very wrong, you know," he said softly. "I hope you don't learn it the hard way."

"Everything of value that I know, I've learned the hard way." She meant to be hard when she said it, but she knew he wasn't fooled. She hadn't even fooled herself.

They had further fruitless talks, but before long he was saying a short goodbye to her in front of the Earth Central building on Manhattan's East River.

She was wearing Space Board blues and carrying a regulation duffel bag when she took a magneplane to the Newark shuttleport, but she never arrived there; as the saying around the investigative branch had it, she had gone off the scopes.

To disguise herself, she didn't bother with time-consuming and expensive plastic surgery. Surgeons kept records, and there was always the possibility that their greed would not stop with bills for services rendered but might extend to blackmail or betrayal. Instead she drew on an older tradition.

An altered hairstyle or a wig, colored contact lenses, a tuft of cotton under the tongue—sometimes just a spot of color on the cheeks—was enough, when combined with subtle changes of gesture and expression and accent, to make her unrecognizable to anyone but a well-programmed machine. Her first transitory disguise made use of a greasy black hairpiece with a ponytail down to her belt.

In a cosmos of strong and varied perfumes, altering her smell was even simpler. She wore leather pants and a leather jacket around the clock for a week and frequented New Jersey waterfront bars where the occupants mistook her ripe aroma for their own.

It needed a couple of days of stalking, keeping her eyes and ears open—she had very good eyes and ears—and some hours of haggling prices over pitchers of beer, but Sparta managed to acquire two illegally programmable I. D. slivers. She never met the people who'd made them, and the people who sold them to her had no idea who she was.

Less than twenty-four hours later, a pretty redhead named Bridget Reilly showed up at Newark and boarded the supersonic jitney for London.

8

Wearing a conservative dark suit and red silk tie, carrying the large black document case he usually carried, Blake left the fortified lobby of his parents' building at the same hour he had for the previous two weeks and headed uptown, taking one of Manhattan's restored antique subway trains.

He'd deliberately established a predictable pattern, spending the early morning hours on the commlink seeking job interviews and leaving home shortly before the lunch hour. He liked to travel by subway rather than robotaxi; by switching trains he could tell whether anyone was following him on foot.

He got off at his usual stop in the upper sixties and walked two blocks east on sidewalks bustling with happy workers and shoppers. It had rained the night before and the robosweepers had polished the shining marble streets. Now the clouds were breaking up, as Blake and everyone else who'd paid attention to the weather report knew they would, and their ragged remnants were tinged with gold in the noonday light.

Blake walked past the Indian restaurant that he'd made his favorite lunch place, but he didn't go in. He continued to the end of the block and used the public commlink on the corner of First Avenue to make a reservation for a compact hydro coupe, to be picked up in a village north of the city, on the east bank of the Hudson.

Then he caught a swift, quiet, hydro-powered uptown local bus and rode to the 125th Street plane station. The elevated station was the crystalline jewel of its renovated neighborhood, its entrance resplendent in an autumn display of maroon and yellow chrysanthemums.

Blake caught a fast magneplane upriver. He got off one stop before the village where he'd reserved his car and waited on the platform to see who else got off with him. No one worthy of suspicion. Good. Just before the magneplane's doors closed he got back on and rode it three more stops.

Making a reservation from a public infobooth had been a feint. The night before he'd used his father's computer to reserve a different car under a different name, originating from somewhere that would look—to even a determined observer—like a different place.

He picked up the little gray two-seater electric from the curbstand, freeing it from its shackle post by inserting his modified I. D. sliver. He drove slowly around the streets of the tiny town before heading north, into the preserve. He was confident that he had eluded surveillance.

Twelve hours later: it was 1:00 A.M., a cold and moonless night under a sky brightened only by hazy stars and the ring of reflecting space junk that circled the Earth all the way out to geosynchronous orbit. Blake had crept within sight of the outer perimeter of Granite Lodge.

The woods were thick with undergrowth and saplings, with an occasional dark conifer among the bare trunks of red oaks and maples and weedy sumac and the hundreds of other species preserved in the parklands of the Hendrik Hudson Preserve. Blake moved as quickly as he dared across the thick layers of dead leaves, still soaked from yesterday's rain.

He knew there were image enhancers and infrared sensors mounted at intervals around the electrified fence, and he knew there were motion detectors between the fence and the wall. There were chemical sniffers scattered throughout the woods, and organic sniffers—in the form of dogs—prowling the lawns. He knew that he was not going to slither undetected onto these grounds. There were no unguarded secret passages; no daring midnight climb up the cliffs would get him past the sentries.

But he'd prepared for all this. After hiding the rented car he'd shed his clothes and pulled on a full body suit of impermeable clear polymer, which incorporated a total skin-area heat exchange system and a shielded internal heat sink, mounted between his shoulder blades.

The heat sink would be saturated in little over an hour now, whereupon it would automatically vent a stream of superheated gas into the atmosphere behind Blake's head, turning Blake into a walking blowtorch. This would be inconveniently conspicuous, although preferable to the alternative—for if the unit failed to vent, it would go critical and turn Blake into a walking bomb.

Until that spectacular moment, however, Blake would stay as cool as a salamander. Externally he had the temperature of his surroundings—

—which made him invisible, not only to the infrared sensors but, since he was sealed in odorless plastic, to the sniffers as well.

His other preparations depended crucially upon the weather. Clear skies . . . The lightest of cool breezes flowing downriver from an approaching high pressure system . . . Right about now . . .

Yes, there they were, way off to his right, a fleet of orangy-pink glowing globes drifting among the stars—

—drifting down the wind, drifting toward the cluster of buildings on the center of the grounds, which were dominated by the stone mansion itself.

Lights blazed in the big house and across the grassy lawns. Barely visible human and animal shapes spilled out of darkened doorways and spread to the sides, keeping to lanes of shadow in a well-rehearsed defensive pattern.

No sirens sounded, however. Blake knew from experience that the folks at Granite Lodge didn't want to wake their neighbors unless they thought they had something really serious on their hands. Which is why there'd been no sirens the night he tried to break Linda out of there.

Blake caught the faint but frantic hum of multiple step-monitors as the nearest railguns bobbed and swung, searching the skies, but no hypersonic chunks of steel were launched at the glowing globes overhead. The globes were virtually invisible to a very confused AARGGS, the anti-aircraft railgun guidance system—

—because the targets were only twenty meters off the ground, unreflective, and so small that at radar wavelengths software written for targets no smaller or lower or slower than parasails and hang-gliders couldn't resolve them.

Blake was attacking Granite Lodge with a fleet of stealth balloons. It would have been overkill to shoot down toy balloons with hypersonic missiles. Still, if the radars found their targets and the railguns fired, it would ruin Blake's scheme.

There were a dozen of the gossamer silk dirigibles, each powered by nothing higher-tech than a bit of burning parafin—a fat candle, bright in the infrared—but steered by feathery vanes and gill-like vents that opened and closed according to instructions from sophisticated guidance chips—preprogrammed for tonight's weather. Slowly, silently, the dirigibles tracked their targets with microscopic visual sensors, drifting in like a fleet of stinging jellyfish.

Too late for AARGGS. Now the human defenders of the lodge opened fire on the aerial fleet—but like the radars, they misjudged the size and range of their targets.

Blake kept still in the darkness, taking long seconds to observe; these defenders were skittish killers, if they were killers at all. Their weapons were silenced, and they weren't using tracer bullets. And their noise suppressors played havoc with accuracy. Without tracers they had no way of knowing where their bullets were going in the night sky. They might even be so scrupulous, Blake thought, as to be using rubber bullets, as they had the night he tried to escape.

Someone got lucky: a burst from an automatic weapon hit one of the little balloons.

There was a blinding flash and a terrific report. Spectacular streamers of light shot out of the blazing balloon as it fell to the wet lawn, where—in an effect so weirdly counterintuitive as to seem alien— it erupted in frenzy, sending little balls of pinkish yellow fire skittering across the damp grass like tiny creatures desperately running for cover. At the uncanny sight, well trained guard dogs howled and fled.

If Blake hadn't been so involved in the moment, he would have laughed. Those bouncing, scurrying points of pink light were a handful of BBs of sodium metal, fizzing into tiny rockets upon contact with the wet grass.

Now the rest of the fleet found their objectives. White, pink, and yellow fireworks erupted on the roof of Granite Lodge. A couple of balloons floated under the porch roof and flashed into incandescence, setting the big wooden beams and the knotty pine planks ablaze.

The three little airships that had been targeted for the garage landed almost simultaneously. Less than a minute later the garage's hydrogen reservoir went off like a real bomb, blowing the walls out of the old carriage house and reducing the vehicles inside to vigorously burning wreckage as a great ball of flaming hydrogen rose into the night sky.

So much for waking the neighbors.

Blake figured he'd created about as much diversion as he could. He went swiftly through the remaining strip of woods. The electrified fence yielded to clips and cutters from his pack. As he crossed the ten meters to the low stone wall he hoped the guardians of the lodge were really as benign as he supposed, for this was the right place for antipersonnel mines in the ground and fléchette booby traps in the trees.

He reached the wall without incident. The orange flames from the porch and garage cast dancing cross-shadows on the side lawn. The area ahead of him was lit only by floodlights. He clambered over the wall, careful of the thin plastic skin that was all he had between him and the black, angular stones. He moved into the white light, walking confidently upright. May as well be confident. Nothing could hide him now, until he reached the triangular shadows beneath the walls.

Once into the darkness near the house he ducked and ran and vaulted onto the side porch. Doors were open where the staff had run out to defend the place. A human shape passed him at the corner of the veranda, shouting back over a shoulder. Blake ducked inside the nearest door.

He went through the darkened library, into the entrance hall. The plans he'd studied, although he knew they lied, had nevertheless revealed the location of the lodge's nerve center. While the huge curving main staircase left an impression of massive foundations, Blake knew there was a room under the stairs, a big room, no doubt acoustically silenced and furnished with consoles and flatscreens and videoplates, perhaps comfortable couches and chairs.

With his clock running out fast he didn't have a lot of time. He found the lock, hidden in the carved wooden paneling, and packed it with plastic. He stepped back seconds before the door crashed inward. He tossed a gas grenade into the room, waited a few seconds, and as he ducked into the room he dropped another grenade behind him in the hall. Why not, *he* wasn't breathing the stuff!

Inside the room, a lone young woman in a white uniform was already sound asleep in her contour chair in front of the display screens, her head thrown back and her long blond hair spilling almost to the carpet. Her right arm hung over the chair and her fingers trailed on the carpet.

As Blake pulled her chair back, away from the console, his gaze was snagged by the ring she wore on the middle finger of that trailing hand, a gold ring set with a garnet carved in the shape of an animal. Later he was to realize that if some recent, separate thought hadn't formed an association in his mind, he would have forgotten the ring as quickly as he noticed it.

Blake looked at the screens and determined that the defense forces were outside diligently putting out fires. He studied the board and realized this was nothing but an I/O layout; the processors were elsewhere.

He took a moment to absorb the room's plan, following the electrical buses and cooling lines . . . *there* were the main computers, inconspicuous in an equipment rack against the short end of the room, where the ceiling descended steeply under the stairs. He didn't have time to stay and play— he tore them out of the rack, breaking their connections, and stuffed them into his pack. He took the trays of chips he found nearby and emptied them in on top before he sealed the pack's flap.

He was out of the room and through the smoke-filled hall—

—he was into the darkened library and through it, and through the doors, and onto the porch—

—he was vaulting the porch rail, hitting the soft grass running . . . running and running across it, catching sight of other running shapes out of the corners of his eyes . . . over the wall, through the fence, into the woods. . . .

He took care to slow his pace, to move with caution and stealth through the damp woods. Behind him, the night sky was aglow with the burning. Sirens and amplified squawks from commlinks and the guttural roar of high-powered, hydrocarbon-burning engines approaching up the main drive drifted on the night, covering the squish of wet leaves underfoot and the scraping of branches as he worked his way through the woods.

His car was parked some twenty minutes' walk ahead through the night woods, well off the road, but a glance at his plastic-covered watch showed he had a wider time margin than he'd planned, so he kept the plastic suit on; it was all that protected him from the bitter cold.

He found the car without trouble—he was a confident nighttime navigator—and tossed his pack into the forward luggage compartment. He slammed the hood down upon it, then opened the door on the driver's side. He reached in and fetched his sliver from under the seat. He inserted it in the ignition; the board showed power to the wheel motors.

He reached to rip open the front of his plastic suit, which would disable the heat transfer system. Once he was safely away, he could dump the stored energy in the suit's heat sink. Before he got his hand on the seam sealer, they came out of the woods—

—three of them in white uniforms, all young, all blond, none looking very happy.

''Hands up,'' said the leader softly. He was a tall kid with a blond crewcut so short he looked bald.

They had him on three sides, and all of them were pointing assault rifles at him. At this range it didn't matter whether the bullets were rubber or not. They could still rupture his spleen or put out his eyes or break something else valuable.

Baldy looked at Blake, naked inside his clear plastic suit, and sneered. ''Fetching outfit.''

''Glad you like it,'' Blake said, his words muffled through the plastic film that covered his mouth. What could you do when you were wearing nothing but sandwich wrap, except try to hold on to your sense of humor?

Baldy gestured to his two companions. They bundled into the cramped back seat of the little electric while Baldy kept his rifle pointed at Blake's lower middle section. ''You drive,'' he said.

''Four people weigh a lot,'' Blake mumbled. ''I don't know if I have enough charge for all of you.''

''We're not going far. Get in.''

Blake eased himself into the driver's seat, hunched forward because of the heat-sink unit between his shoulder blades, intensely aware of the gun muzzles pointed at his neck from the back seat. Baldy slid in beside him. Blake eased off the clutch; the motors whirred and engaged and the car slithered over the muddy track. When he reached the paved country road, Blake turned in the direction of the lodge's main drive.

They drove slowly and silently, until Blake asked, ''How did you happen to get to my car ahead of me?''

''Not something you need to know.''

''Okay, but are you sure you want me to drive you all the way back to the lodge in this thing?''

''Just drive.''

Blake glanced at the pale blue digital display on his left wrist. ''I have to get out for a minute. Just for a minute.''

Baldy smirked at him. ''It will have to wait.''

''It won't wait.''

A muzzle pressed Blake's neck, and an intimate whisper sounded close to his ear. ''We don't care if you fill up your whole body-baggie,'' said the boy behind him. ''You're not getting out of this vehicle until we tell you to.''

Blake shrugged and drove on, down the tree-crowded road, his headlights illuminating bare tree trunks like ghosts in the darkness.

The little electric car was slowing for the lodge's double steel gate when Blake's heat sink went critical. The unit started to whistle.

''What the hell's that?''

''I need to get out of the car right now,'' Blake said, groping for the door handle.

''Watch it!'' yelled the boy in the back seat. ''Hands on the wheel.''

In seconds the whistle was a shriek.

''Let him out,'' said the girl in the back. ''Let me out too.''

Too late. A high-pressure column of blue flame erupted from the unit between Blake's shoulders; from the back it must have seemed that his head was a volcano. The plastic upholstery burst into flame, releasing acrid black fumes. A hole opened in the thin sheet metal roof of the car.

Spouting a spectacular plume of flame, Blake stumbled and staggered out of the car, a man burning alive. His terrified captors scrambled out of the vehicle behind him, staring at him in horror.

Reeling from the awful heat, dying before their eyes, Blake stumbled back toward the smoking vehicle and collapsed into the driver's seat. With a last agonized spasm, an unconscious reflex of escape, he threw the pots into reverse high. The burning car jerked away and spun around, throwing flaming bits across the wet roadway, careening crazily off into the forest.

But somehow the car stayed on the road. Blake hadn't watched all those action-adventure holoviddies, with stuntmen lunging around cloaked in flame, without getting the technique down pat.

9

Blake tugged the knot of his silk tie and smoothed it to lie flat against his white cotton shirt. He snugged his suit jacket neatly around his shoulders and, a moment later, rose as the magneplane slowed for the Brooklyn Bridge station. Someone looking closely might have noticed the red welt across the back of his neck, but a quick glance around reassured him that no one was watching.

He stepped off the plane, briefcase in hand, and briskly marched to the escalator. Minutes later he was on his way back uptown on a restored antique subway train. A century ago it would have been rush hour, but the bright, clean subways were never crowded these days. He got off at a midtown station. As he emerged from underground, the rising sun was touching the tops of the glittering towers around him with pale yellow light.

The physical exhilaration of the attack and narrow escape had drained away, and he experienced a moment's dejection. He wasn't even sure who or what he'd been fighting—or why, now that Ellen had rejected him, except for some vague sense of his own injured pride. Simple fatigue is a great discourager of pride. With self-hypnotic effort, he regained at least a temporary feeling of confidence.

He was on the way to another job interview, and this was for a job he wanted.

The offices of the Vox Populi Institute occupied a three-story brick building in the east 40s, within walking distance of the Council of Worlds complex on the East River. Plain as it was, the building was worth a fortune.

Inside, the decor was even plainer—steel desks, steel chairs, steel filing cabinets, crumbling bulletin boards, crumbling paint (institutional green to shoulder height, institutional cream above), and aggressively plain and surly office help, one of whom finally agreed to show Blake the general direction of Arista Plowman's office. Dexter was not in today.

Arista, it was said, was less tolerant of human foibles than Dexter—theirs was a prickly partnership—she being as far out on one end of the political spectrum as he was on the other. Arista championed humanity at large, Dexter championed the individual human with an actionable grudge. Their differences hardly made a difference to anyone but them, since Dexter's favored weapon in defense of the individual was the class-action suit, and Arista's tactic in defense of the People was to take up the cause of a single, symbolic Wronged Innocent.

She glanced up when Blake appeared at her door and knew instantly she was not dealing with a Wronged Innocent. She growled something like "siddown" and made a pretense of studying his resume.

Arista was a bony woman with heavy black brows and grayish black hair that was contracted into tight waves against her long skull. Her severe dress, black with white polka-dots, hung askew from her wide shoulders, and the way she leaned her elbows on her desk top and perched her skinny bottom on the edge of her chair conveyed her desire to be somewhere else. She shoved the resume to one side of her desk as if it had offended her. "You worked for Sotheby's, Redfield? An auction house?"

"Not on staff. They frequently retained me as a consultant."

Her mouth twisted sourly at the sound of his Brittainted accent. Her own accent was good American, pure Bronx—even though she'd been born and raised in Westchester County. "But you were an *art* dealer." The emphasis alone neatly conveyed her opinion of those who sold things, especially expensive, decorative, useless things.

"In a manner of speaking. Rare books and manuscripts, actually."

"What makes you think you have anything to offer us? We're not here to serve the whims of the rich."

He indicated the scrap of fax she'd brushed aside, his resume. "Extensive research experience."

"Well, we have no shortage of researchers in this office." She started to rise, intending to terminate the interview after thirty seconds.

"Also the work I've already done on a case of utmost interest to your Institute."

"Redfield . . . *Mister* Redfield . . ." She was at the office door now, opening it and holding it open.

He remained sitting. "Powerful agencies of the Council of Worlds have been infiltrated by a pseudo-religious cult, which seeks to take over world government in the name of . . . of an alien deity."

"A *what?*"

"Yes, it's crazy. These people believe in an alien deity. I managed to join an arm of that cult. I can recognize several of its members and at least one of its leaders. Because of what I know, several attempts have been made on my life, the most recent only last week."

Arista let the door swing closed, but she remained standing. "What sort of cult did you say? UFO nuts?"

Perhaps he'd been lucky after all. Arista Plowman's fascination with conspiracy had engaged her attention. Her brother might have just laughed and referred him to the police.

"They call themselves the *prophetae* of the Free Spirit, but they have other names and cover organizations. I penetrated a branch working out of Paris and helped put it out of business"—after all, no reason for modesty—"They worship a being they call the Pancreator, an alien creature of some kind who is supposed to return to Earth to grant the enlightened—meaning themselves—eternal life, and carry them off to some sort of Paradise. Or perhaps establish Paradise right here on Earth."

"I'm not vulnerable to every conspiracy theory that comes down the pike, Redfield."

Oh, I think perhaps you are, he thought happily, keeping a straight face. "I can document everything I'm telling you."

"Well, but what possible interest do you suppose Vox Populi might have in this bunch?"

"The *prophetae* are crazy, but they are numerous and extremely influential. Less than ten years ago, members of the Free Spirit started the Multiple Intelligence program inside North America's Security Agency. That program ceased operations—and its leaders disappeared—when the subject of one of their illegal experiments escaped their control. But not before they had murdered a couple of dozen people. Burned them to death in a sanatorium fire."

"Ten years ago, though. A dead issue by now, unfortunately."

"Less than a month ago, the Space Board discovered an interplanetary freighter, the *Doradus*, which had been converted to a kind of pirate ship. The chief of one of the largest corporations on Mars was implicated. Jack Noble. He's disappeared."

"I heard about that. Something to do with the Martian plaque."

"I was there. I'll give you whatever details you want." Blake leaned back in his chair and looked up at her as she thoughtfully returned to her desk. "Doctor Plowman, you're supposed to be in the business of getting government back into the hands of the governed—after people like my father, if I may speak off the record, helped take it away from them. This is exactly the kind of group I should think you'd want to put out of business."

"Your *father* is a member of this Free Spirit?"

"I assure you he is not." He couldn't tell whether the prospect appalled her or further whetted her appetite. "He is just a well-meaning . . . aristocrat."

Arista Plowman resumed her seat behind the steel desk. "Your resume doesn't say anything about the things you've just described to me, Redfield."

"I'm a marked man, Doctor Plowman."

"So with you here, we could be a target."

"You've been a target for so long that your defenses are excellent. I made sure of that before I came here."

She smiled thinly. "Are you safe in your own home?"

"My parents have had so much *money* for so long that their defenses are almost on a par with yours."

"Why didn't you go to the Space Board in the first place?"

Blake's smile was grim. "Why do you think?"

"Are you implying that the Board of Space Control itself . . . ?"

"Exactly."

Her eyes glazed over with the possibilities, and her feral smile made him feel sure he had a job offer. But it wasn't to be quite that easy. Long experience had taught Arista Plowman caution.

"Interesting, Redfield, very interesting. I'll talk to my brother. He'll want to meet you in person. Meanwhile, don't call us. We'll call you. . . ."

Outside, Blake realized that the interview—not to mention the night's events—had left him exhausted. Exhaustion is hard on the reflexes. When a tall, emaciated young man crossed the street in front of him and darted into the nearest infobox, throwing a hurried glance over his shoulder, Blake thought nothing of it. Indeed, he hardly noticed, until he'd come within a few meters and the man suddenly wheeled and raised his arm.

Blake spun on his heel, in that instant finally recognizing the man, and threw himself backward toward the curb.

The bullet blew a crater in a marble slab on the side of the building, just about where Blake's head had been. More bullets—real metal bullets, fired with zeal and accuracy that, if less than perfect, was too great for even a split second's complacency on the part of the target—following Blake's breathless roll and scramble along the gutter until he reached the shelter of a parked robotaxi. People were screaming and running—this sort of thing *never* happened in Manhattan—and in seconds the block was deserted.

Blake swore at himself for not spotting his assailant sooner, for he knew him quite well. Leo—former wimp—one of his buddies from the Athanasian Society. Blake wished he had a gun. He didn't carry one, not just because they were strictly illegal in England, where he'd resided for the last two years, and not because he had any qualms about defending himself, but because he'd looked at the statistics and calculated the odds and figured he had a better chance of staying alive without one.

Deliberate assassination wasn't included in the odds. He reached up to open the front door of the cab. He slipped inside, keeping his head low, and shoved his I.D. sliver into the meter.

"Where to, Mac?" the cab asked, in a good imitation of early 20th-century New Yorkese.

Blake stuck his head under the dash and spent a few seconds fiddling with the circuitry. Still crouched on the floor, he said, "Is there a skinny long-haired guy in the infobooth on the next corner, to your left?"

"He just left the infobooth. Now he's in the doorway this side of it. Looks like he's thinking about coming this way.''

''Run into him,'' Blake said.

''You puttin' me on?''

''There's a twenty in it for you.''

''Twenty what?''

''Twenty thousand bucks. You don't believe me, take the credit off the sliver now.''

''Yeah, well . . . look, Mac, I don't do stuff like . . .''

Blake poked savagely at the circuitry.

''*Yo*,'' said the taxi, and leaped forward, onto the sidewalk. Bullets splintered the windshield of the Checker—then a grinding jolt threw Blake hard against the firewall.

He kicked the door open and rolled out onto the sidewalk. He vaulted onto the big square trunk of the Checker and threw himself across the cab roof like a runner diving for home plate.

The taxi hadn't touched Leo, but it had him trapped in the recessed doorway with only millimeters to spare. Leo was frantically trying to lift his big feet past the mangled bumper when Blake flew over the roof, into his face, knocking the big nickel-plated .45 revolver sideways and out of his hand. Leo's head crashed backward into the building's art deco stainless steel door, and when he tried to jerk away from Blake's hand around his throat he found that Blake's other hand held a black knife, poised rigidly upright under the angle of his jaw.

''Rather have you alive, Leo,'' Blake gasped. ''So tell me.''

Leo said nothing, but his round terrified eyes said he'd rather stay alive too—although Blake got the impression he'd been ordered to die instead of letting himself be captured.

The flutter of helicopter rotors sounded high above the urban canyon, and the scream of sirens converged at street level.

''Tell me why, Leo, and I'll let you run. If the

cops get you, the *prophetae* won't let you live even one night in jail.''

''You *know*. You're a *Salamander*,'' Leo croaked.

''What the hell's a salamander?''

''Let me go,'' he croaked. ''I won't come back, I promise.''

''Last chance—what's a salamander?''

''Like you, Guy. Initiates once—now you're traitors. The ones who know you best . . . we're sworn to kill you.''

''You bombed my place in London?''

''Not me. Bruni.''

''Yeah, she always had more guts.''

''You didn't even hide, Guy. If you're gonna let me go, please do it now.''

''My name's Blake. Might as well get it straight.'' He released his grip on Leo's throat, but held the knife ready. ''Cabbie, back up a little,'' he yelled. ''Go slow.''

As soon as the Checker had backed far enough away from the doorway, Leo bolted. Blake slipped the knife into its sheath at the small of his back and slid down from the cab's hood. ''We need a story,'' he said, sticking his head in the taxi's window.

''It'll cost you more than twenty thou,'' the taxi said sourly.

''Charge what you think is fair.''

''Okay, Mac. What do you want me to say?''

Blake reached into the taxi and retrieved the briefcase he'd dropped on the floor. ''The guy tried to rob me. You came to my rescue—that's when he shot at you. You almost had him trapped, but he got away.''

''What about all the extra dough on my meter?''

''The truth—I let you charge off my sliver as a reward for saving me. Also to patch your dents.''

''Sure, Mac. Think they'll buy it?''

''You're programmed for gab, aren't you?''

''Hey! Am I a Manhattan cabbie, or what?''

The first police car, a sleek powder blue hydro—no quaint antiques here—whistled to a halt as the police chopper settled in to hover overhead. Blake watched the cops approach, faceplates down, shotguns leveled. At this rate, who knew which side they were on?

After almost two hours' interrogation, the police let Blake go. He got off the subway in Tribeca and walked toward his parents' home, past columns of steam issuing from manhole covers, down deserted asphalt streets where the robotaxis prowled like jungle beasts. Manhattan had become a showplace in this century, an exclusive enclave of the wealthy, and here and there the atmosphere of old New York was maintained for amusement's sake.

Things were busier at the waterfront entrance to his parents' building. Blake nodded at the guard captain as he punched the code into the lock of the private elevator to the penthouse. The other guards were out of public view.

Avoiding his mother—his father was on business in Tokyo, business which required his physical presence—Blake went straight to his room.

He stripped off his torn jacket and soiled shirt and tie and gingerly applied Healfast salve to his blistered neck. The growth factors went to work immediately. By afternoon there would be little evidence of his second-degree burns.

Comfortably dressed in baggy pants and a blousy, Russian-peasant-style shirt, he took his scarred briefcase into his father's office and emptied its contents across the top of the desk—the loot from his raid on Granite Lodge.

A scatter of tiny black chips and two micro-supercomputers, their housings cracked where he'd pulled them out of the system . . . he hoped he hadn't fried them in their own heat. For micro-supers—not unlike men encased in impermeable plastic suits—generated copious amounts of heat; if they weren't vigorously cooled by water or some other fluid, they could burn in seconds.

It took Blake a quarter of an hour to get the first of

the two little machines operating; for input he used his father's keyboard, and the output was displayed on the desktop via his father's holo unit. But after another hour's concentrated tapping Blake gave up trying to extract anything from that machine. Nothing he tried got more than a scramble of standard code symbols on the holo projection, and he suspected that the thing was indeed fried.

He had more luck with the other machine, but only just: after forty minutes of increasingly frustrating play—it kept telling him he was an unauthorized user—he got up and went to stand in front of the window, staring with unseeing eyes into the haze, looking across the lower Hudson to the smoky Jersey shore. He tried to empty his mind of everything except the experiences of the night. It was a species of self-hypnosis, in which he tried to see and hear again everything he had seen and heard inside the lodge.

He went back to the desk and typed a word. A few millimeters above the green leather surface of Edward Redfield's desk, the air glowed.

No message appeared, however, neither a welcome nor a warning. Instead, an animal writhed there in three dimensions. It was a lizardlike creature with a thick tail and a wide triangular head, with tiny gleaming round brown eyes. Its awkward thin legs had splayed toes ending in thick pads. The thing's moist skin was coppery brown, with a bright yellow underbelly.

The string Blake had entered into the machine was SALAMANDER, the term Leo had used to accuse him—and the creature he had seen carved on the unconscious girl's garnet ring.

Nothing encourages persistence like a minimal reward. Blake persisted for another two hours, trying all the chips he'd stolen, one after the other. He got nothing more. Nothing but that writhing salamander.

Bone weary from the night's exertions and the morning's concentrated effort, hunched over an unyielding machine, Blake fell asleep.

* * *

He was awakened by the beat of wings.

No, not wings, rotor blades.

He sat bolt upright, and as soon as he remembered where he was and what he had been doing, he threw himself flat on the floor. But the steady *whuff whuff whuff* of the helicopter outside the window neither increased nor diminished. He crept across the floor and raised his eye to the level of the sill.

A black silhouette, a hole in the sky, diffuse and without detail against the bright haze in the west; the thing just hung there in space, eighty-nine stories above the streets of Manhattan, twenty meters away and exactly opposite the window of his father's office. A Snark. A Snark as Boojum.

As Blake watched, the machine slowly rotated on its axis, until its strut-mounted rocket launchers and twin Gatling guns were pointed straight at him through the window.

Blake didn't move. There was nowhere to run or hide. The Snark carried enough firepower to wipe the penthouse right off the skyscraper on which it sat. The metropolitan police should have been here by now, within seconds of the Snark's arrival. That they were nowhere in evidence spoke volumes. Blake could reach for the controls to the apartment's private defenses—they were inside his father's desk—but even if he reached them alive, he doubted the rooftop rockets could put a dent in a Snark.

Blake stood up, exposing himself to the full view of the machine's pilot. *If you are here to kill me, do it cleanly*, he said without words.

The Snark bobbed its nose. *Yes, we understand each other. Yes, we could do that. Yes, we know it was you, and now you know we can kill you and the people you love, any time we want to.*

Then the machine lazily arched into the air and slid away, peeling off toward the river. Within seconds Blake had lost sight of it in the dazzling bounce of light from the plain of wet algae. It left an unspoken message in its wake: *The next move is yours.*

Blake walked back to the desk. He carefully unplugged the functioning computer and put it and the machine he'd probably scragged into an express envelope, along with all the stolen black chips. He took a thick pen from his father's drawer and wrote in bold block letters across the face of the envelope, "ATTENTION SALAMANDER, C/O NORTH AMERICAN PARK SERVICE, GRANITE LODGE, HENDRIK HUDSON PRESERVE, NEW YORK ADMINISTRATIVE DISTRICT." The address wasn't complete but it was more than sufficient. If they controlled the police, no doubt they had some clout with the postal service.

He swung a windbreaker over his arm, covering the envelope, then left the penthouse and took the elevator to the bottom of the tower. If anything went wrong, he wanted it to go wrong at some distance from his parents' building. This package he would mail from some anonymous neighborhood box.

As he walked the windy streets toward uptown, Blake faced the fact that he was not a happy man. The woman he'd thought he loved wanted nothing to do with him. All the physical possessions he'd valued had been destroyed.

So the Salamanders were former Initiates, were they? Heretics. Rivals to the *prophetae*, and like them, deep into the workings of the system. Blake had thought he could make himself so visible he couldn't be hit without scandal. A forlorn hope. Even if the Plowmans offered him that job at Vox Populi, he owed it to them not to accept.

He'd dragged his own parents into danger, a degree of danger he had foolishly underestimated. Whatever else he did or didn't do, he had to move out of his parents' penthouse. Fast.

10

Sparta found a job at J. Swift's, a large travel agency in the City of London whose computers were rather better connected—for someone of Sparta's leanings—than the firm's managers suspected. They readily hired the girl with the sparkling green eyes and the Irish lilt who called herself Bridget Reilly, and who produced an impressive resume of service in the travel industry.

For the next weeks and months her life was too tedious to contemplate: long hours in front of a flatscreen, speaking into a commlink with clients and other agents, booking and endlessly rebooking flights and rooms and ground transportation for people who couldn't seem to make up their minds or abide by their agreements, and cheerfully accepting responsibility for atrocities over which she had no control—many of them stemming from the middle-class, middle-aged English tourist's desire to experience foreign culture as if through a tea-room window, most of the rest resulting from the young English tourist's conviction (like that of youth everywhere) of personal blamelessness and immortality.

Bridget Reilly was the soul of friendliness at work, but her coworkers, male and female, soon learned that she had not the least interest in getting to know them better than her job required. When the workday was over, Ms. Reilly rode the underground to a tiny, ugly apartment in a dirty, ugly neighborhood, where prudence suggested she keep indoors, away from her neighbors and other strangers. She thawed dinner each night in an autochef; after she ate she went straight to her narrow bed. Six hours later the room's tiny videoplate would brighten the predawn darkness with the BBC's morning news, waking her to another day.

Her inward life was richer and stranger by far.

By night, there were dreams. Night after night she descended into the vortex of lurid clouds. She knew they were the clouds of Jupiter; more than that she did not know. The wind sang to her in a language she could not name, and although she seemed to understand it perfectly she could never remember a word of what had been said when she woke up. All she could remember were the tumbled emotions of ecstasy and fear, of ego-dissolving hope, of poisonous self-hatred.

By day, her intellect was the very edge of Occam's razor. While she booked group tours to Port Hesperus and Labyrinth City with one hand on the keyboard, her other hand rested with PIN spines extended, penetrating her computer's ports, running other programs in the interstices of processing. She needed no screen except the one in her head.

Not even the commander knew where she was or who she pretended to be. She maintained tenuous contact with him through untraceable circuits to his office at the Board of Space Control—somehow he was never in his office—but on the rare occasions they actually conversed, she made little pretense of heeding his suggestions; she was not running *his* programs. Indeed, although she said nothing of this to the commander, she had deferred her researches into Howard Falcon's affairs while she investigated a deeper mystery, the contents of her own mind. . . .

Seated at her travel agency computer, she absorbed whole encyclopedias of neuroanatomy, neurochemistry, drug lore. Using the infolinks, she arranged prescriptions for women who did not resemble each other and did not resemble Bridget Reilly in the least; late at night, in neighborhoods filled with people of wealth or people of color, these women collected their medicines. Sparta's pill and patch collection grew into a pharmacopeia.

At the safe house they'd used drugs on her in an attempt to penetrate her dreams. But she'd refused to work with the commander on his terms; perhaps because of that, perhaps for some deeper reason, the commander had refused to share everything they'd learned from that part of herself she could not reach. Now she used drugs on herself, trying to crack her own subconscious.

Amphetamines and barbiturates and psychedelics acted on her just as a century's documentation said they would; they were useless. Metal salts changed her behavior and threatened to poison her internal organs and left her mind reeling. Alcohol increased the rate of dreaming but reduced the cogency of the dreams and left her nauseated in the morning, with burning eyes. The known neurotransmitters—dopamine and the rest—seemed to add vivid flourishes to familiar dream scenes, but did nothing for her insight or her memory.

Her researches took her farther afield. One taste of a chemical on her tongue and she knew what she was ingesting, for its precise formula spread itself across the screen of her mind. Of the estimated 30,000 significant proteins and peptides in the brain, a comparative handful had been characterized. Still, it was a long list. Methodically she worked her way through it. She recorded the effects of her self-experimentation with clinical accuracy.

But she became ever more isolated. Her coworkers thought she disdained them, and they developed a cordial, low-temperature hatred for her in return. Still, her sacrifices were not in vain. After weeks of horrific nights, she stumbled upon a result.

A short-chain peptide, some nine amino-acid residues long, known to play a role in the formation of the striped columns of the visual cortex, seemed to release an image from her dreams, allowing it to be held in memory.

With the image a word was associated, perhaps two words, whose meaning she did not recognize: "moonjelly."

She took more of the peptide, a cheap and simple preparation that in the previous decade had been a favorite of some aggressively inclined psychotherapists, the type who liked roughing up their clients in the name of love and were inclined to become impatient with the slow unfolding of the talking cure. Cutely, they'd called the stuff Bliss. Bliss had started in the designer drug labs on L-5 as an analogue of controlled substances, not itself illegal. But it quickly made its way to Earth, where it soon developed that Bliss had unfortunate "side effects." A few suicides were enough to get it banned for all but controlled experiments. A single pharmaceutical company manufactured it for the use of researchers, under the brand name Striaphan.

Each successive night that Sparta took Striaphan, the dream word and the dream image became more closely associated, the vision more focused. The "moonjelly" took on a precise form: as if a miniature of the containing dream, the thing she envisioned was itself a fleshy vortex, which pulsed rhythmically in the center of the vortex of clouds. It could have been a terrible sight, but to her it seemed exquisitely beautiful.

She no longer awoke in terror. The conviction grew in her that there was some *thing* in the eye of the Jovian vortex that sang to her, called to her, welcomed her . . . home.

She forgot what she knew of Striaphan's history and contraindications. In the midst of her thrilling discovery, Sparta's extraordinary capacity for self-analysis, for self-awareness, failed her, having dissolved away without her notice. She never noticed the moment when she became dependent upon the stuff.

PART
3

THE
CARNIVAL
OF THE
ANIMALS

11

The ramjet from London began its final approach to Varanasi; steady deceleration pushed the passengers forward against their seat harnesses. Sparta looked much like the Indian women who crowded the jitney: delicate, dark-skinned, black-haired, and swathed in colorful cotton. From her seat window she could see a distant rise of snow-covered peaks, defining the curve of Earth. Then the plane was into the smog.

Her ears popped. She shook a white wafer from a thin plastic tube containing a stack of them. She sucked it silently, urgently; the taste of it was like honey and lemon on her tongue.

A slender woman wrapped in a gauzy cotton sari threaded with gold rose from her chair and smiled as Sparta entered the room. "Welcome, Inspector Troy. Doctor Singh will be free shortly. Please make yourself comfortable."

"Thanks. I'm comfortable standing." Sparta stood at something resembling parade rest. She was wearing dress blues now, with ribbons for marksmanship, good conduct, and extraordinary heroism—the only ribbons she possessed—in a thin colored line above her left breast pocket. The Space

Board uniform made for high visibility; voluntarily, she had made herself a walking target.

"Would you like tea? Other refreshments? These are rather good." The woman touched one of her long polished fingernails to a silver tray that held bowls of colorful sweets, marble-sized balls of ground nuts and coconut milk and pistachios wrapped in silver foil, the foil being part of the treat. The tray rested on the corner of an elaborately carved teak table, as low as a coffee table, which carried nothing else except a discrete imitation-ivory flatscreen and commlink.

"Nothing, thanks." Sparta saw the red dot in the center of the woman's brown forehead and thought of her own "soul's eye," the dense swelling of brain tissue behind the bone of her forehead. She walked to the window and stood with legs braced and hands clasped behind her. "You have quite a view here."

The reception room was on the fortieth floor of the Space Board's Biological Medicine Center, a sprawling glass polygon that rose on the edge of Ramnagar, on the right bank of the broad Ganges; the modernist building had started as a conceptual cube, so savagely sliced and carved by its architect that it might have been chipped from a block of glacial ice that had wandered too far south from the Himalayas. Through the tall windows Sparta could see northwest to the holy city of Varanasi, to its spiked temples rising from the smog and its riverbank steps crowded with bathers descending to share the brown water with drifting flotsam.

The Indian woman resumed her chair, but she seemed to have nothing very much to do. "Is this your first trip to our facility, Inspector?"

"My first trip to India, in fact."

"Forgive me, I hope I am not prying, but you are rather famous"—the woman's voice was clear and musical; perhaps her principal job was to entertain visitors waiting on Dr. Singh—"for you have already been to the moon, to Mars, even down onto the surface of Venus.''

Sparta half turned from the window and smiled. ''I've seen very little of our own exotic planet.''

''What one can see today is mostly haze, I fear.''

''Does the city still use fossil fuel?''

''No, our fusion plant works well. That is wood smoke from the funeral pyres on the *ghats.*''

''Woodsmoke?'' Sparta focused her attention on a stepped terrace beside the river. Her right eye enlarged the scene telescopically, and she could see the flames rising from the stacked logs, see the blackened shape lying atop them.

''Much of the wood is imported from Siberia, these past several decades,'' said the woman. ''The Himalayan forests have been slow to recover.''

Sparta's telescopic view darted to another *ghat*, and another. On one, the partially burned remains of a body were being wrapped in bright cloth; it made a bundle like those floating in the river.

''Perhaps you are thinking, what a strange place for a biological research facility,'' the secretary said cheerfully. ''The holiest city in India.''

Sparta turned her back to the window. ''And you? Do you regard it as strange?''

''Many of our visitors do.'' The woman deftly evaded the question. ''Particularly when they learn that some of our distinguished researchers, very thoroughly grounded in microbial biology, I assure you, are also good Hindus who believe that drinking from the sacred waters of the Ganges purifies the body and unburdens the soul.'' The commlink chimed and the secretary, without answering it, curved her wide red lips in a smile. ''Doctor Singh will see you now.''

The woman who came out from behind the desk might have been her secretary's sister. She had a graceful red mouth, huge brown eyes, and straight black shining hair pulled tightly back behind her neck. "I'm Holly Singh, Inspector Troy. I'm pleased to meet you." The accent was pure Oxbridge, however, without a trace of Indian lilt, and the costume was polo: silk blouse, jodhpurs, and polished riding boots.

"It was good of you to make time for me on short notice." Sparta shook hands firmly and, in the momentary exchange, studied Singh in ways the woman might not have enjoyed knowing about, had she sensed them—the sort of scrutiny one was likely to receive from inquisitive machines upon seeking entry to a military base, or the upper floors of the Board of Space Control's Earth Central headquarters in Manhattan. She focused her right eye on the lens and retina of Singh's left, until its round brown circles filled her field of view. From the retinal pattern, Sparta saw that Singh was the person the files in Earth Central said she was. Sparta analyzed the aroma of Singh's perfume and soap and perspiration, and found in it hints of flowers and musk and tea and a complex of chemicals typical of a healthy body in repose. Sparta *listened* to the tone of Singh's voice, and heard in it what she should have expected to find, a mixture of confidence, curiosity, and control.

"You wish to ask me about ICEP, Inspector? Some questions not covered in the records?"

"Implied by the records, Doctor."

Singh looked rueful. "I suppose the prose in those reports is rather dry. With a few minutes' notice, I might have been able to save you a trip halfway round the world."

"I don't mind travel."

"So I have heard." The hint of a smile.

Sparta had prolonged her inspection an extra few seconds. At first glance—and sniff and listen—Holly Singh appeared to be no more than thirty years old, but her skin was so smooth and her visage so regular that it was evident that she had had most of her physiognomy reconstructed. Yet there was no record of trauma in her file. A disguise, then. And her body odor, too, was a disguise, a compound of oils and acids intended to reproduce just that very smell of a relaxed thirty-year-old female.

Sparta briefly flirted with the notion that Singh was not human at all, but that mythical creature, an android. But who would bother to build a machine that looked like a human, when what was wanted was humans with the capacities of machines?

No, Singh was human enough, someone who wanted to seem other than she was and who knew that nonverbal cues were as important as verbal ones. Her overtrained, impossibly relaxed voice revealed that just as surely as the faint but sharp odor of adrenaline that underlay her customized bodyodor, announcing that her nerves were strung tight.

"Please sit down. Did my assistant offer you refreshments?"

"Yes, thanks. Nothing for me." The white wafer was still a bittersweet memory on her tongue.

Sparta sat in one of the comfortable armchairs facing Singh's desk and adjusted the line of her trouser creases over her knees. The doctor sat in the armchair opposite. The room was shadowed, its glass wall curtained; dappled warm light shone from lamps of brass filigree.

Singh gestured to a cluster of framed holographs on the table between them. "There they are—Peter, Paul, Soula, Steg, Alice, Rama, Li, Hieronymous—their graduation pictures."

"How old were they when these were taken?"

"All young adults, fourteen to sixteen years old. Peter, Paul, and Alice were acquired as youngsters in Zaire—in accordance with local law and Council regulations regarding trade in endangered species, of course. The others were born here at our primate facility." Singh's gaze lingered on the holos. "Chimps have a limited range of expressions, but

I like to think there is considerable pride to be seen in those young faces.''

"You were fond of them," Sparta said.

"Very. They were not experimental animals to me. Although that's how the program began.''

"How *did* it begin?" Sparta coaxed more warmth into her tone; she was surprised at the effort it cost her. "I don't mean officially. I mean, what inspired you, Dr. Singh?''

Singh found the question flattering, as Sparta had hoped, and returned the compliment by favoring Sparta with the steady gaze of her dark eyes—as she no doubt favored everyone on whom she decided to expend valuable time. "I conceived of the program at a time when nanoware technology had finally begun to show the promise that we had dreamt of since the 20th century. It was the middle '70s . . . has it really been almost fifteen years ago now?''

Perhaps a little more than fifteen, Sparta thought—you must have thought up the chimp experiments before someone decided to try them on a human subject as well. . . .

Singh continued. "You may be too young to remember the excitement of the '70s, Inspector, but they were glorious days for neurology, here and at research centers everywhere. With the new artificial enzymes and programmed, self-replicating cells we learned to repair and enhance damaged areas of the brain and nervous system throughout the body . . . to arrest Alzheimer's disease, Parkinson's disease, ALS, and a host of other diseases. To restore sight and hearing to virtually all patients whose deficits were due to localized neurophysical damage. And for those in high-risk jobs''—Singh's glance flickered to Sparta's dress blue uniform, with its thin line of ribbons—''the benefits were even more immediate: a cure for paralysis due to spinal cord injury, for example. The list is long.''

"You made progress on all those fronts simultaneously?"

"The potential benefits were great and, by comparison, the risks were small. Once we were armed with the informed consent of our patients—or their guardians—nothing stood in the way of our research. Other areas were more problematic."

"Such as?"

"We also saw opportunities—and we have yet to achieve our goals here—of making subtler improvements. Restoring memory loss in some cases, correcting certain speech defects, certain disorders of perception. Dyslexia, for example."

Sparta leaned forward, encouraging Singh to expand.

"But you can see the ethical problems," Singh said, confiding in Sparta as if she were a fellow researcher. "A dyslexic can learn to function within the normal range through traditional therapies. Some of the older literature even suggested that dyslexias might be associated with higher functions—what used to be called creativity, the writing of fiction and so on. We were in a position where we really didn't understand the hierarchical relationships. We were possessed of very powerful neurological tools but inadequate knowledge of the organization of the brain itself."

"And of course you couldn't experiment with humans."

"Some of our own researchers were reluctant even to experiment with higher primates."

"Not you."

"I'm sure you've heard many stories about India, Inspector. Perhaps you've heard of the Jains, who sweep the ground before them so as not to step on a flea? Well, I have been known to crush mosquitos—even on purpose." For a moment Singh's wide red lips stretched into a smile, and her white teeth gleamed.

Sparta was reminded more of the Hindu Kali than of the peaceful deities of the Jains.

"But I have a healthy respect for life, and especially for its most evolved forms," Singh went on. "First we exhausted the possibilities of computer modeling—it was from this research, incidentally, that many features of the modern organic micro-supercomputers arose. Meanwhile we pursued neuroanalytical work on species other than primates—rats, cats, dogs, and so on. But when finally it came to the subtler questions I've mentioned, questions of language, questions of reading and writing and remembered speech, no other species could stand in for humanity."

Singh rose with quick grace and went to her desk. She took another, smaller silver-framed holo from the desk and handed it to Sparta. "Our first subject was an infant chimp—her name was Molly—with a motor disorder. The poor thing couldn't even cling to her mother. In the wild she would have died within a few hours of birth, and in captivity she would have developed severe emotional problems and probably would not have reached maturity. I had no qualms about injecting her with a mix of organic nanochips designed to restore her primary deficit . . . and at the same time, quite conservatively, to test some other parameters."

"Language parameters?"

Sparta handed the holo back to Singh, who replaced it on the desk. "Questions concerning the evolution of language, rather." Singh sat down again, attending Sparta as closely as she had before. "A chimp's brain is half the size of a human's but shows many of the same major anatomical structures. Fossil skull casts of the earliest hominids, now extinct but rather more closely related to chimps than we are, show development in the traditional language centers of the brain. And there are no inherent neurophysiological barriers to language, however stringently you might wish to define that term, in the organization of a chimp's brain.''

''The anatomical obstacles to speech were corrected surgically, weren't they?''

''We did no surgery on Molly. That came later, with the others. And certainly there were anatomical problems—but the corrections were minimal, and we made sure they were painless.'' Singh had tensed almost imperceptibly, but now relaxed again as she got back to reciting the good news. ''That initial and quite unofficial neurochip experiment on Molly showed astonishing results. Her motor control improved rapidly, until she was indistinguishable from the average infant chimp. And as I'm sure I don't need to tell you, the average infant chimp is an Olympic athlete compared to the average infant human. This one, even with her primitive natural vocal equipment, started making interesting sounds. 'Mama' and so forth.''

Sparta smiled. ''A good Sanskrit word.''

''A good word in most languages.'' Singh bared her teeth again. ''We knew we'd done something extraordinary. We had bridged the gap between our species, something the first animal-language researchers in the 20th century had tried so hard to do but without clear results. We had done it decisively and without much effort at all. I will never forget that morning, when I went to Molly's cage and 'interacted' with her—orthodox behaviorist terms are rather dry, I fear—when I simply held out my hand and gave her the food pellet. And she said 'Mama' to me.''

Singh's eyes were shining in the textured lamplight. Sparta did not break the silence.

''Looking back, I believe it was in that moment I conceived ICEP, the Interspecies Communication Enhancement Program.'' Singh suddenly frowned. ''Incidentally, I hate the term 'superchimp' only a little less than I despise the word 'simp.' '' The frown dissolved, although her expression remained brusque. "Our first enhanced subjects, these eight, were ready for training a year later. The details of the program, our evaluation of the results, are of course on record."

"The record says nothing about your decision to abandon the program," Sparta said. "Yet no continuing proposal was filed."

"I'm afraid you can put that down to the media-hounds—or perhaps I should say, to the will of the people, who become hysterical when expertly manipulated. It was plain there would be no more funding for ICEP after all of our subjects were lost in the crash of the *Queen Elizabeth IV*."

"All? I found no record of the death of the chimpanzee named Steg."

"Steg?" Singh looked at Sparta carefully. "I see you have read the files carefully." She seemed to come to some unspoken decision. "Inspector, I'm scheduled to fly to Darjeeling as soon as our interview is completed here. I run a sanatorium near there, for my private patients. It's on the grounds of the family estate. Would you care to be my guest this evening?"

"That's gracious of you, Dr. Singh, but I won't keep you long. I think we can complete our business here shortly."

"You misunderstand me. I'm not concerned with the time. I thought you might like to meet Steg. The last of the so-called superchimps."

12

"Everything you remember about that night is true," the commander said, "except it wasn't her in the chopper."

"A stand-in? An actress?" Blake asked.

"Nobody."

"How about the guy who tied me up?"

"He was real."

They were walking side by side through the woods, with the distant cliffs on the far side of the Hudson barely visible through the trees. Their breath made clouds in front of them. All around, autumn blazed.

They came to the edge of the woods. The mansion was to their left, across a wide back lawn already turning brown with approaching winter. Ellen's window and the pantry window Blake had broken in his escape attempt were visible in the near tower; the one still had fresh putty around it, and around the other the new leading of the stained glass was as bright as pewter.

"We were going to catch you in her room—that's about as far ahead as we were thinking. You almost got away. Came through that window, charged the chopper. Complete surprise. If the guy in the Snark hadn't been getting the injection ready, you could have made a mess of us."

"Ellen reached for me, pulled me in. You say that memory's a fake? You can do that?"

"With the right subject."

They resumed walking toward the lodge. After a moment Blake said, "Can you erase my . . . chip? Give me back the truth?"

"Afraid not." The commander laughed, a single sharp expulsion of breath. "If you want, we could give you our version of what you might remember if we hadn't messed with you. It would be just as fake."

"Never mind."

"Raises interesting questions, doesn't it?"

"Like, how will I know tomorrow we really had this little chat?" said Blake.

"Others too."

"Like, why—if this is true—are you bothering to explain? When before, you just wanted to get me out of the way."

"You're dangerous, you know." The commander nodded toward the house. Thick plastic covered the charred porch; more scaffolding stood against the ruins of the carriage house, farther on. "And that was before you knew about Salamander."

Blake's laugh was sour. "What difference does it make? You can rewrite the last week of my life . . . wipe all that mayhem away."

"Before you knew about us, we justified the deception. A temporary lie, we said . . . and Ellen could tell you the truth later."

"She's in on it?"

"She wouldn't have agreed, Redfield, you know her better than that. We didn't ask her. After, when she heard our reasons, she went along."

Blake shook his head angrily. "I don't know how you guys decide where to draw the line. Playing God."

"We're not God. We couldn't rewrite the last

week of your life if we wanted to. An hour or two, if that. Try more, and bad things happen."

"How do you know bad things happen?"

"We didn't invent the technique, Redfield," he said sharply. "They did."

"You use it. The results of their experiments."

"What you asked before"—the commander let the accusation pass, *nolo contendere*—"Human memory's not on a chip. It's distributed in lots of parts of the brain. You'd have to talk to the neuro people about that, it's too complicated for me."

"Sure," Blake said.

"I understand the practical side. That it's easier to blank out something somebody heard or read than something they saw happen. Harder still to blank out something involving the body." The commander eyed him. "You seem to get your body into most of the stuff you learn, Redfield." It sounded almost like a compliment.

"That doesn't exhaust your options, Commander."

"I don't blame you for thinking it, Redfield, but we like to believe we're the good guys. So we don't kill other good guys. We don't hold their friends and relatives hostage. Only two options for us."

"Which are?"

"Well, we could take your word of honor you won't betray us."

Blake was caught by surprise. After a moment he shook his head. "I couldn't give it. If they caught me, tortured me . . . or used those drugs on me again. Or if they took Ellen, or my parents . . ."

"Good. You know yourself." The commander nodded. "We'd take your word anyway."

Some resistance broke inside Blake and he looked at the older man with new respect. "What's your other option?"

"Recruit you."

"I already turned you down."

"Not the Space Board—Salamander."

"I can't be one of you."

They had reached what was left of the porch. The commander paused on the first step. "Why not?"

"You really were one of the *prophetae* once, weren't you?"

The commander stared at him. He nodded once, slowly.

"All of you were, all these scrubbed kids," said Blake.

"That's right."

"I never was. I never believed in that crap, that alien savior business. I only pretended."

"We'll make an exception in your case," the commander said hoarsely.

"You've got it backwards," Blake said.

The commander, watching him with basilisk eyes, did not move, hardly seemed to breathe. Then he relaxed. "Okay. Before I fly you back to the city," he said, "there's somebody I want you to meet."

J. Q. R. Forster, professor of xenopaleontology and xenoarchaeology at King's College, London, was engrossed in a leather-bound volume from a shelf of 19th-century classics when Blake and the commander entered the library. Forster was a tiny bright-eyed fellow whose expression immediately put Blake in mind of an excited terrier. When the commander made the introductions, Forster stepped forward and gave Blake's hand a jerk.

"My dear Redfield, let me congratulate you on the first rate job you and Inspector Troy did in recovering the Martian plaque. Splendid to have it safely back where it belongs."

"Thank you, sir. Ellen spoke of you often." Blake hesitated. "Uh, excuse me for saying so, but you're a lot younger than I expected."

Indeed Forster looked no more than thirty-five, instead of his true fifty-plus years. "If I continue to

INFOPAK
TECHNICAL
BLUEPRINTS

On the following pages are computer-generated diagrams representing some of the structures and engineering found in *Venus Prime:*

Pages 2-6: *Kon-Tiki* Manned Jupiter probe—wire frame overview; nose cone doors open, instrument booms deployed; re-entry shell cutaway views; plan views.

Pages 7-11: *Snark* Twin rotor attack helicopter—wire frame overview; rotation; weapons systems; plan views.

Pages 12-16: *Falcon* Bio-mechanical reconstruction project—standing configuration; sitting configuration, front and back views; side, front and top plan views.

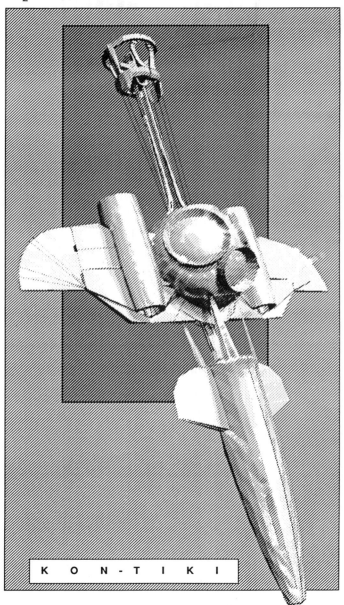

KON - TIKI

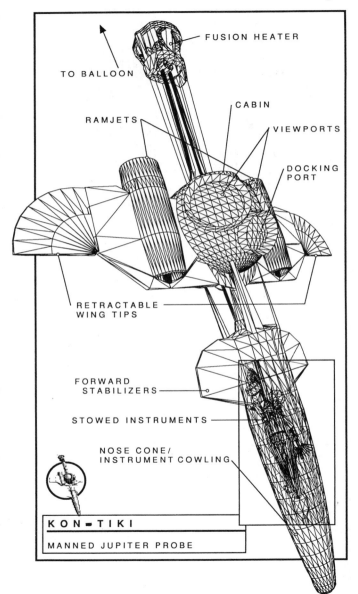

FUSION HEATER

TO BALLOON

RAMJETS

CABIN

VIEWPORTS

DOCKING PORT

RETRACTABLE WING TIPS

FORWARD STABILIZERS

STOWED INSTRUMENTS

NOSE CONE/ INSTRUMENT COWLING

KON-TIKI

MANNED JUPITER PROBE

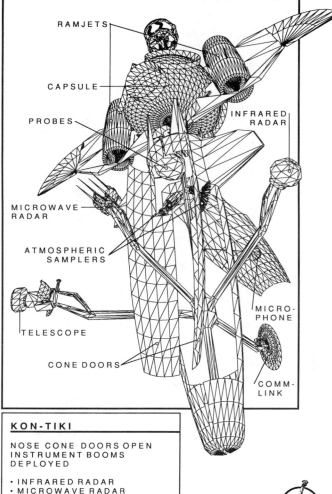

RAMJETS

CAPSULE

PROBES

INFRARED
RADAR

MICROWAVE
RADAR

ATMOSPHERIC
SAMPLERS

MICRO-
PHONE

TELESCOPE

CONE DOORS

COMM-
LINK

KON-TIKI

NOSE CONE DOORS OPEN
INSTRUMENT BOOMS
DEPLOYED

• INFRARED RADAR
• MICROWAVE RADAR
• ATMOSPHERIC SAMPLERS
• MICROPHONES
• VIBRATIONLESS TELESCOPE
• COMMLINK

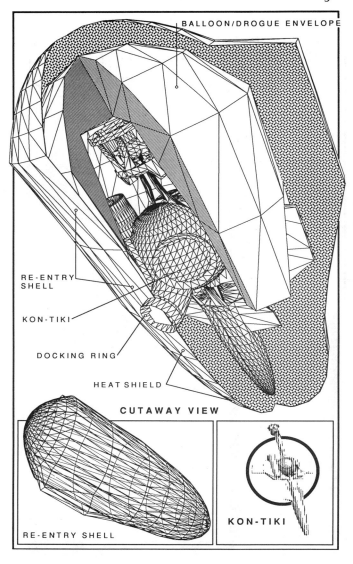

BALLOON/DROGUE ENVELOPE

RE-ENTRY
SHELL

KON-TIKI

DOCKING RING

HEAT SHIELD

CUTAWAY VIEW

RE-ENTRY SHELL

KON-TIKI

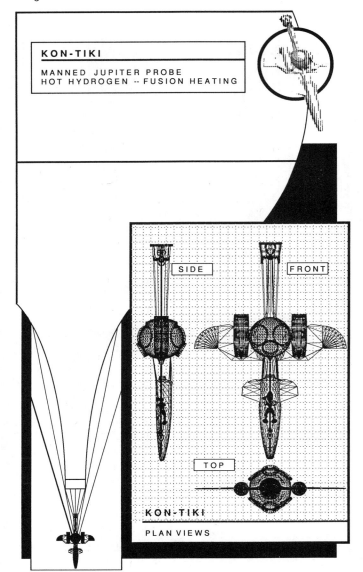

KON-TIKI

MANNED JUPITER PROBE
HOT HYDROGEN -- FUSION HEATING

SIDE

FRONT

TOP

KON-TIKI

PLAN VIEWS

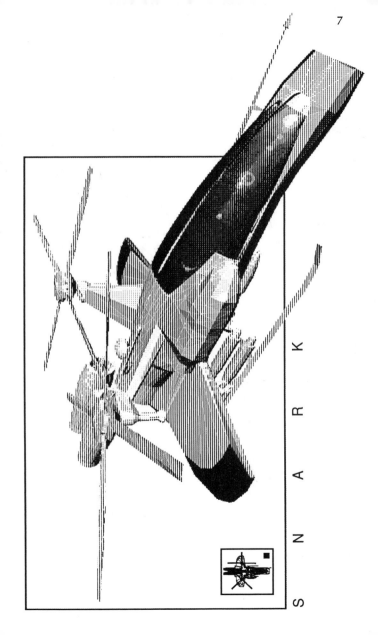

SNARK

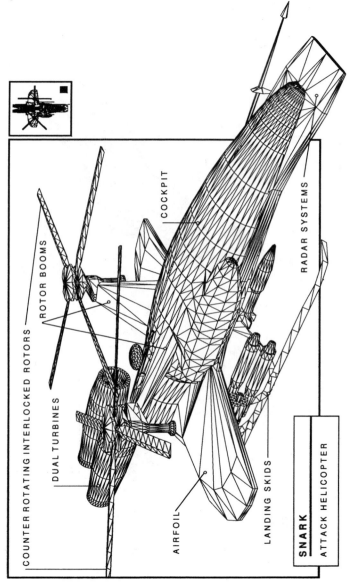

COUNTER ROTATING INTERLOCKED ROTORS

ROTOR BOOMS

DUAL TURBINES

COCKPIT

RADAR SYSTEMS

AIRFOIL

LANDING SKIDS

SNARK

ATTACK HELICOPTER

SNARK

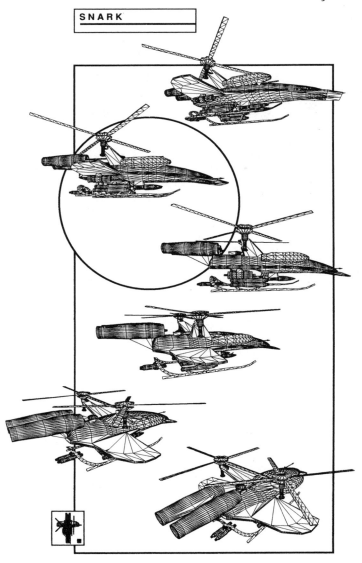

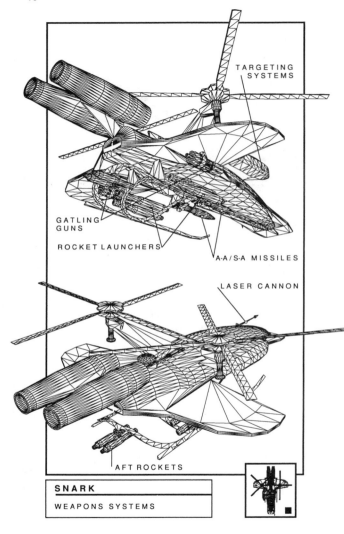

TARGETING SYSTEMS

GATLING GUNS

ROCKET LAUNCHERS

A-A/S-A MISSILES

LASER CANNON

AFT ROCKETS

SNARK

WEAPONS SYSTEMS

11

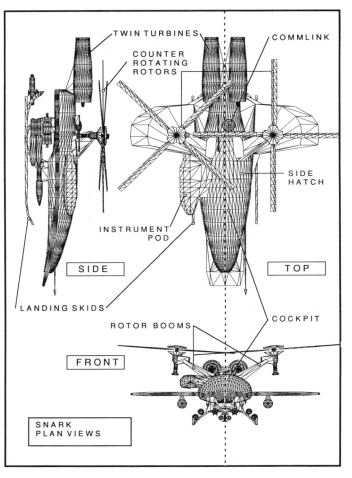

TWIN TURBINES

COUNTER
ROTATING
ROTORS

COMMLINK

SIDE HATCH

INSTRUMENT POD

SIDE

TOP

LANDING SKIDS

ROTOR BOOMS

COCKPIT

FRONT

SNARK
PLAN VIEWS

SNARK

TWIN ROTOR
ATTACK HELICOPTER

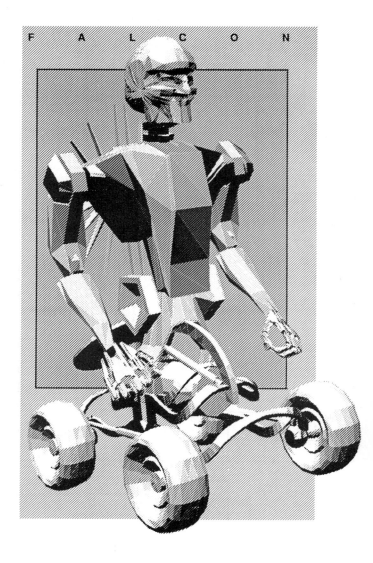

FALCON

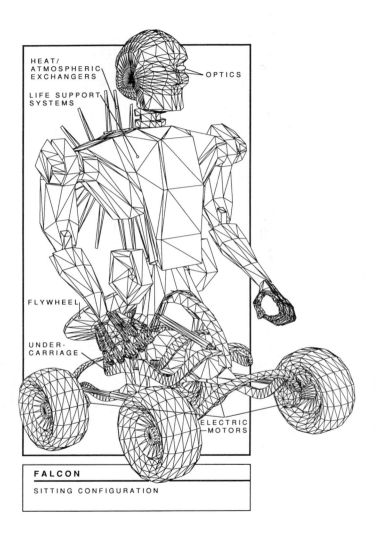

HEAT/
ATMOSPHERIC
EXCHANGERS

OPTICS

LIFE SUPPORT
SYSTEMS

FLYWHEEL

UNDER-
CARRIAGE

ELECTRIC
MOTORS

FALCON

SITTING CONFIGURATION

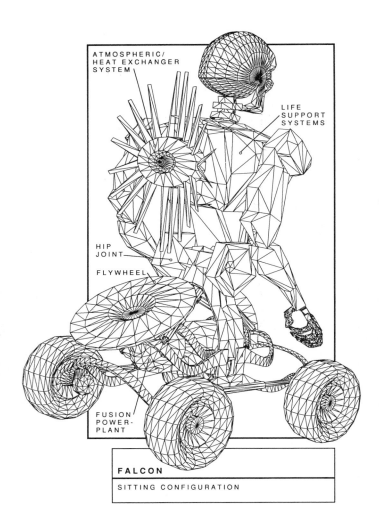

ATMOSPHERIC/
HEAT EXCHANGER
SYSTEM

LIFE
SUPPORT
SYSTEMS

HIP
JOINT

FLYWHEEL

FUSION
POWER-
PLANT

FALCON

SITTING CONFIGURATION

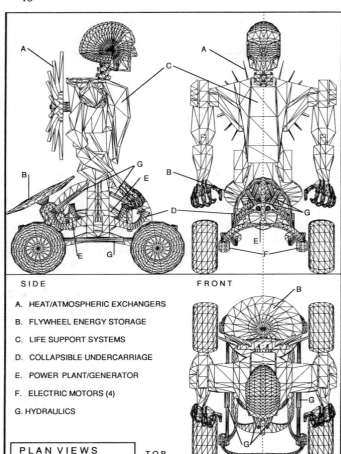

SIDE

A. HEAT/ATMOSPHERIC EXCHANGERS

B. FLYWHEEL ENERGY STORAGE

C. LIFE SUPPORT SYSTEMS

D. COLLAPSIBLE UNDERCARRIAGE

E. POWER PLANT/GENERATOR

F. ELECTRIC MOTORS (4)

G. HYDRAULICS

FRONT

PLAN VIEWS   TOP

FALCON

BIO-MECHANICAL
RECONSTRUCTION
PROJECT

have frequent scrapes with death requiring visits to the plastic surgeon, I shall soon be a boy like yourself," he said. "They said they replaced seventy percent of the skin."

"Sorry," said Blake, embarrassed. He'd forgotten about the Free Spirit bomb, the explosion and fire that had been intended to kill Forster and destroy his life's work.

Forster coughed. "Not really necessary of course . . ."

"Sir?"

"After all, I've studied the thing for so many years I could sit down at a terminal and recreate it from memory."

"The Martian plaque, you mean?"

The commander closed the hall library doors. "Mister Redfield hasn't been briefed, Professor."

Forster looked at Blake with suspicion. "Do you consider yourself a scholar of Culture X, Redfield?"

"Not at all," he said, surprised.

"Isn't this the person you spoke of?" Forster asked the commander, raising a bushy eyebrow.

"Redfield's work relates to yours, Professor. I think after we've talked you'll see the connections pretty clearly."

Blake glanced at the commander. Just before he'd sent him and Ellen to Mars to find the missing plaque, the commander had referred to the assignment as having to do with "archaeological stuff." As if he'd had no idea why anyone would be interested.

"Shall we get on with it, then?" Forster said fussily.

The commander gestured to the library's well-stuffed leather-upholstered chairs. After some moving of furniture, they found that they had moved their seats to the corners of an invisible equilateral triangle, facing inward.

"If you don't mind starting, Professor," said the commander.

''I'm eager.''

''I'll ask them to bring tea—and something stiffer for you,'' he said, catching Forster's look. He fingered his wrist unit. It chimed softly in confirmation.

Forster had brought a flat holo projector from the inside pocket of his tweed jacket, placed it on the lamp table beside him, and keyed its pad. Several dozen sculptural shapes appeared in midair above the unit, seemingly quite solid, as if cast in type metal.

''I presume that by now both of you know of my discovery that the Venus tablets constitute a more spectacular linguistic and philological discovery than the fabled Rosetta stone itself,'' Forster said brightly. His lack of modesty was so transparent Blake found it almost charming. ''Not only were the tablets laid out so as to deliberately reveal the sounds associated with each of the signs you see here—which I have arranged in the frequency of their occurrence, by the way—but the texts, over a dozen different ones, were written phonetically in the Bronze Age languages of Earth. Moreover, they were matched to their translations in the language of Culture X.'' Forster cleared his throat grandly. ''Thus in a single stroke we were able to obtain not only a sizeable sample of the Culture X language, written and phonetic, but also, as a windfall, sample texts of several lost languages of Earth never before deciphered. Tragically, all copies of these tablets were destroyed on that terrible night.''

''But the original Venus tablets still exist?'' Blake asked.

''Yes, buried where we left them on the surface, and I certainly intend to return to excavate them''—Forster hesitated—''someday. When the necessary funds can be raised. But meanwhile I've made a more pressing discovery.'' His bright eyes and pursed lips expressed a curious mixture of emotions. The little boy in him craved approval, the professor in him demanded it. "I've translated the Martian plaque!"

"Congratulations," said Blake, trying to sound sincere. In his business, purported translations of untranslatable old manuscripts were almost as common as plans for perpetual motion machines at the patent office.

"If you'll bear with me just a moment," said the professor, fiddling with the holo unit.

Beneath the floating sculptural signs there appeared other signs, plain Roman letters and world-standard linguistic marks.

"These are the sounds of the signs." He touched the pad, and the signs, paired with their phonetic equivalents, briefly glowed one after the other as the speaker in the unit emitted disembodied phonemes: "KH . . . WH . . . AH . . . SH . . ."

When the machine had gone through the list, Forster said, "The Martian plaque contains many of the same signs—none of the signs borrowed from human languages, of course—and lacking only the three least frequent occurrences in the Venusian tablets." He glanced at Blake. "Because I had memorized it, I was able to reconstruct it during the period when it was missing and all records of its existence had been destroyed. Lying in a bed in the Port Hesperus clinic—amusing myself by thinking, since I could do nothing else—I established that in contrast to the Venusian tablets, which as I said are translations of texts from ancient Earth, the Martian plaque makes only a glancing reference to Earth. An Earth far too young to have evolved creatures that made intentional sounds, much less spoken languages."

He fingered the unit and a full-size image of the Martian plaque appeared, floating above the other signs and marks like a piece of shattered mirror.

"Does that seem an accurate rendition to you, Mister Redfield? It's from memory."

"I have to say that I wouldn't be able to tell the difference."

Forster took that as a compliment. "As one might guess by looking at it, the plaque is not really a plaque. It is but a fragment of a much longer document, most of which is missing. This is what it says."

The speaker spewed forth a broken string of hisses and booms and clicks, reading off the incomplete lines of the plaque in the voice Forster had reconstructed for the long-gone aliens who had inscribed the metal plaque.

Blake tried to seem fascinated. He snuck a look at the commander, whose stone face conveyed nothing.

After the hissing stopped, Forster said, "Here it is in English." This time the voice was sexless and ingratiating, the standard voice of the 21st-century general-purpose computer:

> place on ZH-GO-ZH-AH 134 of WH-AH-SS-CH 9 . . .
> down upon a salt world of EN-WE-SS 9436 . . .
> were designated came humbly and peacefully to do . . .
> leader. Beneath the shore of the dark salt they . . .
> one thousand stadia of this place they . . .
> places of power and their places of production and . . .
> study and their places of rest. Later generations . . .
> over all the salt and land of this world, and . . .
> of WH-AH-SS-CH they did the work assigned to . . .
> the designates labor on this, the first of the . . .
> of EN-WE-SS 9436-7815. Their greatest . . .
> TH-IN-THA. Chariots flowed like a river from the east . . .
> great encampments. The designates honored . . .
> accomplishments. The creatures multiplied . . .

and diversity. In their many kinds . . .
netted together. At the same time other desig-
nates . . .
second and third salt worlds. Then, finally . . .
AH-SS-CH 1095, all those who were . . .
salt worlds to await the success-signaling . . .
the cloud-dwelling messengers where they live . . .
great world. The chariot-riders left this inscrip-
tion . . .
their great work. They await the reawaken-
ing . . .
of waiting at the great world. . . .
Then all will be well.

Blake listened to these broken fragments of odd speech with increasing stupefaction, until the final words startled him from his trance. *"All will be well?"* he blurted.

"The untranslated terms are proper names, of course—possibly names of individuals, certainly the names of stars and planets, including, I'm confident, Earth, Venus, Mars, and the sun," Forster said. "And of course the Bronze Age terms—chariots and stadia and so forth—were the closest equivalents the Venus texts could provide for the original words of the plaque. Their meaning is easy enough to guess."

"It really said 'All will be well'?" Blake repeated.

But Forster was still happily expounding: "Trains or cars, perhaps even vessels of some sort—but not ships, there were perfectly good words for that—and miles or kilometers, some unit of measurement. That sort of thing."

Blake recovered enough to realize the commander was signaling him with a look. *Forster doesn't know.*

" 'Salt world' isn't a Bronze Age term, is it?" the commander remarked coolly, inviting Forster to go on.

"No, but they obviously intended 'ocean world.' Dissolved salts may have interested them as much as water. For whatever reason. Historical, perhaps." Forster had obviously anticipated the question. "Consider that we call galaxies galaxies. If one were to translate that word without the necessary context, one might wonder about the etymology of a term such as 'milkies.' "

"Especially if one weren't a mammal," Blake said.

"Hmm, yes." Forster eyed him from under a gingery brow.

"And the 'great world' . . . ?" prompted the commander.

"*Is Jupiter,*" Forster said triumphantly.

Blake tried again. "Your translation renders the last phrase as, 'Then all will be well.' "

"Yes?" Forster frowned at Blake, an inquisitive frown.

" 'All will be well' is one of the mottos of the people who stole the Martian plaque," Blake said. "The same people who tried to kill you."

Forster looked at the commander, and comprehension dawned. "Ah, this is why you wanted me to meet Mr. Redfield."

"Uh, why I wanted Redfield to meet you." It wasn't a contradiction, exactly, and since tea arrived at that moment, along with a bottle of Laphroaig, Forster's favorite, the commander was saved the trouble of explaining himself more fully.

"Remember the star maps I looked at in the Athanasian Society?" It was twilight. Blake and the commander were walking across the grass toward the white Space Board helicopter that had brought them to Granite Lodge.

"You mean the one you stole from the Louvre?"

"There were others; they already had them. What they had in common was a particular planetary alignment."

The commander raised a grizzled eyebrow.

"The common alignments correspond to a date," Blake said.

"Yes?"

"Which seems to correspond to the scheduled rendezvous of *Kon-Tiki* with Jupiter."

"What do you make of it?"

"You already *know* something's going to happen on Jupiter?" Blake asked, curious.

"So we were taught. We *prophetae*."

"What's between you and Forster?"

"He's got a research scheme; I offered to pull what strings I could. No more questions, Redfield, I'm about to shake your hand goodbye for the last time . . . unless you tell me otherwise."

"Where's Ellen now?" Blake asked.

"I swear I wish I knew," said the commander.

"All right," Blake said quietly. "I'm with you."

13

As the foothills grew rapidly closer, Holly Singh recovered control from the autopilot of her quick little Dragonfly helicopter and manually guided its swift, silent ascent of the terraced ridges. A macadam road and a shining pair of tracks wound like coiling pythons beneath the open craft. An antique train was tortuously making the same ascent, puffing white steam into the mountain air.

Singh nodded toward the bright green terraces that fell away below like so many stairsteps. "Tea plantations. Darjeeling grows the world's best, of its type. So we like to think."

The helicopter crested the ridge at 2,500 meters. The Himalayas, hidden behind the ridges until now, sprang forward in the crystal air. Sparta's breath caught at the sight of the glacier-hung peaks, thrusting like broken glass into the dark blue sky. Katchenjunga, second highest mountain on Earth, dominated all the others; still seventy kilometers away, it nevertheless towered above the darting helicopter, in perspective so starkly carved as to seem close enough to touch.

Suddenly they were buzzing a town, which clung to the crest of the ridge and spilled down its sides. The helicopter flitted over green lawns and old trees, past stone church towers.

"The English—including a round dozen of my great-great-grandparents—developed Darjeeling as a retreat from the heat of the plains," Singh said. "That's why half the buildings look like they were transplanted from the British Isles. See that one, the one that looks like an Edinburgh church? It was a movie house for a few decades. Half the rest of the town could be in Tibet. A colony of Tibetans settled here after fleeing China in the mid-20th century. What remains, including the marketplace, is pure India. We've tried to preserve it pretty much as it was a century ago."

The helicopter skimmed along the ridge, past the town.

Singh noticed the direction of Sparta's gaze and smiled. "Mountain people spend a lot of time praying, one way and another." The barren heights were prickled with poles carrying prayer flags, pale banners hanging limp in the still air.

The helicopter flew on until a broad green lawn opened before it, bordered with massive oaks and chestnut trees. For the merest fragment of a second Sparta searched her eidetic memory: there was something familiar about this wide lawn, these brooding trees, the snowy Himalayas above the cloud-filled valleys beyond.

"Howard Falcon landed a balloon here," she said.

"Indeed, Howard landed here many times," said Holly Singh. "Howard's roots in India are almost as deep as mine. Although none of his very proper British ancestors ever went native." Her mood seemed genuinely cheerful, as if the sharp mountain air had refreshed her. "You must have seen this view in one of the documentaries they made about him. When he was trying to raise money to build the *Queen Elizabeth*, Howard's favorite trick for winning friends and influencing people was to take them up in his fusion-powered hot air balloon—they'd leave from Srinagar and stay aloft for several days, drifting the length of the Himalayas and landing here—right where we're setting down.''

The helicopter settled gently to the grass. Back among the trees Sparta glimpsed a white house with wide verandas and broad eaves, flanked by enormous flowering rhododendrons—bushes as big as trees, holdovers from the last age of dinosaurs.

''And whenever Howard touched down we'd invite our neighbors over and wine and dine and flatter his guests.'' Singh unstrapped her harness and stepped lightly from the helicopter. Sparta tugged her duffel from behind the seat and followed, her shoes sinking into the springy sod.

''No party for us tonight, I'm afraid,'' said Singh. ''Just a quiet dinner at home.''

On the broad lawn, two peacocks carefully picked their steps, displaying enormous fans of blue and green plumes to the peahens that wandered on the lawn. High in a towering cedar, Sparta saw a plumed white egret. To their left, the snow-clad mountains were turning ruddy in the evening light.

The two women walked toward the big house, the doctor in her riding outfit, the policewoman in her trim blue uniform. A tall man in puttees and jacket hurried across the lawn toward them, stopping a few meters away and inclining his turbaned head.

''Good evening, madame.''

''Good evening, Ran. Will you see to the helicopter, please? And take the inspector's valise to her room.''

''At once.''

Sparta handed the tall Sikh her duffel. His nod was as sharp as a military salute.

''I'll take you to your quarters later, Inspector,'' said Singh. ''There's something I want to show you before it gets dark.''

Sparta followed Singh into the cool shadowed aisles beneath the chestnut trees. Through the neat rows of old trees and decorative bushes she saw other white buildings. A few people moved slowly in the courtyard they enclosed, heads down, showing little interest in their surroundings.

"My mother's paternal grandfather—his father having made his fortune in tea—established this place as a tuberculosis sanatorium," said Singh. "Now that tuberculosis is a thing of the past, we treat neurological disorders here . . . those we can. Despite all the progress I spoke about before, some mysteries are beyond us. Though we do try to provide a good home for the people we can't help."

Singh turned off the gravel path and led the way past tall hedges of fragrant camellia. It did not take Sparta's specialized senses to anticipate what they were coming to next; the smell of animals grew stronger with each step.

"My grandfather established this menagerie, which my father agreed to maintain when he married my mother." She smiled. "Dowry arrangements could be rather complex in the old days. I have renovated it and added to the professional staff. Now it is used for research purposes."

Low masonry barns stood among the trees. Sparta identified the sharp smell of cats coming from one, the ripe odor of ungulates from another, and a dry, autumnal whiff of reptile from a third. In a four-story-high wrought iron cage she saw wings flap as an eagle momentarily silhouetted itself against the darkening sky.

"Many rare species from the subcontinent are represented here. You are welcome to spend as much time here as you like, tomorrow"—Singh was leading her past the aviary toward another open structure—"but this evening . . ."

Monkeys and lemurs leaped and screamed in their segregated cages. Singh led Sparta to the end of the row, to the largest cage.

The design was simple and familiar: a floor of sloping concrete several feet below ground level, edged with a system of drains for easy flushing, and a hatch in the corner leading to the long stone barn that backed all the primate cages.

Less familiar were the aluminum struts and spars that crisscrossed the cage, from a couple of meters above the floor all the way to its high roof.

"Is that from the *Queen Elizabeth?*" Sparta asked.

"It's a piece of the mock-up we used for training the chimps. The training was done at the center in Ramnagar, but I salvaged this bit and had it installed here."

Sparta would have asked why, but she had already surmised the answer.

Singh looked in the direction of the rear hatch and called sharply, "Steg! Holly is here."

For a moment nothing happened. The air was filled with the hoots and cries of the other primates. Then a timid face, brown eyes wide and thin lips parted in apprehension, peered out of the shadows.

"Steg! Holly is here. Holly wants to say hello."

The animal hesitated several seconds before slowly emerging from hiding. It swung up onto the nearest of the aluminum spars and sat there, studying Sparta intently.

Sparta knew the face well—that of the terrified chimp Howard Falcon had met face to face during the *Queen*'s last moments. Apparently Falcon's order—"*Boss—boss—go!*"—had saved this one's life after all, although not those of the others.

"Every time I look a chimpanzee in the face, I'm reminded that this is my closest evolutionary relative," said Singh. "I think it is safe to say that none of us understand in a fundamental, cellular, molecular way, why chimps don't look and behave just as we do. After more than a century of sophisticated research we still don't fully understand why we and they have different shapes—although we recognize the utility of the differences—and we still don't understand why we and they can become infected by the same viruses but not get sick in the same ways. We don't understand how humans can read and write and talk in complex sentences, and they, in their natural state, can't. In genetic terms we are so nearly identical that probably only we humans ourselves could tell the difference.'' Singh turned slightly toward Sparta, again favoring her with that thin smile. ''I doubt that an alien, some visitor from another star, would be able to make the distinction at all—not on biochemical grounds, or at least not without very sophisticated instruments. Which suggests that vast evolutionary differences may be achieved by the subtlest physical adjustments.''

''If they are the right adjustments,'' Sparta said, so quietly she might have whispered it.

Singh's eyes widened a fraction of a millimeter before she turned her attention back to the reluctant chimpanzee. ''Steg! Come say hello to Holly.''

Steg crept slowly toward them. He was a fully grown male chimpanzee in the peak years of maturity, with muscles that bulged and rippled beneath his glossy black coat. He outweighed Sparta herself by ten kilos or more. Yet his eyes were dull, his gaze unfocused.

Halfway across, Steg staggered and caught himself on the narrow beam. He froze in place, then seemed almost visibly to steel his nerve, willing himself to continue; his eyes never left Holly Singh's face as he resumed his slow progress toward her.

Finally he caught the wire mesh of the cage in both his leathery hands.

''Say hello to Holly.'' Singh's voice was clear but intimate.

Steg's lips parted in a pained grimace, and a rasping sound came out of his throat. ''Bbbbbb . . . bah, bah . . .''

''That's good, Steg. That's very good.'' Singh reached through the mesh and gave his head a quick scratch. His dark scalp hair was divided by a wide, mottled scar of bare white flesh. She slipped her hand into her jacket pocket and withdrew a chunk of something brown and crumbly.

Steg released his grip on the wire mesh with apparent effort, pulling the fingers of his left hand away one by one, then reached for the food preparation. He shoved it greedily into his mouth and began to chew. Once his mouth was full and his heavy jaw muscles were grinding away, he risked a wide, sidelong gaze at Sparta, his dark pupils rimmed with yellow, his curiosity pathetically mingled with fear.

"He can't speak," said Sparta.

"Not anymore. Nor understand, except a few simple commands, the earliest he learned. And as you saw, his motor functions are impaired. Neurochips can't help destruction of brain tissue that massive." Singh sighed. "Mentally, Steg is roughly equivalent to a one-year-old infant. But not as playful. Not as confident."

Sparta looked up at the rigging that suggested the interior of the vanished *Queen Elizabeth IV*. "Doesn't this setting have painful associations for him?"

"On the contrary. He and the others spent the happiest days of their lives in such a setting." Singh lightly stroked the knuckles of Steg's right hand, which still clung to the cage. "Goodbye, Steg. Holly will come again."

Steg said nothing. He watched them as they walked away.

The light had gone from the sky. Their footsteps crunched the gravel along a barely visible path outlined by low, dimly glowing light fixtures.

"Howard Falcon knew about my work with enhanced chimpanzees from the start," Singh said. "It came up naturally in the course of all those social affairs he precipitated with his ballooning. Indeed, it was his rather casual suggestion that put ICEP on the track to success, although I doubt if he would remember that today. He was always too busy with other matters to take a really personal interest."

"Why was he interested in ICEP at all?" Sparta asked.

"He knew the basics. Normal chimps are superior to humans in almost every physical way. With one or two important exceptions, of course. An adult chimp is quicker and stronger than the quickest and strongest human gymnast, although we are better made for running and throwing—and we have a quantum advantage, not only over chimps but over just about every other living thing, in the construction of our hands. Nevertheless, there was no reason to believe that suitably engineered chimpanzees couldn't join human beings as fully conscious partners, in enterprises of mutual benefit to both."

"Such as the operation of airships?"

"The *Queen Elizabeth IV* was already under construction when Howard casually mentioned the idea to me. I think I surprised him when I took it seriously. Thanks to him, his sponsors readily saw the advantage in supplementing the human crew with intelligent chimpanzees who could handle much of the rigging work inside that vast, open craft. Howard once compared it to a flying cathedral."

"Handle the rigging? Handle the dangerous work, in other words," Sparta said.

"Dangerous to us, not to them." Singh's dark eyes shone in the shadowed night. "Ethical considerations were always important, Inspector, whatever doubts you may entertain on that score. We were not creating a race of slaves. Runs of experiments in the mock-up indicated that chimpanzees were not only comfortable in the *Queen*'s environment but were actually quite happy up there among the spars and rigging. There was not a single near-injury to any chimp during the preliminary tests—some of which were quite strenuous. And those were ordinary lab animals.''

The women came out of the trees, into the open grassy field.

Sparta halted and looked up, considering the night.

Overhead the stars were like fluorescent plankton, four or five thousand of them visible to the ordinary eye in this clear atmosphere, a hundred times that number visible to Sparta's more sensitive eye. To the northwest the glacier-draped mountains—the raw young edges of continental collision—were avatars of the grinding upheavals that had continually reshaped the surface of the spinning Earth.

After a moment she turned to Holly Singh. ''Does Falcon ever come to visit Steg?''

''Falcon is not one of us any longer,'' Singh replied.

''Why do you say that?''

''Since the crash of the *Queen* he's chosen not to live in India. And he no longer seeks company outside the immediate circle of his colleagues on the *Kon-Tiki* project. It's because of what they had to do to save him, I suppose.''

14

Sparta awoke in a high-ceilinged room, gleaming white from centuries of accumulated enamel. Its tall windows were hung with lace and fitted with panes of imperfect glass whose pinhole bubbles refocused the sun into golden liquid galaxies. She didn't know where she was. . . .

She was eighteen years old, a prisoner in a sanatorium, half drunk on the random return of her memory, on the assault of her exaggerated senses. Her heart was pounding and her throat ached with the need to scream, for she could hear the beating wings of the approaching Snark, bringing the assassin.

Sparta rolled out of the bed and slid across the polished wooden floor on her belly, tucking herself naked against the wall below the window sill. She *listened. . . .*

Far down in the deep valleys the night birds called and a million tiny frogs sang to the moon. The light of the full moon was flooding the room through the lace curtains.

It wasn't morning and she wasn't in the sanatorium in Colorado, she was in Holly Singh's house in India, and the air was cold enough that she could see her breath in the moonlight. The sound she heard wasn't a Snark, it was Singh's little two-seat Dragonfly, its tiny fusion-electric engine so silent that all she could hear was the whiffle of the blades—and it wasn't approaching, it was taking off.

Sparta raised her head to the corner of the window and peered out over the sloping lawn. Her right eye fixed on the Dragonfly, already half a kilometer away, as it climbed against a backdrop of moon-shadowed peaks, and she zeroed in until the image of the cockpit filled her field of vision. The angle was bad; she was looking from behind, and could see only the pilot's left shoulder and arm, but the infrared image processed by Sparta's visual cortex was bright as day. The pilot was a woman—Singh, or someone who closely resembled her.

Something in Sparta was not reassured. Was it really Singh in the helicopter? And where was she going in the middle of the night?

Sparta expelled her breath in a short sigh, an angry spasm almost like a snarl, and abruptly she sprang to her feet. For a moment she was exposed to anyone who might be watching her window, but she was defiant. She crossed to the closet where she'd hung her few clothes and slipped on a close-fitting black polycanvas jump suit, then pulled soft black hightops onto her small feet. She returned to the window, this time silently, invisibly.

She disarmed the telltale she'd set on the glass. In the night air the wooden sash had contracted; it came up easily, scraping softly against the frame.

She slipped outside and closed the window behind her. She scampered across the gently sloping roof. At the corner of the veranda she tested the strength of the gutter, then hooked her hands into it, rolled forward and hung from the roof, her feet a meter from the ground. She dropped silently into a bed of decorative Irish moss.

The moonlight through the trees created a blue and black mosaic, but to Sparta's infrared-sensitive eye the ground itself glowed in shades of dull red, the grass and bushes and bare earth giving back the sun's heat in varying degree. She walked quickly along the paths that led to the sanatorium.

She paused once, at the sight of a ghostly white shape moving in the dark cedar branches, but it was only an egret that had sought safety for the night aboveground.

She came to the sanatorium. Four low brick buildings with wide metal roofs formed a compound; in the center of the courtyard stood a gnarled old chestnut. Two of the buildings, facing each other, were dormitories, their individual rooms opening onto verandas. A third building housed the laundry, kitchen, and dining hall.

She *listened* to the deep, drugged breathing of men and women in the dormitories, but passed them by. The fourth structure, the clinic, was her objective.

Except for dim yellow lights illuminating the verandas, none of the buildings showed lights. Sparta circled the clinic slowly, keeping to the shadows. Her close-focused eye traveled along the roofline, around each window and door frame, seeking monitoring cameras and telltales.

It seemed that the building's security was simple, almost primitive. No cameras watched the compound. The windows and doors were wired with conducting strips. She picked a window half hidden by a rhododendron bush and pushed back its shutters. From the thigh pocket of her jumpsuit she removed a slender steel tool; with precisely measured strength she incised a circle in the glass near the latch, tapped it, and let the glass disk fall outward into her hand. She reached through the hole and was about to affix a slack loop of wire to the alarm's conducting strip when she sensed, through her PIN spines, that no current was running in the alarm.

She thought about that for a millisecond, then set the loop anyway, tacking down both ends with aluminized putty. Current could start flowing without warning. Then she twisted the latch. Unlike the bedroom window, it took muscle to lift this sash; crumbs of dirt and old paint fell onto her face and into her hair.

She lifted herself easily onto the sill, tucked her legs, and curled sideways through the narrow opening. Her feet touched the floorboards and she stood up. She was in a small room equipped with a hospital bed and a variety of out-of-date diagnostic equipment. Not what one would expect of an expensive private sanatorium. Leaving the window ajar, she started to explore.

The clinic's offices and examination rooms were arranged on two sides of a long central hall. Moonlight fell through the slatted shutters and doors, most of which stood open, onto a threadbare strip of carpet.

Sparta's heat-seeking eye darted here and there in each of the rooms as she walked along, but she wasted little time, for she expected to find the clinic's records in the administrator's office. With micro-super technology, a century's worth could be stored on a rupee-sized wafer.

At the center of the building, near the front door, she came to a door that was closed. An engraved brass plaque screwed to the flimsy louvered door's crossbrace said "Dr. Singh."

She sniffed the simple magnetic lock. From the pattern of Singh's touch she deduced its sequence. A second later she stepped into Singh's office.

She experienced a peculiar shiver of pride. This had been so easy she'd hardly had a chance to stretch herself. She liked the way she could fool photogram monitors by a dancer's simple tricks of movement; she liked the way she could see in the dark and fool movement sensors by the timing of her steps. She liked the way she could smell who'd been in a room last, and when. She liked the way she could virtually walk through walls.

And she liked the way she could read a computer

system by letting the PIN spines under her fingernails slide into its I/O ports, bleeding it of information—as she did now, to the tiny water-cooled
computer box she found on Singh's office wall.

For a moment she was in trance, her senses overwhelmed by the aromatic tang of large primes
flowing through her calculating organ, her soul's
eye. For her, mathematical manipulation verged on
the erotic. The code key she was pursuing had the
taste and smell of tangerines . . . the feel of a light-
fingered backscratch . . . the sound of a bamboo
flute. Deftly she swam past the databank's safe-
guards, and seconds later found what she was
looking for.

She laughed aloud, not at what she'd found—
hardly funny—but with pleasure at her mastery.
They'd given her powers she'd never asked for or
consented to, powers greater than they knew.

At first it had been frightening to realize that she
could *listen* and hear what other people couldn't,
that she could taste and smell flavors and aromas
that other people couldn't, and not just perceive
them but analyze them in precise chemical detail.
It had been frightening—though convenient—to
discover that she could open electronic locks and
communicate directly with even the most complex
computer systems. Equally convenient were her
boundless memory and her ability to calculate, at
some deep level, far faster than her consciousness
could follow.

Not long ago she had even had the ability to sense
the aether, to cast her very *will* via microwave
beam—action at a distance. More than mere con-
venience, that sensation was one of pure power.

But that had been ripped out of her on Mars. The
life-mimicking organic polymers that had once ca-
pacitated her belly with burning electric power had
been ruptured by a would-be assassin's pulse
bomb. Unknowing surgeons had finished the job.
She had not been raised to depend on these pros-

theses. Her parents had taught her to trust in herself, taught her to believe that simply being human was not only enough, but—if she could be *fully* human—more than would ever be needed. To be human was to be potentially triumphant.

What she now read in Singh's coded files confirmed the conviction that had been building in her since she'd left Mars. A great many human subjects had passed through Holly Singh's ungentle hands. An astonishing proportion of them had died. They were the anonymous, the homeless poor, the orphaned . . . those who would never be missed.

Among them, one stood out.

> *Female subject, 18 years, height 154 centimeters, weight 43 kilograms, hair brown, eyes brown, race: white (English ancestry)/*
> *diagnosis of paranoid schizophrenia by transferring agency confirmed/*
> *patient complains of constant and severe visual and aural hallucinations/*
> *prescribed treatment, GAF neuro-amplification injection/*
> *complications of autonomic nervous system/*
> *apnea/*
> *elevated body temperature/*
> *convulsions/*
> *patient declared dead at 11:31 P.M./*
> *disposition of body according to conclave directive/*
> *shipment to North America contact without incident/*
> *records edited, successfully transmitted on . . .*

On that day, that month, that year. And the dead girl, a nameless runaway washed up in an asylum in Kashmir, appropriated by Singh for her own purposes, could from her appearance have been Sparta's twin. Her appearance was all they had needed from her—the appearance of her dead

body. Singh's treatment of the girl who was un-
lucky enough to look like Linda N. was swift and
deliberate murder.

Eight years ago Sparta had been a patient in a
sanatorium, a building of the same vintage as these
and like them, high in the mountains—the Rocky
Mountains of North America. She'd been trapped
there, mired in her own past, immobilized by her
inability to retain new information for more than
a few minutes. Her short-term memory had been
so effectively eradicated that she could not even remember her doctor's face.

But the doctor she'd had such difficulty remembering had known how to restore her working
memory; he'd done so at the cost of his own life,
giving her precious seconds she'd used to escape—
in the Snark that had brought her intended assassin.

Hardly a coincidence that, at the time, Doctor
Holly Singh should be running a mountain sanatorium, halfway around the globe. Hardly a coincidence that Singh should have developed the
neurochip techniques that the doctor had used to
save Sparta—the same techniques, in part, that had
made Sparta a freak.

One further next-to-impossible coincidence.
When the *Queen Elizabeth IV*, with its crew comple-
ment of neurologically enhanced chimpanzees, had
crashed over the Grand Canyon, and Captain Howard Falcon, Holly Singh's old friend, had been put
back together again, what they could save of his
nervous system had depended on the same neurochip technology. Of course, they'd done more to
Falcon, much more.

Sparta and Falcon and Steg, the crippled chimpanzee, were all cousins under the skull.

Sparta loaded the whole capacious secret file into
her own memory and retracted her spines from the
computer ports. She stood in the moonlit office, listening to the keening cries of exotic birds, the cough

of a tiger, the chatter of sleepless monkeys in the menagerie.

There were powers at loose in the world that intended to render humans as evolutionarily passé as monkeys and chimpanzees—intended to render the distinction meaningless. Holly Singh was working for them, not for the Council of Worlds, not for the Board of Space Control, and certainly not for the welfare of her patients.

Sparta left Singh's office and went down the hall. She removed the wire loop from the alarm circuit and closed the window, leaving the neat hole in the glass, then returned and left by the front door. Whether she confronted them now or in the morning hardly mattered. As an officer of the Board of Space Control, she would arrest Dr. Holly Singh. Singh and her servants were helpless to resist.

Humans and machines had been in growing symbiosis for centuries. Sparta was but a slightly precocious form of what was to come, the inevitable melding of human individual and human-generated mechanism. What was she then but what was once called a cyborg?

No, the dead eighteen-year-old in her cried, *I am human*. A human being corrupted by this *artificial* dependence, these prostheses that made up for no natural or necessary deficiency but were forcibly grafted onto and into her by others with inhuman programs of their own.

Yet she had become dependent upon her prostheses, even while telling herself she used them only for the good, for the sake of humanity, for the sake of discovering what had become of her parents, supposedly murdered, and for the sake of finding those who might have murdered them, and for the sake of eliminating those evil beings who, in giving her these powers, had given her the power to fight back.

And she loved the power.

At this moment she was afraid of nothing.

She walked boldly down the moonlit path, a confident woman who believed that her extraordinary senses protected her from anything the night might hold, and never heard the creature who came out of the shadows behind her.

15

He dropped out of the trees onto her back and for a horrible instant, as her nostrils flooded with the odor of the beast, she thought he would rip her head from her shoulders with his leathery black hands and black-haired muscular arms. Yellow fangs grazed her scalp.

Her strength was a tenth of his and, under ordinary circumstances, her quickness—even enhanced as it was—was a bare match for a chimpanzee's. Desperately she jerked and bent, evading his fangs, breaking his grip on her throat, and rolled, slipping out of the grasp of his clinging, uncoordinated legs. Poor Steg's damaged central nervous system had not prevented him from displaying patience and stealth, but his motor control was severely impaired.

Having failed to kill her immediately, he was at her mercy. He fled, and she sprinted after him. As the terrified chimpanzee ran and stumbled along the path, stretching his arms and vaulting on his knuckles, he hooted and shrieked in anguish, and his hoots and shrieks were immediately taken up by all the sleepless animals caged in Holly Singh's private menagerie.

Something had metamorphosed in Sparta. Her mercy had been strained in these last weeks and days, and she had no more compassion for this miserable half-ape than Artemis for a stag. The grace and speed that would have made a dancer of her had she chosen to be a dancer now bore her in an arc of vengeance.

Ten meters down the path she sprang onto his back and brought him screaming to the ground. The loop of wire she had used to bypass the clinic's alarm system went around his throat and cut off his panic-stricken calls.

She used violent leverage. He died in seconds.

Death. The sucking vortex that beckoned her, which she had resisted with less energy, less conviction, as the months wore on. A trail of death, until this moment none of it of her volition but leading her on, as if she were gravitationally attracted to a moving nexus of destruction. On Earth. Venus. The moon. Mars.

And her parents—dead or not, they were gone. Laird, or Lequeu, or whatever the shadowy figure who dogged her path now called himself, had tried with all his power to murder them. That was enough, and although he was out of her reach, others were not. She anticipated Holly Singh's return, for now she understood very well why Singh had snuck away.

Steg—who understood commands a bit more complex than Singh had pretended—had been ordered to murder Sparta in her bed. He was on his way to do it when she encountered him on the path. To have been killed by him would have seemed a tragic and most regrettable accident. Surely Dr. Singh would have wept copious tears, and the deranged Steg would, sadly, have been put to death. But Singh deserved to die more than Steg.

When Sparta raised herself from the corpse and stood erect there was a moonlight gleam in her eye more savage than any light she had seen in the chimpanzee's. She, who thought she hated killing. She, who lived to prevent murder and to bring murderers to merciful justice. She stood with the blood of a crippled animal dripping from the wire in her hands and with the keening cries of other terrified animals filling the night. In their calls was something less than mourning but more than fear—the advertisement of death.

Sparta found, as she searched her soul and reminded herself of what she had supposed she believed in, that not only could she dredge up no objection to killing Holly Singh, she could even look forward to that event with a certain savor.

With this newfound taste for blood, however, there came a heightened sense of the refined pleasures of the hunt. She decided that, after all, she would defer immediate revenge on Dr. Singh in favor of bigger game.

A long run along the ridge in the thin, cold air brought her to Darjeeling town. The rising sun came up from the mountains toward China, not like thunder but like cold fire; her breath steamed in front of her, and she thought as she watched it that the searing ball of yellow flame was challenging her directly, in the most intimate terms, to cease from patient questioning and to act—that the rising sun had transfigured her. To her right, the roof of this world. To her left, the inhabited universe and its deity, speaking to her in spears of light.

A few purchases in the market and a visit to the latrine behind a sweet shop and she was ready to board the morning's first train. Riding the chugging antique down through the tea terraces toward the plains, she was just another bedraggled tourist girl in search of enlightenment and *bangh*.

By the time the little train reached its terminus, Sparta's thinking had evolved. It seemed to her that her role as Ellen Troy, inspector for the Board of Space Control, had finally and completely outlived its usefulness. For what she was about to do, what was a badge but an encumbrance? She walked across the train platform to the nearest infobooth.

All by itself—as she had so often proved in her short history—it was a ticket to wealth and mobility and invisibility. A smile tugged at her perpetually open lips. She rarely smiled, and this one was not pleasant.

A day after leaving Darjeeling, she walked into the Varanasi shuttleport. Her eyes were liquid brown, her hair was as long and straight and black and sleek as Holly Singh's own, and her sari would have graced a maharani. When she spoke to the cabin attendant on the hypersonic jitney to London, her accent was perfect BBC, enlivened by musical hints of India.

But when she left Heathrow for London by magneplane three hours later, her hair was once more red-gold and curly and her eyes were sparkling green.

The next morning she woke up stiff and cold, to the sound of black rain beating against her apartment's single small window. Winter had come to London.

The videoplate brightened to the image of a young man wrapping his rosebud lips around his words as if he were sucking a lozenge. "Ronald Weir of the BBC reporting. Here is the morning's news. The Board of Space Control has just announced the seizure of the freighter *Doradus*. The vessel was discovered abandoned in a sparsely populated region of the main asteroid belt. The *Doradus* and its crew have been sought for several months in connection with the attempted robbery of the artifact known as the Martian plaque. A Space Board spokesperson notes that the *Doradus* was discovered to have been heavily armed with sophisticated weapons of a type restricted to use by authorized agencies of the Council of Worlds. The registered owners of the vessel have been approached with new inquiries." The announcer shuffled his papers. "In Uzbekistan, South Central

Asia Administrative Region, religious leaders have announced a cease-fire in the nine-year-old hostilities . . .''

Sparta put on one of Bridget Reilly's plainest dresses and sweaters. After a quick breakfast of soy paste on bran, she wrapped her threadbare Burberry around her and made her way through the gray rain to her office in the city.

Without a good morning to anyone, she hung up her coat and umbrella and sat down at her terminal.

To date, no bureaucracy had been safe from her electronic inquiries. Like ivy on a stone wall, her mind had reached into the crevices of every bureaucratic facade, patiently prying loose a flake of information here and a flake there, until massive structures of obstinacy and deceit had crumbled.

The Board of Space Control operated the most sophisticated computer nets in the inhabited worlds; an entire bureau within the Board was devoted to perfecting computer security, and another whole bureau was dedicated to ruining the work of the first. There was a way, only one, to maintain perfect security in a computer: complete isolation, not allowing the machine to talk to any other—and for the Space Board's purposes, that sort of security was useless.

Sparta—although she was not supposed to be— was thoroughly familiar with the intricacies of the Space Board's primal and fractal encryption systems. When all else failed and she chose to take the time, the computer behind the bone of her forehead could break encrypted codewords by sheer number-crunching power. Thus, in the long run, she could peek into any file she wanted to see. Much more easily, she altered files and created new files as she needed them.

Information was an ocean, one she swam in freely.

16

"The Prime Directive states that in any contact between humans and unknown forms of life, the human explorers shall take whatever steps are necessary to avoid disturbing the unknown forms. There follow quite a few footnotes and clarifications, of course, but that's the gist of it."

"An excellent principle; one we lobbied for with great energy." Dexter Plowman looked alarmingly like his sister, with gaunt face, bristling brows, and a tight cap of crimped, gray-black hair. "And successfully, of course."

Blake and the two Plowmans were trudging briskly northeastward along a seemingly endless, garbage-fouled beach. To their right, tired surf the color of tea slumped against the sand. To their left rose the twisted and blackened ruins of Atlantic City.

Arista had tracked her brother to this bleak shore, where he was making a personal inspection—and incidentally providing the mediahounds with photogram opportunities—in preparation for his next big suit against the government. The mediahounds having been reluctant to leave the parking lot and fill their shoes with sand, Blake had Dexter and Arista alone long enough to make his pitch.

"What I'm getting at, sir, is that the Prime Directive was promulgated at a time when there was no clue whatever of surviving life of any kind elsewhere in the solar system. . . ."

"Plenty of evidence for life!" One could almost hear the unspoken *objection!* in Dexter's tone. "All those fossils!"

"Yes sir, at the time a half dozen scraps of fossil had been discovered on the surface of Venus—all confidently dated to a billion years ago, when Venus had oceans, a moderate climate, and an Earthlike atmosphere."

"The whole point, Redfield! Close the gate *before* the pigs get out, isn't that what they say?"

"The horse, Dexter," his sister muttered.

He ignored her. "And sure enough, it wasn't long before the Martian plaque proved they *had* gotten here. And just a few months ago, there were those spectacular discoveries on Venus. . . ."

"Yes, sir, I was on Port Hesperus at the time," Blake said.

"Oh, really?"

"My question is different. I'm wondering just what motivated . . ."

"Motivation!" Dexter vigorously kicked at a cluster of used syringes. "A space station worker came to us with evidence that he had been infected with extraterrestrial microorganisms."

"What a fiasco!" Arista sneered. "You couldn't produce a shred of evidence at the trial."

"While we may have lost the horseshoe, dear"—he wasn't looking at her when he said "dear"—"we saved the nail."

"You lost the case," she muttered.

"We won the *principle*. No contact between humans and aliens. Quarantine established as the baseline. A resounding victory for exo-ecology. None of this going in and mucking about with things we don't understand." He paused long enough to scrape a gob of tar from his foot.

"Yes sir. While the worker's lawsuit didn't succeed, the Space Board did not resist your subsequent initiative campaign to write the Prime Directive into administrative law," Blake said.

Dexter gave him an appreciative glance—what a bright lad! "In fact, their Long Range Planning office had already come over to our side. Given friendly testimony."

Blake hesitated, approaching the delicate moment. "The worker whose grievance you undertook . . ."

"A class action, as a matter of fact. On behalf of all employees of the Board of Space Control who had been exposed to disease-causing extraterrestrial organisms."

"Nonexistent extraterrestrial organisms," Arista muttered.

"No attempt was made to punish or discipline the worker because of his legal action," Blake said.

"We made damn sure of that!"

"In fact, he was given a raise and promoted within a year after losing his suit against his own employers."

Dexter's bushy eyebrows jumped—oh, really?—but he said nothing.

"I was curious as to where the actual text of the Prime Directive originated," Blake continued. "I managed to uncover a draft of a memo from Brandt Webster, who as you may know is now Deputy Chief of Staff for Plans. . . ."

Dexter erupted. "How?"

"Sir?"

"How did you discover this draft memo?"

"I used a, uh, home computer. Webster's memo spells out the wording of the Prime Directive virtually as it was adopted more than a year later. I'm wondering. . . ."

As Dexter's thick brows drew closer together he stumbled over a seagull carcass.

". . . if possibly Webster worked with your people at Vox Populi in drafting the proposal to the Council of Worlds.''

Dexter's glance flickered to his sister. ''Certainly it's *possible*. I'm not sure, at this late date.''

''Sir, Webster's superior initially rejected his proposal on several grounds, mainly that in unprecedented situations astronauts should be allowed the greatest possible scope of judgment and action. Further, that there was no evidence of extraterrestrial life in the solar system at the time and plenty of evidence against its existence under any but Earthlike conditions. All that happened five months *before* the Space Board worker came to you with his complaint.'' Blake patted the polycanvas briefcase he had lugged up the beach. ''I have the holocopies here.''

''Mm. Later, Mr. Redfield.''

''I also have copies of the documents the worker, Mr. Gupta, showed you when he came to you with his complaint. And holos of the recovered Jupiter probe that supposedly brought an infectious organism back to Ganymede Base. And microphotograms of the supposed alien organism. And the doctor's report of the worker's CNS infection . . .''

''I remember all those perfectly well,'' Dexter said irritably, but the fire had gone out of his *objection*.

Arista smiled nastily. ''Then Mr. Redfield won't have to show you the documents that proved the so-called alien organism was ordinary *S. cerevisiae*—yeast—mutated by exposure to gamma radiation and antibiotics.''

''That didn't come out until much later,'' said Dexter.

''And his nervous-system infection turned out to be a mild case of herpes,'' said Arista.

''So the defense contended,'' said Dexter.

''So the jury believed,'' said Arista.

''By then we had dominated the media for months,'' Dexter said. ''The larger issue was well understood by the public—dangerous alien life-forms *could* exist. As I said at the time, bugs in the bushes—"

"Birds," Arista muttered.

"—are worth a timely stitch. And I still firmly believe that."

"Sir, this Gupta may be a member of the group I mentioned earlier, the Free Spirit . . ."

Dexter's eyebrows shot up. "Ah, I see it now! A conspiracy!" He made a sharp left turn, leading the little group around the outfall from a sewage pipe. "You are implying that I was duped into helping create a political climate in which the Prime Directive would pass over the objections of Space Board higher-ups. Yes, yes, Redfield, now I see why my sister swallowed your sugar-coated argument. But you've skipped something."

"What would that be?" asked Arista.

"Motivation!" *Objection!* "What possible motivation could this Free Spirit cult of yours have for protecting human explorers from extraterrestrial germs!"

"None, sir."

"F. O. B.!" Dexter crowed.

"Q. E. D.," muttered Arista.

"That's not what the Prime Directive primarily does, sir," Blake said mildly. "The Prime Directive in effect requires an explorer to sacrifice himself or herself before harming or causing distress to an extraterrestrial."

"Even an extraterrestrial *bug*," Arista said sourly. "Dexter, shut up a minute. Stop defending yourself and just listen."

Brother and sister locked gazes. Dexter blinked first.

"Go ahead, Redfield," Arista said.

"When I infiltrated the Free Spirit I learned that their beliefs are based on historical texts which they think are records of alien visits to Earth. This so-called Knowledge indicates the approximate location of the alien home star. It also indicates when and where they think the alien Pancreator will return."

"Which would be . . . ?" Dexter grumbled.

"Jupiter. Two years from now."

The little group came to a halt. The beach ahead was crowded with small purplish shapes like abandoned baggies. "What are those?" Dexter demanded, horrified. "Leftovers from somebody's lunch?"

"Jellyfish, sir. Don't step on them. They could sting."

"As you say." Dexter shoved his hands deeper into his overcoat pockets. Standing still, the wind seemed stronger. "Redfield, why should Vox Populi or anyone else be concerned with the beliefs of these moonies?"

"Loonies," muttered Arista.

"For a couple of reasons, sir. They've taken over the machinery of government—spending the people's money on their religion, if you want to look at it that way. Within the last century there have been three hundred and twenty-six probes into the clouds of Jupiter. Two years from now the *Kon-Tiki* expedition is scheduled to send the first human explorer to Jupiter."

"Yes, yes, it's a big waste, but that's what science *is*, isn't it? Cons and crazy people fleecing the public."

Blake let the proxmirism pass. "What if some alien thing *is* waiting in the clouds of Jupiter. The Prime Directive prohibits approaching it."

Dexter shook his head. "This is nuts!"

"The Free Spirit *are* nuts," Blake said. "That doesn't mean they're not right. What I've seen of the Knowledge looks pretty convincing."

"Right or wrong, they need to be stopped," Arista put in.

"How do *you* propose to do it, Redfield?"

"I'm glad you asked, sir. . . ."

They turned and walked back down the beach. The frigid smoke-filled wind which had been at their backs now stung their cheeks and burned their eyes and numbed their ears, and Blake had to shout over it to outline his plan.

By the time they reached the parking lot, where a few shivering reporters still waited to hear Dexter's next antiestablishment salvo, he was more than a convert; he was already preparing to take credit for Blake's scheme.

"As I've always said, Redfield," he expounded, "you can't break eggs without a loose cannon."

"That's me, sir," Blake cheerfully agreed, while Arista's eyes rolled skyward.

PART
4

THE WORLD
OF THE
GODS

17

Two years later . . .

The fueling tender blew its hoses a little rougher than it should have, spilling a quick blizzard of freezing oxygen into space. On Captain Chowdhury's board, the numbers bounced. No alarms went off, no vital pieces were broken off, but *Garuda* would have to spend more fuel than it should, keeping station.

The captain swallowed a curse. "*Garuda* to *Sofala*, that was an execrable separation. Please learn your job before you come back."

"It is our opinion that it is your loadmaster who needs to learn his job," the *Sofala*'s captain replied sharply. "Do you insist upon arbitration?"

Chowdhury hesitated—his mass-to-fuel ratio was only minutely on the down side—before he replied, as coolly as he could, "Leave the mouse-pushers out of it. Just go easy, will you?"

Sofala did not deign to answer. The fuel tender slid smoothly away, climbing toward Ganymede.

Chowdhury keyed off. He'd have to have a word with his loadmaster. Meanwhile, no harm done, and there were plenty of more important things to worry about.

But he wondered which demon he had failed to propitiate before lifting this grandly named bus from Ganymede a month ago. What should have been a routine job, despite the hoopla about the fancy cargo—after all, all he had to do was keep his converted tug on station behind Jupiter's little moon Amalthea—had plagued him from the start with all the accumulated glitches and gremlins and bugs he'd somehow managed to avoid in an error-free, twenty-year career, jockeying ships among the big planet's satellites.

The gremlin in the works was Sparta. She had shoved her PIN spines into one of the fuel-control microprocessors and messed up its timing; a second later she had readjusted it. Chowdhury's system check would reveal nothing amiss.

Sparta hovered in the shadows of the loading manifold, *listening* to the quick exchange between the two captains—filtering their distant voices out of all the multiple vibrations of the ship—before scurrying further back into the dark.

She used the narrowest of access passages to climb toward her lair in one of the ship's auxiliary power bays. From her grease-blackened face her sunken eyes shone starkly. She squeezed through the cramped shadows, finding her way by acute hearing and smell, seeing the dull red glow of *Garuda*'s metal guts in the infrared. She made it to her nest while the tug was still wobbling from the bad disconnect.

In a space station or a satellite colony, whose populations often exceeded 100,000, she could easily have disappeared in the crowd—as she'd done on Ganymede Base—but in a ship with twenty-eight people aboard, her only choice was to hide. She disguised her slight but anomalous extra mass by arranging numerous little "accidents" in refueling and resupply.

For a month, ever since *Garuda* had launched from Ganymede, she'd been living the life of a homeless refugee, secreting herself in the tiny space behind the AP unit service hatch. In that time she'd

grown gaunt and filthy, with few opportunities to
sponge her body or dry-wash her hair and none to
clean her clothes. Twice she'd risked stealing bits
of laundry from the recycler, substituting her own
grimy underwear and coveralls. She'd filched food
from stores when she could and rescued scraps
from recycling; her meager diet had a high proportion of nutrients in forms others didn't want: pow-
dered grape drink, salted yeast extract, freeze-dried
tofu chips—

—but she carried her own supply of Striaphan,
in a tube filled with hundreds of little white disks
that melted like fine sugar under the tongue.

Garuda was *Kon-Tiki*'s mother ship. A ten-year
veteran of service in near-Jupiter space, until eighteen months ago *Garuda* was an unprepossessing
heavy-lift tug with spartan facilities for the usual
crew of three. Now its builders wouldn't have rec-
ognized it. *Garuda*'s cargo holds had been replaced
with a complex of crew facilities, tiny but luxuri-
ous—private cabins, dining room, game rooms,
clinics, commissary—and its life support systems
had been enlarged, its onboard power units made
multiply redundant, its chemical fuel tanks tripled
in capacity. Amidships, *Garuda* bristled like a sea
urchin with antennas and communications masts.

The most obvious and striking change was *Kon-
Tiki* Mission Control itself, the big circular room
that sliced right through *Garuda*'s middle, belting
the ship's equator with dark glass windows below
the smaller dome of the bridge. Once *Kon-Tiki* had
been launched, a flight director and five controllers
would man the Mission Control consoles, in three
shifts around the clock.

And now that *Sofala* had topped off *Garuda*'s pro-
pellant tanks, that launch was only hours away.

Sparta lay curled like a fetus, weightless in the
dark, *listening* to the final countdown. . . .

With the main airlocks of the two craft mated, the *Kon-Tiki* module had been carried into Jupiter orbit on *Garuda*'s bow. Now Sparta heard the sealing of the locks and the clang of the hatches, felt the shudder of shackles springing back in precise sequence and the final bump of separation. She heard the hiss of *Garuda*'s attitude-control jets compensating almost imperceptibly for the gentle push *Kon-Tiki*'s own jets had given the mother ship as it separated.

Sparta imagined the *Kon-Tiki* module, its intricacies hidden beneath gleaming cowlings and heat shields, carefully increasing its distance from *Garuda*.

Now both craft hung virtually motionless a thousand kilometers above the desolate rocks and ice of Amalthea, in the radiation shadow of that modest satellite. For *Kon-Tiki*, Jupiter would soon rise above the rim of the little moon, but the great planet would remain hidden from *Garuda* throughout the mission. When orbital separation was complete and all systems had been checked, *Kon-Tiki* would fire its retrorockets and begin its long fall.

Howard Falcon's quest was about to reach its culmination.

Sparta's quest over the past two years had been more private and more tortured. She lay *listening* as his moment of triumph approached, while her consciousness phased in and out of dark dreams and distorted memories. . . .

"Are you all right, dear?"

The solicitous questioner is a wide woman with the broad hands and bright cheeks of a former milkmaid, whose round Rs betray her Somersetshire origins. Her arms are filled with bundled sheets.

The girl blinks her blue eyes and smiles apologetically. "Was I at it again, Clara?"

"Dilys, I warn you that you'll never work your

way out of the laundry if you keep falling asleep standing up.'' Clara pushes the armful of dirty sheets into the maw of the industrial-sized washing machine. ''Be a good girl and pull those others out of the hamper, will you?''

Dilys bends to drag the sheets up from the depths of the cart. Above her head opens the maw of the laundry chute, which reaches three stories up to the top floor of the country house.

Clara lifts an eyebrow. ''If I didn't know you for an innocent, I'd suspect you of listening in. That chute's a fine telephone to the bedrooms, as you've no doubt discovered.''

Dilys turns wide eyes on her. ''Oh, I wouldn't do that.''

Clara's ample bosom shakes with a hearty laugh. ''Not that it would do you any good at this hour of the morning. Nobody upstairs but Blodwyn and Kate, stuffing these down the hole.'' Clara takes the sheets from Dilys, pushes the slept-on-once linen into the machine, and closes the round glass door on it. Her brown eyes glint with mischief. ''You'd learn more about our guests from these. See here, Miss Martita's sheets haven't been slept in at all. Why not?'' She pulls open a used expanse of bedding. ''Here's a clue: that fellow Jurgen is not the ox he appears.''

''I don't understand,'' Dilys said.

''I mean the difference between an ox and a bull, dear.''

''Clara!''

''But perhaps a miner's daughter shouldn't be expected to understand country matters.'' Clara crumples the sheet and shoves it into the washer. ''No more daydreaming, now. See that the towels and napkins are pressed and folded by the time I get back.''

Dilys watches Clara's broad back and broader hips disappear up the stairs. Rather than attend to the ironing, the slim, dark girl immediately falls back into trance. Although she isn't standing near the laundry chute now, she is doing just what Clara has accused her of doing. She is *listening.* Listening not to bedroom antics, in which she has no interest, but to the casual conversations of Lord Kingman's weekend guests. Voices come to her from the hall. . . .

"The hunting is rather good to the west—let's leave it to the others, what do you say?" Kingman's voice, an older man's, ripe with good breeding.

"I'm sure you'll find us something worth shooting, Rupert." A middle-aged man, whose every utterance so far has betrayed a terrible impatience underlying his charm.

"I won't disappoint you . . . ahh"—Kingman's voice drops, his inflection sours—*"here's the German now."*

Downstairs in the laundry room, the dark-haired girl stands rapt. Her peculiarities will be tolerated in the household for the sake of the centuries-old, romantic, mystical reputation of the Welsh—not to mention that old Lord Kingman seems to have a special fondness for a *merch deg.* But under her brunette wig her hair is blond and her eyes are not as dark blue as they seem, and Kingman would be profoundly shocked to discover the bitterness in this particular pretty girl's heart.

Sparta—but for Kingman and his cronies, alone in all the worlds—knows that Kingman was the captain of the *Doradus.*

PIRATE SHIP IN SPACE, the newsheads had screamed. There were no pirates in space, of course. Putting aside practical matters of pursuit and conquest, where could they possibly hide? Not near inhabited planets and moons, and the Mainbelt was not the Caribbean: the asteroids were small and airless and unable to support life, without huge and obvious investments of capital.

The *Doradus* had not been a pirate vessel, but a secret warship, intended to be held in reserve against some future conflict with the Council of

Worlds. In all the solar system, less than a dozen fast Space Board cutters were authorized to carry offensive weapons; the *Doradus* was a formidable force. How well guarded had been the secret of that ship! How chagrined the Free Spirit must be at its loss!

As the news media recounted in great detail, the registry of the mystery ship was aboveboard and normal: the ship was owned by a most respectable bank, Sadler's of Delhi, which had loaned the capital for its construction. The builders had gone bankrupt and forfeited, and Sadler's had acquired the ship and hired a reputable shipping line to operate it, a firm which had subsequently leased *Doradus* to an asteroid-mining venture that made regular voyages between Mars and the Mainbelt. For five years the ship had turned an unremarkable but respectable profit.

Yet every one of the ten recorded officers and crew of *Doradus*, it soon developed, were fictitious identities. Even though four bodies had been left on Phobos when *Doradus* had blown its cover, their true identities could not be established.

Still, not a glimmer of evidence linked the ship's phony crew with any wrongdoing on the part of the mining company that had apparently hired them in good faith, or the shipping line that had contracted with the mining venture, or the bank that had contracted with the shipping line, or the bankrupt shipbuilders who had lost their investment.

Sparta knew that such a complex deceit could never have been successful without the complicity of people deep within the Board of Space Control itself. Through her own access to electronic media she had leveraged her way into the Space Board's investigations branch, learning the results of the search of *Doradus* almost as soon as Earth Central did.

Among the armaments found on board were "12

each passive-target missiles of SAD–5 type, no serial numbers; 24 each high-impulse torpedoes with proximity-fused HE warheads, no serial numbers, design previously unknown; 4 each Tooze-Olivier space-adapted repeating shotguns; 24 cases, 24 rounds per case, antipersonnel shells for same; 2 each miscellaneous 9–mm copper-point bullets, possibly of antique manufacture . . ." Along with the heavy stuff, two old pistol bullets—somebody on board the *Doradus* had been a gun collector.

As it happened, one of the directors of the Sadler's Bank who had been active in arranging the bankruptcy and leasing arrangements of the *Doradus* was an enthusiast of antique weapons, an Englishman of rather distinguished ancestry—name of Kingman.

It was the sort of obscure fact that Space Board investigators would have gotten around to checking sooner or later, by way of doggedly tracking down every possibility. Whether the investigators would have been able to make anything of it was less certain. Sparta's approach was more intuitive and direct. Her carefully constructed resume was borrowed freely from a real girl from Cardiff named Dilys, and it withstood the intense scrutiny of Kingman's household manager; Sparta had seen to it that a position had opened shortly before.

Soon after arriving at Kingman's estate, Sparta had confirmed her guess, learning from her voluble belowstairs colleagues of Kingman's famous ancestor and of a pistol taken off a German soldier in the battle of El Alamein, a pistol that accepted the rounds Kingman, in his haste, left aboard his abandoned warship.

Now "Dilys" stands listening until the voices she hears through the walls fade away, one by one. Kingman and his weekend guests are leaving the house for their afternoon of shooting. She turns back to the mountain of linen that needs ironing. By tonight, she knows with a certainty she would not be able to explain, she will learn the final secrets of the *prophetae*. . . .

Aboard *Garuda*, Sparta stirred fitfully and roused herself from sleep. A steadily increasing intake of Striaphan—for almost two years now—had shrunk her emotional life to a black knot of rage, but it had not diminished her powers of perception and calculation . . . so long as she was awake enough and strong enough to focus them. But her head throbbed and her mouth was dry. It took long seconds for her to recall where she was, why it was so cold and dark and foul-smelling in this cramped little space.

Then the glow of remembered anger once more began warming her from inside. *Kon-Tiki* had awakened her.

Kon-Tiki was on its way down.

18

The fall from Amalthea's orbit to the outer atmosphere of Jupiter takes only three and a half hours—plus a few minutes to gain an extra modicum of orbital inclination, thus avoiding the wide stretch of the planet's diaphanous, rubble-filled rings. Even with the detour, it's a short trip.

Few men could have slept on so swift and awesome a journey. Sleep was a weakness that Howard Falcon hated, and the little he still required brought dreams that time had not yet been able to exorcise. But he could expect no rest in the three days that lay ahead, and he must seize what he could during the long fall down into that ocean of clouds, some 96,000 kilometers below.

Thus, as soon as *Kon-Tiki* had entered her transfer orbit and all the computer checks were satisfactory, he tried to prepare himself for sleep. Viewed coldly, it was the last sleep he might ever know— so it seemed appropriate that at almost the same moment Jupiter eclipsed the bright and tiny sun, as his ship swept into the monstrous shadow of the planet. For a few minutes a strange golden twilight enveloped the ship; then a quarter of the sky became an utterly black hole in space, while the rest was a blaze of stars.

No matter how far one traveled across the solar

system, the *stars* never changed; these same con-
stellations now shone on Earth, millions of kilometers away. The only novelties here were the
small, pale crescents of Callisto and Ganymede.
There were a round dozen other moons somewhere up there in the sky, but they were all much
too tiny and too distant for the unaided eye to pick
them out.

"All's nominal here," he reported to the controllers far above him on *Garuda*, drifting in safety
in Amalthea's shadow. "Closing down shop for
two hours."

"That's a roger, Howard," the flight director replied. The bit of jargon from the early days of the
American space program might have sounded
strange once, pronounced as it was in Thai-
accented English, but certain phrases of American
and Russian had long since become as familiar in
interplanetary space as ancient nautical terminol-
ogy on the seven seas of Earth.

Falcon switched on the sleep inducer and fell
swiftly into that aimless musing that is prelude to
unconsciousness. His brain, which stored information willy-nilly and produced it by free association at moments like this, now reminded him of
the etymology of the name Amalthea: it meant
"tender," as in gentle and caring. Amalthea the
goat-nymph had been nursemaid to the infant
Zeus—whom the Romans fondly equated with Jupiter—in his hiding-cave on Crete.

For a long time after Jupiter's inner moon was
discovered it was known simply as Jupiter V, the
first to be found after the four satellites made famous by Galileo—their names also borrowed from
mythological associates of Zeus. If it served no other
caring purpose, Amalthea was a cosmic bulldozer
perpetually sweeping up the charged particles
which made it unhealthy to linger close to Jupiter.
Amalthea's wake was almost free of radiation and
chunks of flying matter, and there *Garuda* could

park in perfect safety while death sleeted invisibly all around it.

Falcon idly pondered these matters as the electric pulses surged gently through his brain. While *Kon-Tiki* fell toward Jupiter, gaining speed second by second in that enormous gravitational field, he slept—at first—without dreams. The dreams always came when he began to awake. He had brought his nightmares with him from Earth.

He never dreamed of the crash itself, though he often found himself face to face again with that terrified superchimp, seen in those moments when they were both descending through the collapsing gasbags. The simps hadn't survived, except one, he didn't really know which; most of those who were not killed outright were so badly injured that they'd been painlessly euthed. He didn't know if that holdout survivor was the same one he'd confronted in the wreck, but Falcon—in his dreams—always had that one's face in front of him. He sometimes wondered why he dreamed only of this doomed creature and not of the friends and colleagues he had lost aboard the dying *Queen*.

The dreams he feared most always began with his first return to consciousness. There had been little physical pain; in fact there had been little sensation of any kind. He was in darkness and silence, and he did not even seem to be *breathing*—

—strangest of all, he could not locate his limbs. He felt them there; he had all their sensations. They seemed to move, but he did not know where they were. . . .

The silence was the first to yield. After hours, or days, he had become aware of a faint throbbing, and eventually, after long thought, he deduced that this was the beating of his own heart. That was the first of his many mistakes.

Next there had been faint pinpricks, sparkles of light, ghosts of pressure upon those still ghostly limbs. One by one his senses had returned, and pain had come with them. He had had to learn everything anew.

He was a baby, helpless, and about as cute as sour milk and dirty diapers; probably there would have been lots of desperate smiling at Mom, if he could have figured out how to smile, and who was Mom. But soon he was a toddling infant: lots of cheers from everybody as he lurched half the length of the room before he folded abruptly. Folded up time after time. Physical therapy, they called it.

Though his memory was unaffected—it didn't *seem* to have been affected, for he could certainly understand the words that were spoken to him—it was months before he could answer his interrogators (why did they always lean over him with those damned lights overhead, those bright lights in a circle?) with more than a flicker of an eyelid.

Vivid now were the moments of triumph when he had uttered the first word . . . first pressed the pad of a book chip . . . and then, finally, *moved*. Moved through space (the space of a hospital room), and not in his imagination but under his own power. *That* was a victory indeed, and it had taken him almost two years to prepare for it.

A hundred times he'd envied the dead superchimps. They had tried and died. He hadn't died, so he had to keep trying—he was given no choice in the matter. The doctors, his close friends, had made their deliberate decisions, deliberately.

And now, years later, he was where no human being had ever traveled, falling planetward faster than any human in history.

Sparta was falling with him, toward the bright planet, if only in her blazing imagination. Her eyes burned and her heart throbbed painfully in her chest. She hadn't slept for twenty hours, yet all her senses, the ordinary and the extraordinary, were tuned to a bright pitch.

The *pain* of that brightness, the crashing pain of

perception and imagination, cried out for relief. Her weak fingers fumbled for the precious vial. She snapped off the cap and tried to extract a wafer, nestled close to the others in their tube, but they were obstinate in the microgravity. She extended her PIN spines and prized one out.

Slowly the wafer melted under her tongue. The brightness softened; imagination dissolved into memory—dreamed memory, or perhaps remembered dream. . . .

Dilys pauses to listen.

Except for the night watchman and his assistant, out prowling the grounds, the staff of the great house are deep in exhausted sleep. Upstairs the last of the guests are finally asleep too.

The shooting parties had set out and had not returned for several hours. Kingman and the man called Bill had taken the east side of the estate; the west side was left to the big, loud German fellow—whose partner was Holly Singh.

Singh had not bothered to disguise her looks or her name; Dilys had wondered if the others' identities were as real as hers. When a late guest arrived she knew they were: he was Jack Noble from Mars, who had vanished after the failed attempt to steal the Martian plaque.

The hunters had returned when the woods were in shade and October shadows were long on the meadow.

Cook had had dinner for six to contend with, but a butler, maid, and manservant were sufficient to do the service. Dilys, inexperienced in the ways of the household, had been free to sit in her tiny room in the servant's wing and watch the viddie, until exhaustion overcame her.

She'd tried to *listen*, but after dinner Kingman and his guests had seemed to vanish into some utterly soundproof recess of the ancient manor. Through the crashing din of the nearby kitchen she'd filtered the sound of footsteps descending stone stairs—even the whisper of long robes—then a loud screech of iron hinges and the boom of heavy wooden doors. Then nothing.

Nothing to do but sit quietly in her little room, while the rest of the staff bustled about her, and think. Seems there was a place beneath the house that did not appear in the oldest plan, those fragments of parchment dating from the late 14th century, when what was to become Kingman's house had begun as an abbey on the pilgrim road. If the hidden place deep in the earth had been built at that time, its architects and builders had conspired to keep it secret. If it had been dug later, the contractors and workmen were equally discreet.

How was such perfect discretion obtained? By the ancient expedients, no doubt still in use. How many building inspectors and historians and would-be archaeologists had come into sudden wealth or met with untimely death after professing an interest in this significant pile of old stones?

Dilys, truly exhausted after fourteen hours of washing and ironing, had been unable to resist exhaustion. She'd fallen asleep then, and wakened to this deathly quiet moment.

Now she leaves her narrow cell, walks through the big kitchen smelling of grease and soap—moonlight spills through the high leaded windows, reflects from the round bottoms of hanging steel pans and bowls, gleams from racks of knives—moves through the pantry into the service hall beside the main dining room.

Here a door opens upon a narrow stair, those she had heard them descend. Nothing guards the door. She opens it and moves swiftly down the spiraling stone steps into utter darkness.

Infrared radiation seeps from the warm stone walls, enough for her to see by. Empty racks and abandoned casks are shoved back against the walls, but someone has recently been in to dust off the cobwebs. The stone pavement underfoot has been washed and waxed. At the far side of the old wine cellar is another door, again unlocked and unguarded. Here, at the heart of the conspiracy, confidence has overruled caution.

Through the door. More stone steps—cooler now, a cave that keeps a steady temperature all year around. She sees forms in the dim glow of the Earth's faint radioactive warmth.

At the bottom of the steps. The air redolent of perfumes and perspirations; by their various scents she knows Kingman and each of his guests. There—their ghosts hang in midair, six white robes still glowing with the body heat of those who have recently worn them.

In front of her, another door, this one of metal. She touches her tongue to it: bronze, cool and sour. On its surface, only a few handprints, still barely warm and thus visible. Otherwise the door is a slab of black in the dim red darkness.

She sniffs the air, stares at the cooling prints, *listens*.

She eases the door open. Cold air flows gently out of the cavern. From the barely perceptible echoes of her quiet footfalls on the stone she senses the amount of empty space in the chamber.

To see more, even she will need light. She cups her palm over the bright electric torch, making a lantern of her hand's bones and flesh. By the blood-filtered light she sees a severely simple octagonal chamber of pale sandstone, like a church without aisles or transept, higher than it is wide. The floor is of black marble, highly polished, unadorned.

On eight sides slender stone piers soar upward, springing into thin ribs which criss-cross the vault in a star pattern. Between the ribs, a ceiling painted so dark a blue that it is black in the red light. Bright gold eight-pointed stars randomly adorn it, in sizes from nail heads to shield bosses. The biggest star, a kind of gold target, is fixed at the high center.

The architecture is Late Gothic, a style originating in Eastern Europe in the 14th century, in England called Perpendicular. The work is original, no copy, but this vault is no church. The stars overhead are not randomly sprinkled.

This is a planetarium. It depicts the southern sky, and at its center is the constellation Crux. She recognizes the nature of the room from what Blake has told her. The starry vault is an analogue, centuries older, of the last chamber in the underground villa in Paris where Blake's initiation into the *prophetae* had culminated.

She moves slowly about the windowless, utterly sterile room, noting how the golden stars above are reflected in the polished black marble at her feet, as if from the bottom of a deep well.

There, in the center of the black marble floor, is the single decorative feature, directly beneath the bright golden star in Crux. A raised round stone, with a device carved upon it. She uncaps her torch and shines its intense white beam straight down.

A Gorgon's head. Medusa.

Not the classical fancy of a lovely woman with garden snakes for hair, but an Archaic-period horror mask of deeply carved and brightly painted limestone—red and blue and yellow—fused upon the marble: staring eyes, wide-stretched maw, curved tusks, a scalp writhing with vipers.

The Goddess as Death.

The hall in Paris that Blake had told of had been built in the Age of Reason, and the starry chamber which he had attained after many trials was dominated by an enormous statue of Athena, inside of which was housed (O pinnacle of Apollonian calm and exuberance!) a pipe organ. But on the aegis of that same Athena, goddess of wisdom, was an archaic mask of Medusa.

The *prophetae* worship the Knowledge, *Agia Sophia*, Athena and Medusa, Wisdom and Death. To look upon the face of Medusa is to be turned to stone. To resist the Knowledge is to die.

She could be the greatest of us
To resist us is to resist the Knowledge

The gaunt girl who now looks upon the face of the goddess thinks otherwise. Beneath the carved stone mask at her feet rests something of great value, something of deepest significance to the people who put the mask here.

To confront wisdom is to die. The gate of wisdom is death.

The slab is heavy, but it lifts easily away. The crypt below, lined with white limestone, is no wider or deeper than the marble plate above. Something in it is hidden under a linen shroud. She plucks the shroud away and penetrates the dark chamber with a spear of light. She sees. . . .

An iron chalice bearing the figure of the striding storm god. Hittite, older than the carved Medusa, at least 3,500 years old.

A pair of papyrus scrolls. Egyptian, almost as old.

The tiny skeletons of two human infants, yellowed to ivory. Origin unknown. Age indeterminate.

A slim black datasliver, shiny and new.

"Kon-Tiki Mission Control at mission elapsed time three hours, ten minutes, on the mark,'' said flight director Meechai Buranaphorn into the data recorder. ''And here's the mark. . . . Guidance, give us your verbal assessment please.''

''Tracking still nominal for scheduled atmospheric descent.''

''Medical?''

The med controller spoke into his comm unit. ''All nominal. EEG indicates our man is in transition out of stage-two sleep.''

Already there was a lag in signal reception from *Kon-Tiki,* amounting to perhaps a twentieth of a second and steadily increasing. Mission Control was forced to maintain communication with *Kon-Tiki* via comm satellites in temporary orbits, for between *Garuda* and the planet the shield of Amalthea was always upraised, blocking line-of-sight communication.

The half dozen controllers hung comfortably in loose harnesses above their sparkling flatscreens. Through surrounding windows of thick glass a spectacular landscape of pocked and irregular ice and rock reflected feeble sunlight back into the circular room: it was one end of the oblong moon, which stretched away for dozens of kilometers like a striated, convex plaster impression of Death Valley. From the edge of the dirty white horizon an orange-red glow refracted daytime on Jupiter. The planet itself would never be seen through the windows of this room, but *Kon-Tiki*'s triumphant return would be.

For all the relative luxury of its custom-made facilities, *Garuda* was a crowded ship, with five crewmembers and a total of twenty-one mission controllers, scientists, and supporting technicians. When Howard Falcon was aboard, that made twenty-seven people. There was one other passenger on *Garuda*'s official roster, but so far as the professionals were concerned he was worse than useless baggage.

Mister Useless Baggage spoke up now, from a privileged seat peering over the flight director's shoulder—the controllers knew him mainly as someone from a watchdog citizens' group authorized by the Board of Space Control to observe the mission, a place a couple of hundred media types would willingly have shed blood over.

"Consumables, Redfield here, if you can spare a moment. My calculations do not quite jibe with your estimate of oxygen-consumption rates aboard *Kon-Tiki*. Will you kindly reconfirm?" His voice and manners were those of an unfriendly tax collector.

The controller in question objected to nothing,

offered nothing, merely suffered the indignity and tapped a few keys. The Baggage Man had subjected all of them to such indignity in the weeks since *Garuda* had left Ganymede.

Mr. Baggage, Redfield, as he called himself, grunted at the numbers freshly displayed on his screen and said nothing. He was not really paying attention, not even really caring.

Armed with the plans Blake had worked out for them, Dexter and Arista had launched their public-relations blitz. . . . "Quis custodet custodies?" Arista had demanded, as confident of her dimly remembered Latin as only priests and lawyers can be. Dexter had put the matter a little more earthily: Who sets a dog to watch the eggs?

Faced with Vox Populi's persistence and this last bit of untranslatable logic, the Board of Space Control had given in. After much jockeying and negotiating—the Plowmans never hesitating to go public when things bogged down—it was agreed that one or more impartial observers from an organization such as Vox Populi should be allowed free access to every facet of the *Kon-Tiki* program, throughout its operations.

Blake sometimes suppressed a grin when he thought how readily the Space Board had capitulated. The mess was not all that funny, really, when he considered that perhaps a dozen people on this ship knew all about it and were merely awaiting a chance to kill him. And even the innocents wished he would go away.

Yet he stayed and asked harassing questions and watched them, sometimes for two or more shifts at a time without sleeping. What he was looking for, they didn't know. They weren't friendly, and neither was he.

Blake's bitter reverie was broken by the comm controller. "Flight, we have Howard on line."

19

Kon-Tiki was just emerging from shadow, and the Jovian dawn was bridging the sky ahead in a titanic bow of light, when the persistent buzz of the alarm dragged Falcon up from sleep. The inevitable nightmares (he had been trying to summon a nurse, but did not even have the strength to push a button) had swiftly faded from consciousness. The greatest—and perhaps last—adventure of his life was before him.

He called Mission Control, now almost 100,000 kilometers away and falling swiftly below the curve of Jupiter, to report that everything was in order. His velocity had just passed fifty kilometers per second (given that he was within the outer fringes of a planetary atmosphere, that was one for Guinness), and in half an hour *Kon-Tiki* would begin to feel the resistance that made this the most difficult atmospheric entry in the entire solar system.

Scores of probes had survived this flaming ordeal, but they'd been tough, solidly packed masses of instrumentation, able to withstand several hundred gravities of drag. *Kon-Tiki* would hit peaks of thirty Gs, and would average more than ten, before she came to rest in the upper reaches of the Jovian atmosphere.

Very carefully and thoroughly Falcon began to

attach the elaborate system of restraints that would anchor him to the walls of the cabin. No simple webbed harness here—when he'd finished making the last connections among the struts and tubes and electrical conduits and strain sensors and shock absorbers, he was virtually a part of the ship's structure.

The clock on the console was counting backward. One hundred seconds to entry. For better or worse, Falcon was committed. In a minute and a half he would hit palpable atmosphere and would be caught irrevocably in the grip of the giant.

The countdown proceeded: minus three, minus two, minus one, on down to zero.

Nothing happened. At first.

The clock began counting up—plus one, plus two, plus three—and then, from beyond the walls of the capsule, there came a ghostly sighing that rose steadily to a high-pitched, screaming roar. The countdown had been three seconds late, not at all bad, considering the unknowns.

The noise was quite different from that of a plunging shuttle on Earth or Mars, or even Venus. In this thin atmosphere of hydrogen and helium, all sounds were transformed a couple of octaves upward. On Jupiter, even thunder would have falsetto overtones.

Squeaky thunder. Falcon would have grinned if he could.

With the rising scream came mounting weight. Within seconds he was completely immobilized. His field of vision contracted until it embraced only the clock and the accelerometer. Fifteen Gs and four hundred and eighty seconds to go. He never lost consciousness; but then, he had not expected to.

Kon-Tiki's flaming trail through the atmosphere was surely spectacular, viewed by the photogram cameras feeding Mission Control, or by any other watcher—many thousands of kilometers long by now. Five hundred seconds after entry, the drag began to taper off: ten Gs, five Gs, two . . . Then the sensation of weight vanished almost completely. Falcon was falling free, all his enormous orbital velocity dissipated.

There was a sudden jolt as the incandescent remnants of the capsule's heat shield jettisoned. The aerodynamic cowlings blew away in that same instant. Jupiter could have them now; they had done their work. Falcon released some of his physical restraints, giving himself a bit more freedom to move within the capsule—without diminishing his intimacy with the machinery—and waited for the automatic sequencer to start the next and most critical series of events.

He could not see the first drogue parachute pop out, but he could feel the slight jerk. The rate of fall diminished immediately. Soon *Kon-Tiki* had lost all its horizontal speed and was going straight down at almost fifteen hundred kilometers an hour.

Everything depended on what happened in the next sixty seconds.

And there went the second drogue. He looked up through the overhead window and saw, to his immense relief, that clouds upon clouds of glittering foil were billowing out behind the falling ship. Like a great flower unfurling, thousands of cubic meters of the balloon's fabric spread out across the sky, a vast parachute scooping up the thin gas until finally it was fully inflated.

Kon-Tiki's rate of fall dropped to a few kilometers an hour and remained constant. Now there was plenty of time. At this rate it would take Falcon days to fall all the way down to the surface of Jupiter.

But he would get there eventually, if he did nothing about it. Until he did, the balloon overhead acted merely as an efficient parachute, providing no lift—nor could it do so while the density of the gas inside and out was the same.

Then, with its characteristic and rather disconcerting *crack*, the little fusion reactor started up, pouring torrents of heat into the envelope overhead. Within five minutes the rate of fall had become zero; within six, the ship had started to rise. According to the altimeter, it leveled out a little over four hundred kilometers above the surface—or whatever passed for a surface on Jupiter.

Only one kind of balloon will work in an atmosphere of hydrogen, the lightest of all gases, and that is a hot-hydrogen balloon. As long as the fuser kept ticking over, Falcon could remain aloft, drifting across a world that could hold a hundred Pacifics. After traveling in stages some five million kilometers from Earth, the last of the watery planets, *Kon-Tiki* had begun to justify her name. She was an aerial raft, adrift upon the fluid currents of the Jovian atmosphere.

Falling toward Jupiter, Falcon had emerged from his painful dreams into triumphant sunlight. In her stinking hiding hole aboard *Garuda*, in the shadow of Amalthea, Sparta still lived inside hers. . . .

"Dilys" has no means of reading a datasliver without an interface. Five minutes after discovering the crypt she is back upstairs in Kingman's kitchen, at the household computer. The terminal has been placed too near the gas range, its flatscreen hazy and its keypad slick with grease. Nevertheless, she enters the terminal with her fingerprobes and feels the tingling flow of electrons. She inserts the stolen chip. Its contents spill directly into her forebrain.

She rolls the spiky ball of information in multidimensional mental space, seeking a key to entry. The mass of data is gibberish, although not without formal regularities. But the key is nothing so simple as a large prime; its complex geometric quality eludes her for long seconds. Then an image comes unbidden into her mind. It is familiar indeed, the swirling vortex of clouds into which her dreams have so often led her—

—but seen from higher up, so that the peculiarly curdled patterns of Jupiter's clouds are as plain and sharply defined as a slowly stirred paint can, drops of orange and yellow paint spiraling into the white.

Vistas of information split open before her.

She is falling into and through those bottomless clouds—no, she is soaring through them like a winged creature. Intense waves of radio emission seep through her, fill her with thrilling warmth, a sensation so familiar it causes her sweet pain—for the memory that she once could experience such sensations in her own body.

She is dazzled, disoriented, made a little drunk. She struggles to retain an objective outlook, to make sense of what she is seeing.

This is data from a Jupiter probe. A tag on the file, accessed by her objective mind, gives its designation and date. She is experiencing what the probe "experienced" through all its sensors, its lenses and antennas and radiation detectors.

The file terminates. With a jump, like a cut in a viddie, she is inside another experience.

An operating theater. A swirl of lights overhead. A tingle of dulled pain throughout her body, radiating from her belly to the tips of her toes and fingers. Is this *herself* on the table? Is she reliving her agony on Mars through some monitor's data record? No, this is another place, another . . . patient. The physicians take their time.

They are invisible behind their masks, but she can smell them. Not much left of the flesh and blood human under the lights, and what there is is supported by an intricate fretwork of plastic and metal . . . instruments where organs should be. Temporary support systems? Permanent prostheses?

Jump. New file.

Falcon. She *is* Falcon. She/he is testing her/his restored limbs, her/his restored sense organs. Grisly business . . . the most primitive sort of physical therapy. Her/his progress monitored by internal implants. . . .

Again she struggles to separate her consciousness from the experience in which she is immersed. These are Falcon's feelings, but Falcon himself does not seem to know that he has been tapped, is being recorded. They've put a bug in him, inside his head.

Fascinated, she immerses herself in his therapy, the painful stretching and flexing of his patched limbs and organs—his restored and enhanced powers. Of his eyes—capable of microscopic and telescopic vision, of sensitivity to ultraviolet and infrared. Of his sense of smell—capable of bringing instant chemical analysis to consciousness. Of his sensitivity to radio and particle radiation. Of his ability to *listen* . . .

He was her. But better. New and improved. Better sensors. Better processors. She felt a surge of anger, of stark jealousy.

Jump. New file.

Flight simulation, down into the swirling clouds of the gas giant, a planet which could only be Jupiter. Visuals and other data, lifted from probes. Supersonic winds. Hydrocarbon slurry. Temperature shifts, pressure shifts—all seen from inside Falcon's head. And she is there, swimming in it with him.

A hot beam of radio—

—and then a sound, a song, a booming choir, coming right into his/her breast, bursting from it with a swelling joy and a shocking, necessary urge. For the Song is the Knowledge, and the Knowledge is that, in the end, All Will Be Well. . . . Despite and because of the sacrifice. The necessary and joyfully-to-be-contemplated Sacrifice. A voice as of that of the God of Heaven sounds all around: ''Remember the Prime.''

She gives herself up to the luxury and ecstasy of the simulation. Falcon loves it. Falcon seeks it as she does, the giving, the final surrender. . . . "Remember the Prime."

Then she understands. Her rage and jealousy soar as she identifies with Falcon, the one who has taken her place, the one who is made better than she.

She breaks the link and pulls the chip from the terminal, pulls her spines from its ports, cuts all contact. She is consumed with a rage that could kill her.

20

Though a whole new world was lying around Falcon, it was more than an hour before he could examine the view. First he had to check all the capsule's systems and test its response to the controls. He had to learn how much extra heat was necessary to produce a desired rate of ascent, and how much gas he must vent in order to descend. Above all, there was the question of stability. He must adjust the length of the cables attaching his capsule to the huge, pear-shaped balloon, to damp out vibrations and get the smoothest possible ride.

Thus far he was lucky. At this level the wind was steady, and the Doppler reading on the invisible surface gave him a "ground" speed of 348 kilometers per hour. For Jupiter, that was modest; winds of up to 2,000 klicks had been observed. But mere speed was of course unimportant; the danger was turbulence. If he ran into that, only skill and experience and swift reaction could save him. And these were not matters that could yet be programmed into *Kon-Tiki*'s computer.

Not until he was satisfied that he had got the feel of his strange craft did Falcon pay any attention to Mission Control's pleadings to hurry the checklist. Then he deployed the booms carrying the instrumentation and the atmosphere samplers. The capsule now resembled a rather untidy Christmas tree, but it still rode smoothly down the Jovian winds while it radioed torrents of information to the recorders on the ship so far above. And now, at last, he could look around.

His first impression was unexpected and even a little disappointing, based as it was on naive personal memories of Earth. As far as the scale of things was concerned, he might have been ballooning over an ordinary cloudscape in India. The horizon seemed at a normal distance; there was no feeling at all that he was on a world eleven times the diameter of his own. He smiled and made the mental shift—for a mere glance at the infrared radar, which sounded the layers of atmosphere beneath him, confirmed how badly human eyes could be deceived.

Now his memories were of a different sort. He saw Jupiter as it had been seen by hundreds of unmanned probes that had preceded him this far. That layer of clouds apparently about five kilometers away was really sixty kilometers below. And the horizon, whose distance he might have guessed at about two hundred, was actually almost 3,000 kilometers from the ship.

The crystalline clarity of the hydrohelium atmosphere and the enormous curvature of the planet would have fooled the untrained observer completely, who would have found it more challenging to judge distances here than on the moon. To the earthbound mind, everything seen must be multiplied by at least ten. It was a simple business for which he was well prepared. Nevertheless, he realized there was a level of his consciousness that was profoundly disturbed—which, rather than acknowledge that Jupiter was huge, felt that *he* had shrunk to a tenth his normal size.

No matter. This world was his destiny. He knew

in his heart that he would grow used to its inhuman scale.

Yet as he stared toward that unbelievably distant horizon, he felt as if a wind colder than the atmosphere around him was blowing through his soul. All his arguments for a manned exploration of Jupiter had been disingenuous, and he realized now that his inner conviction was indeed the truth. This would never be a place for humans. He would be the first and last man to descend through the clouds of Jupiter.

The sky above was almost black, except for a few wisps of ammonia cirrus perhaps twenty kilometers overhead. It was cold up there on the fringes of space, but both temperature and pressure increased rapidly with depth. At the level where *Kon-Tiki* was drifting now it was fifty below zero Centigrade, and the pressure was five Earth atmospheres. A hundred kilometers farther down it would be as warm as equatorial Earth, and the pressure about the same as at the bottom of one of the shallower seas. Ideal conditions for life.

A quarter of the brief Jovian day had already gone. The sun was up halfway in the sky, but the light on the unbroken cloudscape below had a curious mellow quality. That extra six hundred million kilometers had robbed the sun of all its power. Though the sky was clear, it had the feel of an overcast day. When night fell, the onset of darkness would be swift indeed; though it was still morning, there was a sense of autumnal twilight in the air.

Autumn was something that never came to Jupiter. There were no seasons here.

Kon-Tiki had come down in the center of the equatorial zone—the least colorful part of the planet. The sea of clouds that stretched out to the horizon was tinted a pale salmon; there were none of the yellows and pinks and even reds that banded Jupiter at high altitudes. The Great Red

Spot itself—most spectacular of all of the planet's features—lay thousands of kilometers to the south. It had been a temptation to descend there, where the probes had hinted at such spectacular vistas, but the mission planners had judged that the south tropical disturbance had been "unusually active" these past months, with currents reaching over a thousand million kilometers an hour. It would have been asking for trouble to head into that maelstrom of unknown forces. The Great Red Spot and its mysteries would have to wait for future expeditions.

The sun, moving across the sky twice as swiftly as it did on Earth, was now nearing the zenith; it had become eclipsed by the great silver canopy of the balloon. *Kon-Tiki* was still drifting swiftly and smoothly westward at a steady 348 klicks, but only the radar (and Falcon's private, instantaneous calculation) gave any indication of this.

Was it always this calm here? Falcon wondered. The scientists who had analyzed the data from the probes spoke persuasively of the Jovian doldrums; they had predicted that the equator would be the quietest place, and it seemed they'd known what they were talking about after all. At the time, Falcon had been profoundly skeptical of such forecasts. He'd agreed with one unusually modest researcher who had told him bluntly, "There are no experts on Jupiter."

Well, there would be at least one by the end of the day. If he survived until then.

Aboard *Garuda*, flight director Buranaphorn released his harness catch and floated smoothly away from his console. Moments later his relief, Budhvorn Im, slipped gracefully into the harness. She was a petite Cambodian woman wearing the uniform of the Indo-Asian Space Service, with a colonel's firebirds on her shoulders.

"So far it's less exciting than a simulation," said Buranaphorn.

"That is very nice," said Im. "Let us hope it stays that way." She checked in her colleagues one by one as, throughout the circular room, the first-shift controllers handed off to the second shift.

Garuda's internal commlink crackled with Captain Chowdhury's tired voice. "Bridge to *Kon-Tiki* Mission Control."

"Go ahead, Captain," Im replied.

"I've got a permission-to-come-aboard request from a Space Board cutter now leaving Ganymede Base. Two people to board. Their ETA is at our MET nineteen hours, twenty-three minutes."

"What is the reason for this visit?" Im asked, puzzled.

"No reason given." He paused, and she heard the crackle of a commlink in the background. "Cutter repeats this is a request."

"No reflection on either crew, but I would prefer not to risk misalignment during docking procedures."

"Shall I say you ask me to refuse permission, then?"

"I suppose if they really want to come they will make it an order," said Im. When Chowdhury didn't reply, she said, "No point in antagonizing them." Or putting Chowdhury on the line. "Please stress to the cutter's captain the delicate nature of our mission. Also please keep me informed."

"As you wish." Chowdhury keyed off.

Im had no idea why a cutter would choose to descend upon *Kon-Tiki* Mission Control in the middle of the mission, but they certainly had the right to do so. And she had no real fear of a mishap. Only a docking accident—highly unlikely—would interrupt communications with the *Kon-Tiki* capsule.

It was only when she glanced at the controllers—their consoles arrayed in a neat circle before her—that Im noticed one or two faces wearing apprehensive expressions—worried looks that couldn't be explained by the nominal status of the mission.

Sparta's consciousness of the dark world around her returned in a red haze of pain. She *listened*, long enough to determine the status of the mission. She heard Im and Chowdhury discuss the approach of a Space Board cutter. That did not concern her. It was none of her affair. Soon it would all be over.

She scrabbled in the tube and withdrew another white wafer. It melted with exquisite sweetness under her tongue. . . .

She isn't "Dilys." She is Sparta again. Inside the black tightsuit she doesn't feel the cold, except on her cheekbones and the tip of her nose. She is a shadow in the dawn woods, her short hair hidden under the suit's hood, only her face exposed.

She waits in the woods for the low sun to rise, bringing the color of October to the dewy woods. The smell of rotting leaves reminds her of an autumn in New York. With Blake. When things started to split.

The smell of leaves . . . That was what Earth had that no other planet in the solar system had. Rot. Without rot, no life. Without life, no rot. Was it really Them who had made all this messy life, started it or at least coaxed it along on Venus and Mars and Earth? On Mars and Venus life had dried up, frozen or gotten pressure-cooked, washed away in the hot acid rain or blown away in the cold CO_2 wind. Only on Earth had it taken hold in its own filth.

And now it was spreading fast, trying to keep one step ahead of itself. Rot spreading to the planets. Rot spreading to the stars.

All this nasty stew a gift of the *Pancreator*—the *prophetae*'s peculiar way of referring to Them. Those who were out there "waiting at the great world," according to the Knowledge—she had remembered it all, now; it had all been encoded in Falcon's programming—and the Knowledge said they were waiting among "the cloud-dwelling messengers" for "the reawakening"—of which the *prophetae* were the sign-bearers. . . .

She had been chosen by them to carry the sign, *made* to carry it. She had been built to find the messengers in the clouds, to listen and speak with them—with the radio organs that had been ripped out of her on Mars—to speak in the language of the signs the *prophetae* had taught her and whose memory they had imperfectly erased when they had rejected her.

The sun rises. A shaft of orange light penetrates the dew-laden forest and finds Sparta's pale eyes, striking fire.

She resists our authority
To resist us is to resist the Knowledge

But the Free Spirit were those who resisted, mocking their own name for themselves. These false *prophetae* were trapped in their ambition and blind to their own tradition. What they could not see was that she had indeed yielded to the Knowledge, and in her it had flowered. Flowered and ripened and eventually burst, like a fig hanging too long on the branch, splitting open to expose its purple flesh, heavy with seed. They were too stupid to see that they had wrought better than they knew, too stupid to see what she had become. For Sparta was the Knowledge Incarnate.

When she would not follow their false path, they had turned against her. They had tried to cut the Knowledge out of her head, burn it out, drain it out of her with her heart's blood.

She had escaped them. For these years she had slowly been reassembling herself from the torn and scorched scraps of flesh they had left to her. She was harder now, colder now, and when she had succeeded in resurrecting herself, she would do what needed doing. What the Knowledge—which was Herself—demanded.

But first she would kill those who had tried to pervert her. Not out of animus. She felt nothing for them now, she was beyond rage. But things needed to be cleaner, simpler. It would simplify matters to eliminate those who had made her, starting with Lord Kingman and his houseful of guests.

Then she would have time to kill the usurper, the quasi-human creature they had intended to substitute for her. This Falcon. Before he could take the wrong message into the clouds.

From her vantage in the woods she sees a figure appear on Kingman's terrace. The house is rimmed in light from the rising sun. Morning mist curls across the meadow grass and bracken, rendering the mansion as gauzy as a painting on a theater scrim.

She allows the image from her right eye to enlarge on the screen of her mind. It is incredibly crisp and undistorted, better than new—Striaphan has that effect on the brain.

The man on the terrace is the one named Bill, the one whose smell is such an odd layering of unfamiliar scents. He is staring right at her as if he knows she is here—which is impossible, unless he has telescopic vision to match hers.

Where he stands, he looks to be an easy target. Unfortunately the shot is impossible, even with her rifled target pistol. The bullet's gyroscopic spin, precessing as it resists gravity's arc, will have pulled it into a wide spiral by the time it reaches the terrace. At this range not even the fastest computer in the world—the one in her brain—can predict where the bullet will strike, except to within a radius of half a meter.

On the other hand, with the bullets she is using, if she catches a piece of flesh, even half a meter is as good as dead.

But no, let Bill wait.

Now Kingman comes out of the tall doors, wearing his shooting jacket and carrying his gun. He recoils at the sight of Bill—but though he clearly wants to avoid him, it is too late. She *listens.* . . .

"Rupert, I really didn't intend to . . ."

"If you'll excuse me, I believe I'll have another go at that tree-rat. Maybe I'll get him this time."

Kingman's voice is clipped, soft, he never looks the other man in the eye. The shotgun rests in the crook of his arm, rests there so casually it is obvious it must pain him not to raise the muzzle and blast this species of rat who stands right in front of him. But instead he turns and marches past, down the stairs to the wet lawn, and sets out across it—straight toward her.

No dogs with him. He must consider dogs a nuisance when it comes to potting tree-rats.

Kingman first. Let him come halfway. Then if this Bill creature is still exposed . . .

Still she *listens,* to the squish and slither of Kingman's Wellingtons across the rank grass. The sun is full behind the leaves at the edge of the woods, turning them bright red and yellow, silhouetting the tracery of their veins.

Better to take him in the woods. Then go back toward the house, into it if necessary, taking the rest one by one. Quietly. Privately. Head shots are best.

Kingman is in the bracken now, the stiff wet fronds of the autumn-brown fern soaking his twill trousers to the knees. The near trunks come between her and him, although now and then she can glimpse him between them, moving through the mist.

She is still *listening,* tracking his progress through the bracken, on the verge of breaking her trance, stepping off to intercept him—

—when she hears the other.

Vibrations at the edge of her enhanced sensibility, way off to her right. Delicate footsteps in a slow, intricate rhythm, like the last drips of rain from the eaves, after the storm has passed.

A deer. Two of them, does probably, stepping slowly and lightly through the woods, searching the undergrowth for fodder.

But there is another step as well, slower yet, and heavier. Not an animal, but moving almost like one. Footsteps faint and oh-so-cautious. The moves of a professional stalker.

Kingman's gamekeeper? No, as of half an hour ago, the old gaffer was sleeping off last night's binge, in his room in the west wing.

This is a new player.

She gets a vector on the sound, then ceases *listening* and relaxes into movement. Though she can no longer hear as well, she can imagine the stranger's stepwise moves.

Now comes Kingman on her left, pressing through the wet brush like an elephant, walking with the unthinking confidence born of a lifetime's familiarity with these woods. She moves right, not wanting to cut off the unknown player but rather to come in behind, to have a look. She goes through the brightening forest with all the grace and alertness she can muster.

She catches herself—barely—just before she walks into him. Had she not had the advantage of knowing he was there . . . Well, he is very good. She trembles motionless against the rough bark of a bent old oak.

Then he moves, and she sees who he is. Curly red hair, camel's hair coat, pigskin gloves—among the sunlit autumn leaves he is almost better camouflaged than she. His skill comes as no surprise to her.

The orange man. He'd almost killed her on Mars, and again on Phobos. She'd had a chance to kill him then, but out of some misguided impulse—of what, justice? Fair play?—she'd held back. Even though she knew he'd killed the doctor who had

freed her from the sanatorium, even though somehow she knew even then—though she had not
quite made the connection in memory—that he'd
tried to kill her parents. Perhaps succeeded.

She rests her cheek against a cushion of emerald
green moss on the tree trunk, holding her breath
and waiting for him to go on past, down that narrow creek bed choked with fallen leaves. Whatever
scruples she'd had are irrelevant now.

His footsteps stop.

She pushes her face cautiously forward, peering
around the tree trunk. She can not see him. But
Kingman's footsteps keep coming through the
woods.

The loud *crack* of the orange man's pistol splits
the morning calm. Even without the suppressor he
normally uses, she knows the .38 by its sound—

—which startles the deer. They go bounding
deeper into the preserve, crashing through the
brush without pausing to look back, two living
animals not making enough noise, however, to
obliterate the heavy fall of Kingman's dead body—
straight over, he hits the forest floor like a felled
tree. Head shot.

If she could see the orange man she would shoot
him, but he is already moving away from her,
screened by too many tree trunks, walking calmly
in the direction of the house. She creeps after him,
until her view of the meadow and the mansion is
clear.

He's out of the woods now, into the open, making no effort to hide himself. All of Kingman's
guests are gathered on the terrace, chatting calmly
with each other as they watch the orange man's
progress. The one called Bill has turned away from
the rail to face the others. His stance is relaxed,
arrogant.

For fifteen seconds she *listens*. . . .

''So, Bill, on to Jupiter''—Holly Singh speaking, a

smirk bending her red lips—*"But how do we know Linda won't be there ahead of us. As she was on Phobos?"*

Bill takes his time answering. Then he says, *"Actually, my dear, I'm depending on it."*

Her trance takes only an instant. She comes out of it with her mind made up. She aims and squeezes. The orange man's head comes apart, more pink than orange.

To get off her other shots takes time, perhaps a third of a second each. The inherent uncertainty of the extreme range takes its toll. Only two of the first four rounds find targets.

The one aimed at Bill gets Jack Noble instead, in the midsection. The second shot is wasted against the wall of the house. The next one is aimed at Holly Singh, who is ducking. It finds her shoulder, taking the shoulder and half her neck. The fourth shot breaks an irregular block of stone from the balustrade—

—by which time the others are down, hiding behind it. A few seconds later they begin firing back from its cover.

She is already gone, running through the woods more lightly than the deer.

21

That first day, the Father of the Gods smiled upon Falcon. It was as calm and peaceful here on Jupiter as it had been, years ago, when he was drifting with Webster across the plains of northern India. Falcon had had time to master his new skills, until *Kon-Tiki* seemed an extension of his own body. Such luck was more than he had dared to hope for, and he began to wonder if he might have to pay a price for it.

He smiled inwardly. Even within the perfect man, shreds of superstition remain.

The five hours of daylight were almost over. The clouds below were full of shadows, which gave them a massive solidity they had not possessed when the sun was higher. Color was swiftly draining from the sky, except in the west itself, where a band of deepening purple lay along the horizon. Above this band was the thin crescent of a closer moon, pale and bleached against the utter blackness beyond.

With a speed perceptible to the eye, the sun went straight down over the edge of Jupiter almost 3,000 kilometers away. The stars came out in their legions—and there was the beautiful evening star, Earth, on the very frontier of twilight, reminding him how far he was from the place of his origin. It followed the sun down into the west. Humanity's first night on Jupiter had begun.

With the onset of darkness, *Kon-Tiki* began to sink. The balloon was no longer heated by the feeble sunlight and was losing a small part of its buoyancy. Falcon did nothing to increase lift; he had expected this and was planning to descend.

The invisible cloud deck was still some fifty kilometers below, and he would reach it about midnight. It showed up clearly on the infrared radar, which also reported that it contained a vast array of complex carbon compounds as well as the usual hydrogen, helium, and ammonia. Falcon could see all this for himself, with perceptual abilities that were not general knowledge.

The chemists were dying for samples of that fluffy, pinkish stuff; though some of the previous atmospheric probes had gathered a total of a few grams, they had had to analyze the compounds on board, with automated instruments, in the brief time before they'd disappeared into the crushing depths. What the chemists had learned so far had only whetted their appetites. Half the basic molecules of life were here, floating high above the surface of Jupiter. Where there was "food," could life be far away? That was the question that, after more than a hundred years, none of them had been able to answer.

The infrared was blocked by the clouds, but the microwave radar sliced right through and showed layer after layer, all the way down to the hidden "surface" 400 kilometers below. That was barred to him by tremendous pressures and temperatures; not even the robot probes had ever reached it intact. It lay in tantalizing inaccessibility at the bottom of the radar screen, slightly fuzzy, showing a curious granular structure that neither Falcon nor his radar screen could resolve.

An hour after sunset he dropped his first onboard probe. It fell swiftly for about a hundred kilometers, then began to float in the denser atmosphere, sending back torrents of radio signals, which he relayed to Mission Control. Then there was nothing else to do until sunrise, except keep an eye on the rate of descent and monitor the instruments.

While she was drifting in this steady current, *Kon-Tiki* could look after herself.

Flight Director Im announced the end of Day One. "Good morning, Howard. It's one minute after midnight, and we've got green boards all around. Hope you're enjoying yourself."

Falcon's reply came back, time-delayed and distorted by static: "Good morning, Flight. All the boards I'm looking at are green too. Looking forward to sunrise so I can see a little more out the windows."

"Call us then. Meanwhile we won't pester you."

Im keyed the ship's bridge.

"Mangkorn here, Flight." The ship's second mate, a Thai with ten years' service among Jupiter's moons, was the officer of the new day; Captain Chowdhury had gone to his cabin to catch some sleep.

"Good morning, Khun Mangkorn," she said. "Can you give me an update on our VIPs?"

"The cutter is on a ballistic Hohmann from Ganymede. No change of ETA."

"Thank you."

Ten minutes passed without incident. Suddenly graph lines leaped on the screens. Im reached for the command channel. "Howard! Listen in on channel forty-six, high gain."

There were so many telemetering circuits that she could have forgiven Falcon if he remembered only those few which were critical, but he didn't hesitate. Through her commlink she heard the click of the switch on his panel.

He brought up the frequency on his inboard amplifier, which was linked through to the microphone on the probe that now floated 125 kilometers below *Kon-Tiki* in an atmosphere almost as dense as water.

"Put it up on the speakers," Im said. The communications controller immediately switched the loudspeakers to the probe's channel.

At first there was only a soft hiss of whatever strange winds stirred down in the darkness of that unimaginable world. And then, out of the background noise, there slowly emerged a booming vibration that grew louder and louder, like the beating of a gigantic drum. It was so low that it was felt as much as heard, and the beats steadily increased their tempo, though the pitch never changed. Now it was a swift, almost infrasonic throbbing.

Then, suddenly, in midvibration it stopped—so abruptly that the mind could not accept the silence: memory continued to manufacture a ghostly echo in the deepest caverns of the brain.

The controllers exchanged glances. It was the most extraordinary sound that any of them had ever heard, even among the multitudinous noises of Earth. None could think of a natural phenomenon that could have caused it. Nor was it like the cry of an animal, not even one of the great whales.

If Im had not been so engrossed, she might have noticed the barely constrained excitement on the faces of two of her controllers. But she was on the comm to the bridge. "Khun Mangkorn, would you send someone to wake up Dr. Brenner, please," she said. "This could be what he's been waiting for."

The awesome sound came over the speakers again, following exactly the same pattern. Now they were prepared for it and could time the sequence; from the first faint throb to final crescendo, it lasted just over ten seconds.

But this time there was a real echo, not an

artifact of memory—very faint and far away, it might have come from one of the many reflecting layers deeper in the stratified atmosphere.

Or perhaps it was from another, more distant source. They waited for a second echo, but none came.

"Howard, drop another probe, will you? With two mike pickups maybe we can triangulate the source."

"Okay, Flight," came the delayed reply, and over the speakers in Mission Control they heard the nearly simultaneous thump of the robot instrument probe separating from *Kon-Tiki*'s capsule. Oddly enough, none of *Kon-Tiki*'s own microphones was picking up anything except wind noise. The boomings, whatever they were, were trapped and channeled beneath an atmospheric reflecting layer far below.

Olaf Brenner came through the hatch in the center of the control room's "floor," emerging from the corridor that led down to *Garuda*'s living quarters. The pudgy, gray-haired exobiologist was still sleepy, bouncing off the bulkheads in uncoordinated haste, flying almost out of control. He tried to strap himself to his console next to the flight director's, pulling on his sweater at the same time. Im had to help him keep from drifting away.

Brenner didn't bother to say thanks for the save. "What's happening?" he demanded.

"Listen," Im told him.

Over the speakers the boomings were repeating themselves. Falcon's second probe had swiftly dropped through the reflective layers beneath and the bright screens in Mission Control made it clear that the strange sounds were coming from a cluster of sources about 2,000 kilometers away from *Kon-Tiki*. A great distance, but it gave no indication of their intrinsic power—in Earth's oceans quite feeble sounds could travel equally far.

"What does that sound like?" Im asked.

"What does it sound like to you?" Brenner said gruffly.

"You're the expert. But it could be a deliberate signal, maybe?"

"Nonsense. There may be life down there. In fact I'll be very disappointed if we find no microorganisms—perhaps even simple plants. But there couldn't possibly be anything like animals as we know them—individual creatures that move about under their own volition."

"No?"

"Every scrap of evidence we have from Mars and Venus and Earth's prehistory tells us there's no way an animal can generate enough power to function without free oxygen. There's no free oxygen on Jupiter. So any biochemical reactions have to be low-energy."

"You picking up this conversation, Howard?" Im inquired.

Falcon's carefully neutral voice came over the speakers. "Yes, Flight. Dr. Brenner's made this argument before."

"In any case"—Brenner turned his attention to the data on his flatscreen and spoke directly to Falcon through the commlink—"some of these soundwaves look to be a hundred meters long! Even an animal as big as a whale couldn't get that out of its pipes! They *must* have a natural origin, Howard."

"Probably the physicists will come up with an explanation," Falcon replied. His tone was cool.

"Well, think about it," Brenner demanded. "After all, what would a blind alien make of the sounds it heard on a beach during a storm, or beside a geyser, or a volcano, or a waterfall? The alien might easily attribute them to some huge beast."

An extra second or two passed before Falcon said, "That certainly is something to think about."

"Quite," Brenner harrumphed.

There, for the time being, their conversation ended.

From Jupiter, the mysterious signals continued at intervals, recorded and analyzed by batteries of instruments in Mission Control. Brenner studied the accumulating data displayed on his flatscreen; a quick Fourier transform revealed no apparent meaning lurking in the rhythmic booming.

Brenner yawned elaborately and looked around. "Where's the professional busybody?" he asked Im, seeing the empty harness where Blake Redfield often perched.

"Even professional snoops have to sleep sometime," replied the flight director.

Blake was in his tiny cabin, sleeping fitfully. He'd been sleeping about five hours in every twenty-four, and not all at once. He'd spaced his naps, making a point of monitoring the operations of each of Mission Control's three daily shifts. What it had gained him was a pretty good idea who the ringers were, the controllers who controlled themselves too well under his constant needling and prodding.

No matter which side of this multi-sided game they were on, they and he shared knowledge denied the rest of the people on *Garuda*, namely that Falcon had a purpose in the clouds that went well beyond the mission's stated objectives.

Even Falcon himself appeared not to know. Was he pretending? It was a question—one of many—that could only be answered in the event.

In her hiding hole, Sparta stirred from dreams of revenge. Her red eyes opened and she ran a furry tongue over yellow teeth. Reality reemerged only gradually.

She *listened* long enough to confirm mission elapsed time. Soon now. . . . She knew it was time to move, if she were to reach Blake. But did she still want to? She pondered. . . .

Her red eyes had watched from hiding as he went about his officious business, tapping into data without permission, asking rude questions of the off-duty controllers, making a pest of himself. To her, his behavior was transparent. He knew, as she did, that something was rotten in the *Kon-Tiki* mission. But unlike her, he didn't know what. He was scratching and prying at scabs, hoping to irritate the beast into striking back—thus revealing itself.

Some ember of compassion for him still burned in her brain. He had no idea that they were simply biding their time, that he was already marked for death. Blake's efforts were dangerous and useless.

She owed him nothing. Still, she could warn him of the cataclysm to come. She had done her best to behead the Free Spirit. Like the Hydra, it grew other heads.

22

About an hour before sunrise the voices of the deep died away, and Falcon began to busy himself with preparation for the dawn of his second day. *Kon-Tiki* was now only five kilometers above the nearest cloud layer; the external pressure had risen to ten atmospheres, and the temperature was a tropical thirty degrees Centigrade. A fellow could be comfortable here with no more equipment than a breathing mask and the right grade of heliox mixture.

Mission Control had been silent for several minutes, but shortly after dawn bloomed in the Jovian clouds, Im's voice came over the link. "We've got some good news for you, Howard. The cloud layer below you is breaking up. You'll have partial clearing in an hour. You'll have to watch out for turbulence."

"I'm already noticing some," Falcon answered. "How far down will I be able to see?"

"At least twenty kilometers, down to the second thermocline. *That* cloud deck is solid—it's the one that never breaks."

As Falcon well knew. He also knew it was out of his reach. The temperature down there must be over a hundred degrees. This must be the first time a balloonist had ever had to worry not about his ceiling but about his basement.

Ten minutes later he could see what Mission Control had already observed from its orbiting sensors with their superior vantage points: there was a change in color near the horizon, and the cloud layer had become ragged and humpy, as if something had torn it open. Falcon cranked his nuclear furnace up a couple of notches and gave *Kon-Tiki* another five kilometers of altitude so that he could get a better view.

The sky below was clearing rapidly and completely, as if something was dissolving the solid overcast. An abyss was opening before his eyes. A moment later he sailed out over the edge of a cloud canyon twenty kilometers deep and a thousand kilometers wide.

A new world lay spread beneath him; Jupiter had stripped away one of its many veils. The second layer of clouds, unattainably far below, was much darker in color than the first—almost salmon pink, and curiously mottled with little islands of brick red. These were all oval-shaped, with their long axes pointing east-west, in the direction of the prevailing wind. There were hundreds of them, all about the same size, and they reminded Falcon of puffy little cumulus clouds in the terrestrial sky.

He reduced buoyancy, and *Kon-Tiki* began to drop down the face of the dissolving cliff.

It was then that he noticed the snow.

White flakes were forming in the atmosphere and drifting slowly downward. Yet it was much too warm for snow, and in any event there was scarcely a trace of water at this altitude. Moreover, there was no glitter or sparkle about these flakes as they went cascading down into the depths. When, presently, a few of them landed on an instrument boom outside the main viewing port, he saw that they were a dull, opaque white, not crystalline at all, and quite large, several inches across. They looked like wax.

He realized that this was precisely what they

were. A chemical reaction taking place in the atmosphere around him was condensing the hydrocarbons floating in the Jovian sky.

About a hundred kilometers ahead there was a disturbance in the cloud layer; the little red ovals were jostling around and were beginning to form a spiral, the familiar cyclonic pattern so common in the meteorology of Earth. This vortex was emerging at astonishing speed; if that was a storm ahead, Falcon said to himself, he was in big trouble.

And then his concern changed to wonder—and fear.

What was developing in his line of sight was not a storm at all. Something enormous—something scores of kilometers across—was rising through the clouds.

The reassuring thought that it, too, might be a cloud, a thunderhead boiling up from the lower levels of the atmosphere, lasted only a few seconds. No, this was *solid;* it shouldered its way through the pink and salmon overcast like an iceberg rising from the deep.

An iceberg floating in hydrogen? That was impossible, of course, but perhaps it was not too remote an analogy. He focused his telescopic eye upon the enigma—and moments later adjusted *Kon-Tiki's* optics to convey the same image to Mission Control—and he saw that the vast shape was a whitish, crystalline mass threaded with streaks of red and brown. It must be, he decided, the same stuff as the "snowflakes" falling around him—a mountain range of wax.

It was not, he realized, as solid as he had thought. Around the edges it was continually crumbling and reforming. . . .

Mission Control had been pestering him with questions for well over a minute now.

"I know what it is," he said firmly, answering at last. "A mass of bubbles, some kind of foam, hydrocarbon froth. The chemists are going to have a field day . . . *Just a minute!*''

''What's happening?'' Im's calm but unmistakably urgent voice came in on top of the radio delay. ''What do you see, Howard?''

Falcon heard Brenner babbling excitedly in the background, but he ignored the pleas from *Garuda* and concentrated his attention on the telescopic image in his own eye. Belatedly he refocused the mechanical optics. He had an idea . . . but he had to be sure. If he made a mistake, he would be a laughingstock to everyone who was watching the feed from this mission, throughout the entire solar system.

Then he relaxed, glanced at the clock, and cut in on the nagging voice from Mission Control. ''Hello, Mission Control,'' he said, very formally. ''This is Howard Falcon aboard *Kon-Tiki*. Emphemeris time nineteen hours, twenty-one minutes, fifteen seconds. Latitude zero degrees five minutes north. Longitude one hundred five degrees, forty-two minutes, system one. . . . If Dr. Brenner is still standing by, please tell him there *is* life on Jupiter. And it's *big*.''

''I'm very happy to be proved wrong,'' came back Brenner's reply, as quickly as the distance allowed. For all his earlier vehemence, Brenner seemed downright cheerful. ''Guess Mother Nature always has something up her sleeve, eh? Just keep the long lens on and give us the best pictures you can.''

If Falcon had been given to irony he would have asked himself what the hell the exobiologist expected he would be doing besides getting the best pictures he could. But Falcon's sense of irony had never been well developed.

He tweaked the vibrationless telescope and peered at the videoplate image. That should keep Brenner happy. Then he looked as closely as he could with his own eye. The things moving up and down those distant waxen slopes were still too far away for Falcon to make out many details, although they must have been very large indeed to be visible at all at such a distance. Almost black, shaped like arrowheads, they maneuvered by slow undulations of their entire bodies, so that they looked rather like giant manta rays swimming above some tropical reef.

Perhaps they were sky-borne grazers, no more carnivorous than cattle browsing upon the cloud pastures of Jupiter, for they seemed to be feeding along the dark red-brown streaks that ran like dried-up riverbeds down the flanks of the floating cliffs. Occasionally one of them would dive headlong into the mountain of foam and disappear completely from sight.

Kon-Tiki was moving only slowly with respect to the cloud layer below. It would be at least three hours before it was above those ephemeral hills. It was in a race with the sun. Falcon hoped that darkness would not fall before he could get a good view of the mantas, as he had christened them, as well as the fragile landscape over which they flapped their way.

The commlink crackled. "Howard, I hate to leave at a time like this, but it's time to change shifts," said Im. "Dr. Brenner has just ordered another liter of black coffee. I think he plans to be with you awhile."

"Indeed I do," Brenner said jovially.

"Thanks for your help, Flight," Howard said. "And hello, Flight."

"Hello, Howard." The voice that came back was that of David Lum, an ethnic Chinese from Ganymede with long service in the Indo-Asian space program. "We had to pry Budhvorn out of here," said Lum. "She would have hogged all the fun."

The fun was some time coming—a long three hours. During the whole period Falcon kept the external microphones on full gain, wondering if this was the source of the booming in the night. The mantas certainly seemed large enough to have produced it. Once he got an accurate measurement, he discovered they were almost 300 meters across the wings! That was three times the length of Earth's largest whale, although Falcon knew the mantas couldn't weigh more than a few tonnes.

Finally, half an hour before sunset, *Kon-Tiki* was almost above the waxy mountains.

''No,'' said Falcon, again answering repetitive queries from Brenner, ''they're still showing no reaction to my presence. I don't think they're very bright. They look like harmless vegetarians. If they were to try to chase me, I doubt they could reach my altitude.''

Still, he was a little disappointed that the mantas showed not the slightest interest in him as he sailed high above their feeding ground. Perhaps they had no way of detecting his presence. He could see little detail in their structure, and even computer-enhanced photograms through the telescope had detected no sign of anything that resembled a sense organ. The creatures were simply huge black deltas, rippling over hills and valleys that in reality were little more substantial than the clouds of Earth. Though they looked solid, Falcon knew that anyone who stepped on those white mountains would go crashing through them as if they were made of tissue paper.

At close quarters he could see the myriad cellules or bubbles from which they were formed. Some of these were quite large, a meter or so in diameter, and Falcon wondered in what witches' cauldron of hydrocarbons they had been brewed. There must be enough petrochemicals deep down in the atmosphere of Jupiter to supply all humanity's needs for a million years.

The short day had almost gone when he passed over the crest of the waxen hills, and the light was fading rapidly along their lower slopes. There were no mantas on this western side, and for some reason the topography was very different. The foam was sculptured into long, level terraces, like the interior of a lunar crater. Falcon could almost imagine that they were gigantic steps leading down to the hidden surface of the planet.

And on the lowest of these steps, just clear of the swirling clouds that the mountain had displaced when it came surging skyward, was a roughly oval mass, five or six kilometers across. It was difficult to see, since it was only a little darker than the gray white foam on which it rested. Falcon's first thought was that he was looking at a forest of pallid trees, like giant mushrooms that had never seen the sun.

Yes, it must be a forest—he could see hundreds of thin trunks springing from the white waxy froth in which they were rooted. But the trees were packed astonishingly close together; there was scarcely any space between them. Perhaps it was not a forest after all, but a single enormous tree like one of the giant multi-trunked banyans of the East. Once he had seen a banyan tree in Java that was over 650 meters across. This monster was at least ten times that size.

The light had almost gone. The cloudscape had turned purple with refracted sunlight, and in a few seconds that too would vanish. In the last light of his second day on Jupiter, Howard Falcon saw—or thought he saw—something that cast the gravest doubts on his interpretation of the white oval. But it also thrilled him in a way he could not have consciously explained.

Unless the dim light had totally deceived him, those hundreds of thin trunks were beating back and forth in perfect synchronism, like fronds of kelp rocking in the surge.

And the tree was no longer in the place where he had first seen it.

PART
5

A MEETING
WITH
MEDUSA

23

A gleaming white cutter sidled cautiously up to *Garuda*'s main airlock. The diagonal blue band and gold star on the cutter's bow declared its authority: the Board of Space Control was the Council of Worlds' largest agency, many-armed like Shiva, both nurturing and disciplinary, coordinating space development and sponsoring scientific missions such as *Kon-Tiki*, but at the same time acting as police, coast guard, and marines. The white cutter had a strangely aerodynamic appearance for a spacecraft, for the Space Board had designed its fusion-powered ships to pursue their objectives even into the depths of planetary atmospheres.

The cutter was a long way from an atmosphere now. As it hung motionless in space, a docking tube snaked out from its lock and sealed itself to the equally motionless *Garuda*. A few minutes later, a Space Board commander and a big blond lieutenant with a stun-gun on his hip flew expertly onto *Garuda*'s bridge.

They were met by Rajagopal, the first mate. "How can we assist you, Commander?" Somehow, from the woman's glossy red lips, even the simple courtesy sounded arrogant.

"We're here to observe." He was tall, sunblackened man with a rasping, Canadian-accented voice.

"Fine, fine. If you wouldn't mind saying . . ."

"Sorry," he said firmly. "If you'll show us to Mission Control, we'll stay out of everybody's hair."

Her expression hardened. "This way, please."

The passageway from the bridge to Mission Control was short, ending in a hatch in the center of what was, when *Garuda* was accelerating, the control room's ceiling. Six controllers looked up curiously as the uniformed spacers entered the room. Rajagopal curtly announced the arrivals to Lum, the flight director, and returned to the bridge.

A few moments later, the commander and his partner took up different positions, the commander hovering beside the hatch that led to the bridge, the lieutenant moving opposite him to the hatchway in the floor. The silent maneuver had the effect of telling the men and women in this fishbowl of a room that they were under arrest.

Blake Redfield opened his eyes in time to see *her*, swinging silently and weightlessly down from the ceiling of his sleeping cubicle. She perched right on top of him, hunched over him like a nightmare.

He didn't believe it. He blinked, as if that would give the horrid apparition time to go away. When he opened his eyes again, the nightmare began in earnest.

Sparta must have seen the look in his eyes, the fear that shifted through recognition to a calmer, deeper apprehension.

"Are you here to kill me?" He meant to speak boldly, but his words came out in a dry whisper.

She grinned. In the grease-blackened mask of her face, her teeth were gleaming ivory and her tongue was blood red. "You don't have to do anything more, Blake. I've already taken care of it. Guard your own back."

"What do you . . . ?"

"No, don't move," she said.

He pretended to relax, while staring up at her. "What did you do, Ellen?"

"Don't call me Ellen."

Don't call her Ellen?—he took a deep breath; his ears were ringing with the tension—*For years she's insisted I call her Ellen.* "What's your name now?"

"You know who I am. You don't need my name."

"As you wish." She was mad. It was plain as the evil grin on her face. Look at her, starved to bones, those red eyes burning in her head. "What have you done?"

The words hissed out of her in a hot stream. "You don't need to keep trying to trap them. The mission will fail, I've seen to it. When it does, the *prophetae* who are left will show themselves. Then I'll take care of them, too."

"What have you *done*?"

"Don't betray me to the commander," she said, unfolding her legs and pushing lightly against his knees as she lifted toward the ceiling.

"The commander? He's . . .?" Blake broke off, watching in amazement as she slithered into the air-exchange duct, an opening he would have thought too small for a human body.

"Don't betray me." She was already out of sight when her words reached him. "You want to live, don't you?"

"Sorry about this," said Mission Control over Falcon's speakers. "Source Beta is looking iffy. Probability seventy percent it's gonna blow within the next hour."

Falcon scrolled through the chart on the map screen. Beta—Jupiter latitude one hundred and forty degrees—was almost 30,000 kilometers away and well below his horizon. Even though major eruptions ran as high as ten megatons, he was much too far away for the shock wave to be a serious danger. The radio storm that it would trigger was a different matter.

The decameter outbursts that at times made Jupiter the most powerful radio source in the whole sky had been discovered in the 1950s, to the utter astonishment of ground-bound astronomers. Well over a century later their underlying cause remained a mystery. Only the symptoms were understood.

The "volcano" theory had best stood the test of time, although no one imagined that this word had the same meaning on Jupiter as on Earth. At frequent intervals—often several times a day—titanic eruptions occurred in the lower depths of the atmosphere, probably on the hidden surface of the planet itself. A great column of gas, a thousand kilometers high, would start boiling upward as if determined to escape into space.

Against the most powerful gravitational field of all the planets, it had no chance. Yet some traces—a mere few million metric tonnes—might manage to reach the Jovian ionosphere, and when they did, all hell broke loose.

The radiation belts surrounding Jupiter completely dwarf the feeble Van Allen belts of Earth. When they are short-circuited by an ascending column of gas, the result is an electrical discharge millions of times more powerful than any terrestrial flash of lightning; it sends a colossal thunderclap of radio noise flooding across the entire solar system and on to the stars.

Probes had discovered that these radio outbursts were concentrated in four main areas of the planet. Perhaps there were weaknesses there that allowed the fires of the interior to break out from time to time. The scientists on Ganymede now thought they could predict the onset of a decameter storm; their accuracy was about that of a terrestrial weather forecast a century and a half ago.

Falcon did not know whether to welcome or fear

a radio storm, which would certainly add to the value of the mission—if he survived it. At the moment, he simply felt a vague irritability, as if this was all a distraction from some larger purpose. *Kon-Tiki*'s course had been planned to keep it as far as possible from the main centers of disturbance, especially the most active, Source Alpha. As luck would have it, the threatening Beta was the closest to him. He hoped that the distance, almost three-fourths the circumference of Earth, was safe enough.

"Probability now ninety percent," said Mission Control. Flight Director Lum's voice held a distinct note of urgency. "Forget what I said about an hour. Ganymede would have us believe it could be any second."

The radiolink had scarcely fallen silent when the magnetic field-strength graphic shot upward; before it could go off the screen, it reversed and dropped as rapidly as it had risen, in a spike as sharp as an ice pick. Far away and thousands of kilometers below, something had given the planet's molten core a titanic jolt.

Mission Control was late to get the news. "There she blows!"

"Thanks, I already know."

"You can expect onset at your position in five minutes, peak in ten."

He already knew that, too. "Copy." He didn't tell them how.

Far around the curve of Jupiter a funnel of gas as wide as the Pacific Ocean was climbing spaceward at thousands of kilometers per hour. Already the thunderstorms of the lower atmosphere would be raging around it, but they were nothing compared with the fury that would explode when the radiation belt was reached and began dumping its surplus electrons onto the planet.

Falcon began to retract all the instrument booms that he'd earlier extended from the capsule. There were no other precautions he could take. It would be four hours before the atmospheric shock wave reached him, but once the discharge had been triggered the radio blast, traveling at the speed of light, would be here in a tenth of a second.

Nothing yet: the radio monitor, scanning the spectrum, showed nothing unusual—just the normal mush of background. But Falcon noticed that the background noise level was slowly creeping upward. The pending explosion was gathering strength.

At such a vast distance he'd never expected to *see* anything. But suddenly a flicker as of far-off heat lightning danced along the eastern horizon. Simultaneously half the circuit breakers on the main board tripped, the capsule lights failed, and all comm channels went dead.

He tried to move, but he could not do so. The paralysis that gripped him was not psychological. He'd lost control of his limbs, and he could feel a painful tingling sensation throughout the network of his nerves. It seemed impossible that the electric field could have penetrated the shielded cabin— which was effectively a Faraday cage—and yet there was a flickering glow over the instrument board, and he could hear the unmistakable crackle of brush discharge.

Bang. Bang!

The emergency systems—*bang!*—threw themselves into operation—*bang!*—and the overloads reset. The lights flickered on. Falcon's humiliating paralysis disappeared as swiftly as it had come. With a glance at the board, he leaned toward the ports.

No need to try the external inspection lamps, for outside the windows the capsule's support cables seemed to be on fire. Lines of electric blue light glowed against the darkness, stretching upward from the main lift ring to the equator of the giant balloon; rolling slowly along several of them were dazzling balls of fire.

The sight was so strange and so beautiful that it was hard to read any menace into it—although few people, as Falcon knew, could even have seen ball lightning at such close quarters. And certainly none had survived, if they'd been riding a hydrogen-filled balloon in the atmosphere of Earth. He remembered the flaming death of the *Hindenburg*—how could any dirigible pilot forget it, how could any such pilot fail to have memorized the old newsreel frame by frame?—destroyed by a spark upon docking at Lakehurst in 1937. That could not happen here, though there was more hydrogen above his head than had ever filled the last of the Zeppelins; it would be a few billion years yet before anyone could light a fire in the atmosphere of Jupiter, *sans* oxygen.

With a sound like briskly frying bacon, the speech circuit came back to life—it was Lum's frantic voice. "Hello, *Kon-Tiki*—are you receiving? Are you receiving?" Chopped and badly distorted, the flight director's words were barely intelligible.

Falcon's spirits lifted; he had resumed contact with the human world. "I receive you, David," he said, a bit less formally than usual. "That was quite an electrical display. But no damage so far."

"We were afraid we'd lost you. Howard, please adjust telemetry channels three, seven, and twenty-six. Also gain on video two. And we don't quite believe the readings from the external ionization sensors."

Reluctantly Falcon tore his gaze away from the fascinating pyrotechnic display around *Kon-Tiki*. As he worked to recalibrate the instruments he occasionally glanced out the windows. The ball lightning disappeared first, the fiery globes slowly expanding until they reached a critical size, at which they vanished in a silent, almost gentle explosion.

But even an hour later, there were still faint glows around all the exposed metal on the outside of the capsule, and the radio links stayed noisy until after midnight.

"We're changing shifts again, Howard. Meechai will be taking over shortly."

"Thanks for a good job, David."

"Morning, Howard. Welcome to Day Three." Buranaphorn's voice was clear in the radiolink.

"They go by fast, don't they?" Falcon said pleasantly.

Deep inside himself, he felt anything but pleasant. That electrical shock, the paralysis . . . something strange was happening, although he could not say what. Lurid images came unbidden into his imagination, and he imagined that someone was speaking right next to him—was right here next to him in the capsule—but the words were in a language he had never heard, as in a dream where one clearly sees the words on the page but can make no sense of them.

Falcon struggled to maintain his concentration. His mission was far from complete.

The remaining hours of darkness were completely uneventful—until just before dawn.

Because it came from the east, Falcon thought he was seeing the first faint hint of sunrise. Then he realized that it was twenty minutes too early, and the glow that had appeared along the horizon was moving toward him even as he watched.

It swiftly detached itself from the arch of stars that marked the invisible edge of the planet, and he saw that it was a relatively narrow band, quite sharply defined—the beam of an enormous searchlight, swinging beneath the clouds. Perhaps fifty kilometers behind the first racing bar of light came another, parallel and moving at the same speed. And behind that another and another, until all the sky flickered with alternating sheets of light and darkness.

Falcon thought that he must have become inured to wonders by now, and surely this display of pure, soundless luminosity could not present the slightest danger. Nevertheless, it was an astonishing display, an inexplicable display—and despite himself he felt cold fear gnawing at what was otherwise an almost inhuman self-control. No human could look on such a sight without feeling like a helpless pygmy in the presence of forces beyond his comprehension. Was it possible that Jupiter carried not only life, but . . .

His mind reeled. The windows of his capsule spun in front of his eyes as rapidly as the searchlight beams in the vast dark cloudscape outside them.

But also intelligence . . . ?

The thought had literally had to fight its way to consciousness. What could his unconscious know with such fervor and jealousy that it would want to hide it from his own conscious mind, from the spotlight of reason?

An intelligence that only now was beginning to react to his alien presence . . . ?

"Yes, we see it," said Buranaphorn, in a voice that echoed Falcon's own sense of awe. "We have no idea what it is. We're calling Ganymede."

The display was slowly fading; the bands racing in from the far horizon were much fainter, as if the energies that powered them were becoming exhausted. In five minutes it was all over. The last faint pulse of light flickered along the western sky and was gone. Its passing left Falcon with an overwhelming sense of relief. The sight had been so hypnotic, so disturbing, that it could not have been good for anyone's peace of mind to contemplate it too long. He was more shaken then he cared to admit. An electrical storm was something he could understand, but *this* was totally incomprehensible.

Mission Control stayed silent. He knew that the information banks up on Ganymede were being searched; people and machines were turning their minds to the problem. Meanwhile a signal had gone back to Earth, but just getting there and getting a "hello" back would take an hour.

What as this rising unease, this dissatisfaction? Trying to press into his mind like the gathering of another titanic radio blast—it was as if Falcon knew something he did not want to admit to himself that he knew.

When Mission Control spoke again, it was with Olaf Brenner's tired voice. "Hello, *Kon-Tiki*, we've solved the problem—in a manner of speaking—but we can still hardly believe it." The exobiologist sounded relieved and subdued at once. One might think the man was in the midst of some great intellectual crisis. "What you are seeing is bioluminescence. Perhaps similar to that produced by microorganisms in the tropical seas of Earth— certainly similar in manifestation—here in the atmosphere, not the ocean, but the principle seems to be the same."

"That pattern was too regular, too artificial," Falcon mildly protested. "Hundreds of kilometers across."

"It was even larger than you imagine. You observed only a small part of it. The whole pattern was almost five thousand kilometers wide and looked like a revolving wheel. You merely saw the spokes, sweeping past you at about one kilometer per second."

"A *second!*" Falcon could not help interjecting. "Nothing living could move that fast!"

"Of course not. Let me explain. What you saw was triggered by the shock wave from Source Beta, moving at the speed of sound."

"What's that have to do with the pattern?"

"That's the surprising part. It's a very rare phenomenon, but identical wheels of light—a thousand times smaller—have been observed in the Persian Gulf and the Indian Ocean. Listen to this:

British India Company's *Patna*, Persian Gulf, May 1880, 11:30 P.M.: 'An enormous luminous wheel, whirling 'round, the spokes of which appeared to brush the ship along. The spokes were two hundred to three hundred yards long. . . . Each wheel contained about sixteen spokes. . . .' And here's one from the Gulf of Oman, dated May 23, 1906: 'The intensely bright luminescence approached us rapidly, shooting sharply defined light rays to the west in rapid succession, like the beam from the searchlight of a warship. . . . To the left of us, a gigantic fiery wheel formed itself, with spokes that reached as far as one could see. The whole wheel whirled around for two or three minutes. . . .' " Brenner broke off. "Well, they go on like that. Ganymede indexes some five hundred cases. Computer would have printed out the lot if we hadn't called a halt."

"All right then, I'm convinced—but still baffled."

"Can't blame you for that. The full explanation wasn't worked out until late in the 20th century. Seems these luminous wheels result from submarine earthquakes, and always occur in shallow waters where the shock waves are reflected and form standing wave patterns, sometimes bars, sometimes rotating wheels—the 'Wheels of Poseidon,' they've been called. The theory was finally proved by making underwater explosions and photographing the results from a satellite."

"No wonder sailors used to be so superstitious," Falcon remarked. He saw the pertinence of the terrestrial examples: when Source Beta blew its top, it must have sent shock waves in all directions—through the compressed gas of the lower atmosphere, and down through the solid body of Jupiter's core. Meeting and recrossing, these waves canceled here, reinforced there. The whole planet must have rung like a bell.

Yet the explanation did not destroy his sense of

wonder and awe; he would never be able to forget those flickering bands of light, racing through the unattainable depths of the Jovian atmosphere. This was a world where *anything* could happen, and no one could guess what the future would bring. And he still had a whole day to go.

Falcon was not merely on a strange planet. He was caught in some magical realm between myth and reality.

Blake, meanwhile, was squeezed between two clusters of pipe in a space that had never been designed for human occupancy, the sort of space that's left over after the welders have come in and done their job, and the pipefitters have come in and done theirs, and the electricians have come in and done theirs—none of them really expecting to have to come back, but leaving this technically negotiable tiny squeeze-hole in case some poor sap actually had to get in there with a wrench or set of wire-cutters to fix something broken.

What Blake was doing in here was the sort of thing that got people killed. He was hunting a wounded animal.

Linda, or Ellen, or whatever secret name she called herself, was much smarter and quicker than he, and he knew it. He'd seen enough of her uncanny "luck" to guess at what she had in her brain and nerves but never talked about. Probably she could see in the dark and smell him coming, just like a wounded mountain lion.

Nevertheless she must be stopped. She was too dangerous to allow to go free and way too dangerous to underestimate. If she said she had ensured that Howard Falcon's mission would fail, she had reason. Yet he couldn't simply hand her over to the commander, tell him that at last she was back—and wash his hands of the results. Too many things were happening too fast. He had to handle this on his own.

A couple of factors were on his side. With his perverse addiction to sabotage, Blake was a more experienced sneak even than she. With any luck, she wouldn't be expecting him, for she'd gone out of her way to warn him off, when she must have known he didn't suspect she was within three planets of here.

And she was sick. But whether her haunted eyes and wasted body meant she was any less formidable, he didn't know.

He moved slowly through the almost impassable passage until he was next to the AP service bay. He'd already searched the more accessible of the places on his list where she might hide. They'd proved a little too accessible for her to risk.

Through a mere crevice between electrical bus bridges he got a glimpse into the AP service area, dimly illuminated by a couple of glowing green diodes. Nothing was moving in there, nothing visible. Blake listened as hard as he could, but he could hear only the whine and hum and creak of the ship above his own breath and heartbeat. Quiet as they were, they sounded like hurricane wind and surf in his ears.

He inched himself forward, until he was hanging half into the space where he expected to find her.

The madwoman's ill-timed screech was his only warning. She flew out of the deep shadows into the sickly green light, talons outstretched, screaming like a harpy. She could have torn his throat out—but because of her scream he had a fractional moment in which to register her fiery eyes, her gleaming fangs, as he convulsed, twisted—

—and seized her wrist. Her PIN spines, extended beneath her nails, sliced open his arm like razors, but he didn't notice. His calves were still wedged fast in the narrow passage; they gave him the leverage he needed, and . . .

With a single jerk of its neck a leopard seal peels the skin off its prey in a spray of blood. . . .

The effect on Sparta was not so grisly. Whipped upside down by Blake, she did a rag doll's somersault and slammed butt first into the bulkhead, legs splayed. Her foul breath came out in an explosive grunt and she feebly waved her free arm, but Blake's left fist slammed into the point of her chin. Her head snapped back and her eyes rolled up in her head.

His own blood was floating in the little room, little black bubbles in the green light, more of them all the time. He folded his arms around her wasted, filthy body and burst into tears. Sobbing bitterly, he groped with his good hand for the dogged hatch that opened into the maintenance corridor.

He'd been hoping he wouldn't have to turn her in. He'd wanted to get the truth out of her and, if he could think of any way to do it, help her get free.

Too late. He was losing blood fast; he needed to get to the clinic. And she was dying in his arms.

24

When true dawn finally arrived, it brought a sudden change of weather. *Kon-Tiki* was moving through a blizzard; waxen snowflakes were falling so thickly that visibility was reduced to zero. Falcon worried about the weight that might accumulate on the balloon's envelope. Then he noticed that any flakes settling outside the window quickly disappeared; *Kon-Tiki*'s continual outpouring of heat was evaporating them as swiftly as they arrived.

If he had been ballooning on Earth, he would also have had to worry about the possibility of hitting something solid. No danger of that here. Mountains on Jupiter, in the unlikely event that there were any, would still be hundreds of kilometers below him. As for the floating islands of foam, hitting them would probably be like plowing into slightly hardened soap bubbles.

Nevertheless he took a cautious peek with the horizontal radar. What he saw on the screen surprised him. Scattered across a huge sector of the sky ahead were dozens of large and brilliant echoes, completely isolated from one another, apparently hanging unsupported in space. Falcon remembered the phrase early aviators had used to described one of the hazards of their profession, "clouds stuffed with rocks," a good description of what seemed to lie in the path of *Kon-Tiki*. The radar screen made for a disconcerting sight, although Falcon reminded himself that nothing really solid could hover in this atmosphere.

Falcon's conscious mind tried to pigeon-hole the apparition—some strange meteorological phenomenon, then, and still at least 200 kilometers off—but an inchoate emotion welled in his breast. "Mission Control, what am I looking at?" His own tight voice surprised him.

"No help, Howard. All we have to go on is your radar signal."

At least they could see the weather, and Buranaphorn conveyed the welcome news that he would be clear of the blizzard in half an hour.

Yet there was no warning of the violent cross wind that abruptly grabbed *Kon-Tiki* and swept it almost at right angles to his course. Suddenly the envelope was dragging the capsule through the air like a sea anchor, almost horizontally. Falcon needed all his skill and his rattlesnake-quick reflexes to prevent his ungainly vehicle from tangling itself in the guys, even capsizing.

Within minutes he was racing northward at over 600 kilometers per hour.

As suddenly as it had started, the turbulence ceased. He was still moving at high speed, but in still atmosphere, as if he'd been caught in a jet stream. The snowstorm vanished, and he saw with his own eyes what Jupiter had prepared for him.

Kon-Tiki had entered the funnel of a gigantic whirlpool, at least a thousand kilometers across. The balloon was being swept along a curving wall of cloud. Overhead the sun was shining in a clear sky, but far beneath, this great hole in the atmosphere drilled down to unknown depths until it reached a misty floor where lightning flickered almost continuously.

Though the vessel was being dragged downward so slowly that it was in no immediate danger, Falcon increased the flow of the heat into the envelope until *Kon-Tiki* hovered at a constant altitude. Not until then did he abandon the fantastic spectacle and return to considering the problem of the radar signals. They were still out there.

The nearest echo was now only about forty kilometers away. All of the echoes, he quickly realized, were distributed along the wall of the vortex, moving with it, apparently caught in the vortex like *Kon-Tiki* itself. He peered through the windows with his telescopic eye and found himself looking at a curiously mottled cloud that almost filled the field of view.

It was not easy to see, being only a little darker than the whirling wall of mist that formed its background. Not until he had been staring for over a minute did he realize that he had met it before. Quickly he trained *Kon-Tiki*'s optics on the object, so that Mission Control could share the view.

The first time he'd seen the thing it had been crawling across the drifting mountains of foam, and he had mistaken it for a giant, many-trunked tree. Now at last he could appreciate its real size and complexity, could even give it a name to fix its image in his mind. For it did not resemble a tree at all, but a jellyfish, such as might be met trailing its tentacles as it drifted along the warm eddies of Earth's ocean currents. To some early naturalist those trailing tentacles had been reminiscent of the twisting snakes of a Gorgon's head, thus the creature's name: Medusa.

This medusa was almost two kilometers across, with scores of tentacles hundreds of meters long; they swayed back and forth in perfect unison, taking more than a minute for each complete undulation—almost as if the creature were rowing itself through the sky.

The other radar blips were other, more distant medusas. Falcon focused his sight, and the balloon's telescope, on half a dozen of them. He could detect no obvious variations in size or shape; they all seemed to be of the same species. He wondered just why they were drifting lazily around in this thousand-kilometer orbit. Were they feeding upon the aerial "plankton" sucked in by the whirlpool—sucked in as *Kon-Tiki* itself had been?

"Mission Control, I haven't heard anything from Dr. Brenner. Did he go back to bed?"

"Not to bed, Howard," came Buranaphorn's delayed reply. "Just to sleep. He's right beside me, snoring like a baby."

"Wake him up."

"By the . . ." Brenner's squawk came through the link a second later. "Howard, that creature is a hundred thousand times as large as the biggest whale! Even if it's only a gas bag, it must weigh a million tonnes! I can't even guess at its metabolism. It must generate megawatts of heat to maintain its buoyancy."

"It couldn't be just a gas bag. It's too good a radar reflector."

"You've got to get closer." Brenner's voice had an edge of contained hysteria.

"I could do that," Falcon replied—he could approach the medusa as closely as he wanted, by changing altitude to take advantage of differing wind velocities—but he made no move. Something in him had seized up, in a twinge of paralysis like that he'd experienced in the radio storm.

"Falcon, you must immediately . . ."

Buranaphorn firmly interrupted Brenner. "Let's stay where we are for the present, Howard."

"Yes, Flight, let's do that." Falcon's words conveyed relief—and a certain wry amusement at that "we." An extra thousand kilometers or so of vertical distance made a considerable difference in Mission Control's point of view.

But Olaf Brenner offered no apology for his attempt to usurp the flight director's prerogatives.

* * *

Sparta's eyes opened. In her sleep she had been *listening* to the exchange between Mission Control and the fragile balloon whirling through the clouds of Jupiter so far below. Yet there was no comprehension on her ravaged face.

"*Aiingg Zzhhhee* . . ." Her throat was full of sand. "What?"

Three men were peering down at her, two young, one older. She didn't recognize them. Again she tried to focus in, to study them at close range, but her head was about to explode. If she could see into their eyes, read their retinal patterns, she would surely be able to recognize them. . . . But why was her right eye dead? She could form an image only at a fixed, normal angle. She could see no better than any ordinary person.

"I can't see," she said in a whisper, barely more distinctly.

One of the young men waved his hand in front of her face. She tracked it with her eyes. He held up three fingers. "Can you see my hand? How many fingers?"

"Three," she whispered.

"Keep both eyes open," said the man, who must be a doctor. He laid the palm of his hand over her right eye. "How many fingers now?"

"Four. But I can't see."

He moved his palm to cover her left eye. "How many now?"

"Still four."

"Why do you say you can't see?" The doctor took his hand away from her face. "Are you experiencing distorted vision? Shadows? Any abnormality?"

She turned her head aside, not bothering to reply. The fool did not understand what she was talking about, and it occurred to her that it was better not to explain things to him.

"Ellen, we must talk to you," said one of the

others, the old one. Why did he call her that name? It wasn't hers.

She tested her bonds, trying not to be obvious about it, and found them strong. She had been strapped to a cushioned surface, a bed, with wide woven bands around her ankles and wrists and middle. Tubes were running into her arms, and she could vaguely sense more tubes and wires sprouting from her head. Those tubes must be doing something to her head. She couldn't *see*.

But she could still *listen*. . . .

For over an hour now, while *Kon-Tiki* had been drifting in the gyre of the great whirlpool, Falcon had been experimenting with the videolink's contrast and gain, trying to record a clearer view of the nearest of the medusas. He wondered if its elusive coloration was some kind of camouflage; perhaps, like many of Earth's animals, it was trying to lose itself against its background. That was a trick used by both hunters and hunted.

In which category was the medusa? He didn't really expect to answer that question in the short time left to him, yet, just before local noon, and without the slightest warning, the answer came.

Like a squadron of antique jet fighters, five mantas came sweeping through the wall of mist that formed the funnel of the vortex, flying in a V formation directly toward the gray mass of the medusa. There was no doubt in Falcon's mind that they were on the attack; evidently it had been quite wrong to assume that they were harmless vegetarians.

Everything happened at such a leisurely pace that it was like watching slo-mo. The mantas undulated along at perhaps fifty klicks; it seemed ages before they reached the medusa, which continued to paddle imperturbably along at an even slower speed. Huge though they were, the mantas looked tiny beside the monster they were approaching. And when they flapped down upon its back, they looked about as big as birds landing on a whale.

Could the medusa defend itself? Falcon didn't see how the attacking mantas could be in danger as long as they avoided those huge, clumsy tentacles. And perhaps their host was not even aware of them. They could be insignificant parasites, tolerated as a dog tolerates fleas.

No, it was obvious the medusa was in distress.

With agonizing slowness, it began to tip over like a capsizing ship. Ten minutes passed; it had tilted forty-five degrees, and it was rapidly losing altitude.

Falcon could not help but feel pity for the beleaguered monster. The sight even brought bitter memories, for in a grotesque way the fall of the medusa was almost a parody of the dying *Queen*'s last moments.

"Save your sympathies," said Brenner's oddly flat voice over the commlink, as if the exobiologist had been reading his mind. "High intelligence can develop only among predators, not among these drifting browsers—whether they're in the sea or in the air. Those things you call mantas are closer to us than that monstrous bag of gas."

Falcon heard out the scientist's assessment and was moved to dissent. But he said nothing. After all, who could *really* sympathize with a creature a hundred thousand times larger than a whale? Nor did Falcon want to prod Brenner, who must be near utter exhaustion. His remarks were increasingly infected with inappropriate emotion.

Falcon was saved from further brooding upon the state of Brenner's soul—or his own—by the sight of the medusa, whose tactics seemed to be having an effect. The mantas had been disturbed by its slow roll and were flapping heavily away from its back, like gorging vultures interrupted during mealtime. Did they somehow prefer an upright orientation, or was something else, invisible to Falcon, spurring them into action?

They had not moved very far at that, continuing to hover a few yards from the still-capsizing monster, *when there was a sudden, blinding flash of light*—

—synchronized with a crash of static on the radio. Falcon felt the jolt as a sour spasm where his stomach used to be. He watched in close-up as one of the mantas slowly twisted end over end, plummeting straight downward, trailing a plume of black smoke behind it as it fell! The resemblance to a fighter going down in flames was quite uncanny.

In unison the remaining mantas dived steeply away from the medusa, gaining speed by losing altitude. Within minutes they had vanished in the wall of cloud from which they had emerged.

The medusa, no longer falling, began to roll back toward the horizontal. Soon it was sailing along once more on an even keel, as if nothing had happened.

"Beautiful!" Brenner's ardent voice breathed into the commlink, after the first moment of stunned silence. "Electric defenses, like eels and rays. And at least a million volts!" He paused, and resumed with an edge on his voice. "Talk to us, Falcon. Do you see any organs that might have produced the discharge? Anything that looks like an electrode?"

"No," said Falcon. He tweaked the resolution. "Something odd here, though. See this pattern? Run a replay—it wasn't there before."

A broad, mottled band had appeared along the side of the medusa, forming a regular checkerboard, startling in its geometric precision. Each square was itself speckled in a complex subpattern of short horizontal lines, spaced at equal distances in a geometrically perfect array of rows and columns.

"You're right," said Brenner, with something

very like awe in his voice. "That's new. What do you think?"

Buranaphorn didn't give Falcon time to answer the question. "Meter-band radio array, wouldn't you say, Howard?" He laughed. "Any engineer who didn't have a biologist's reputation to protect would know it at a glance."

" 'S why it returns such a massive echo," said Falcon.

"Why, maybe, but why *now*," Brenner demanded. "Why has it just appeared?"

"Could be an aftereffect of the discharge," Buranaphorn said.

"Could be," said Falcon. He paused before he said, "Or maybe it's listening to us."

"On this frequency?" Buranaphorn almost laughed. "Those would have to be meter-, even decameter-length antennas. Judging by their size."

Brenner broke in excitedly. "What if they're tuned to the planet's radio outbursts? Nature never got around to that on Earth, even though we do have animals with sonar and electric senses—but Jupiter's almost as drenched in radio as Earth is in sunlight!"

"Could be a good idea," said Buranaphorn. "The thing could be tapping into the radio energy. Could be it's even a floating power plant."

"All of which is very interesting," said Brenner, his voice trembling with that authoritarian edge again, "but there's a much more important matter to settle. I'm invoking the Prime Directive."

For a long moment the radiolink between Mission Control and *Kon-Tiki* was silent. Even Buranaphorn was quiet.

Falcon spoke first, with leaden effort. "Please state your reasons."

"Until I came here," Brenner began, with cheer that rang false to his listeners, "I too would have sworn that any creature who could have made a shortwave radio antenna must be intelligent. Now

I'm not so sure. This could have evolved naturally. Really, I suppose it's no more fantastic than the human eye.''

''Fine and good, Dr. Brenner,'' Buranaphorn said. ''Why are you invoking the Prime Directive?''

''We have to play safe,'' said Brenner, dropping the false cheer. ''We have to assume intelligence, even if none of us here believes it.''

We, Falcon thought, as he sought to control the roiling emotions that welled up within him. . . .

''Therefore I am placing this expedition under all the clauses of the Prime Directive,'' Brenner said, with a terminal flourish.

A responsibility which he had never consciously imagined had descended upon Howard Falcon. In the few hours that remained to him, he might become another inhabited planet's first ambassador from the human race.

Odd that it came as no surprise—but rather with an irony so delicious that he almost wished the surgeons had restored to him the power of laughter.

Aboard *Garuda*, Buranaphorn gave Brenner a searching look: the gray-haired little man had sagged in three dimensions and was floating in his harness like a ball of dough. Buranaphorn said curtly, ''I wish I'd let you stay asleep.''

When it came to research, the Prime Directive could develop into a prime pain in the neck. Nobody seriously doubted that it was well intentioned. After a century of argument, humans had finally learned to profit from their mistakes on their home planet, or so it was hoped—and not only moral considerations but self-interest demanded that these stupidities should not be repeated elsewhere in the solar system. That's one of the reasons the guy from Voxpop was here, right? To make sure they stuck to it.

Nobody in *this* crew needed reminding. To treat

a possibly superior intelligence as the settlers of Australia and North America had treated their aborigines, as the English had treated the Indians, as practically everybody had treated the tribes of Africa . . . well, that way lay disaster.

Buranaphorn persisted. "Doctor, I'm serious. Don't you think you ought to get some real rest?" After all, the Prime Directive's first clause was *keep your distance.* Make no approach. Make no attempt to communicate. Give them plenty of time to study you—although exactly what was meant by "plenty of time" had never been spelled out. That much alone was left to the discretion of the human on the spot. "Whatever that thing is, we're not going to get any better visuals while it's night down there."

Brenner looked at him oddly. "I couldn't possibly sleep. Do you know how long we've been waiting for this moment?"

"As you say, Doctor." One of *those*, thought Buranaphorn—and up until an hour ago he'd had me fooled. Brenner had seemed so sane, so levelheaded. *He* was the guy who kept saying they might find some germs down there . . . but nothing more.

This mission seemed to have attracted a lot of types who'd invested their life hopes (to coin a phrase) in the clouds of Jupiter—certified engineers, but closet religionists just the same. The type that had called themselves Creation "scientists" back in the 20th century. For his part, Meechai Buranaphorn was an ex-rocket jock and an aeronautical engineer who wore his Buddhism lightly. Not that he went out of his way to squash bugs—and he never ate meat unless, you know, it had been raised to be eaten. But some of these guys . . . you'd think they were expecting instant reincarnation or something. Buranaphorn forced his thoughts back to the status of the mission.

At least the two Space Board heavies had cleared

out of the place; the way they'd been behaving, you'd think they were trying to start trouble. But maybe they'd had a reason to be here after all. Who would have thought . . . ? He keyed the bridge. "What's the word on the stowaway?"

Rajagopal came back at him. "There is no word," she said.

"Come on, give me something, Raj." The first mate had that infuriating haughtiness that, in Buranaphorn's opinion, came naturally to Indian women. Especially those in positions of authority.

But Rajagopal relented. "She and Redfield are locked in the clinic with our Space Board visitors."

"How's the captain taking it?"

Chowdhury himself came on the comm. "Please do your job, Mr. Buranaphorn, and let us do ours. Don't distract yourself with inessentials. Your mission is the reason we are all here."

Thanks for the reminder, jerk, Buranaphorn thought. But he kept the thought to himself.

Inside the ship's tiny clinic, Sparta was unconscious again.

"I didn't hit her that hard," Blake said, for what must have been the hundredth time.

This time the blond doctor—he was from an old Singapore family, Dutch by ancestry—didn't bother to reply. He'd already explained at length that the woman's intercranial blood vessels had been rendered dangerously permeable by her use of the drug Striaphan, found in huge quantity on her person—use which had evidently been massive and prolonged. Even a moderate blow to the head was enough to have caused rapid subdural hematoma.

Blood on the brain was not all that uncommon aboard spacecraft; flying around weightless, people tended to collide with things head first. The clinic's nanosurgical kit could have handled the routine noninvasively, perhaps within a couple of hours, had the patient been in good health, as most space workers were. Unfortunately, this woman was severely malnourished and her lungs were teeming with pneumonia—not overwhelming medical problems, but ones rarely encountered in space and, in combination with the concussion and blood clot, definitely life-threatening.

Things would be a lot easier, thought the doctor, if he could get rid of the kibitzers. The clinic, a wedge of a room off the recreation area, was small enough already without having to share it with this distraught character Redfield and this gray hulk of a Space Board officer—and where the hell had *he* come from, flashing his badge and pulling Council of Worlds rank?

"Stay here, Doctor Ullrich," said the officer. "Mr. Redfield and I will be back shortly."

"There is nothing more I can do for the patient until . . ."

"Stay here."

"But I haven't eaten in . . ." The hatch closed on the young doctor's pained objection.

Outside, in the corridor, the commander turned to his lieutenant. "Anything, Vik?"

"Nothing." The big blond lieutenant had his stun-gun out of its holster.

The commander peered at Blake. "She's been on board at least since Ganymede. You're sure it's not a bomb?"

"Not on *Kon-Tiki*. It would have showed up as extra mass."

"She hid her own mass easily enough."

"On *Garuda* she had a couple of orders of magnitude more mass to slop around in. *Kon-Tiki* was weighed repeatedly before they launched it. Right down to the gram. I watched."

"Yeah, I get the impression you made yourself a perfect pest," the commander grunted. "A pulse bomb, then—something tiny, not explosive, bad enough to fry the circuitry—what they did to her on Mars."

"She's been an outlaw for almost two years, outside anybody's system. How would she get access to anything that sophisticated and expensive?"

"I could ask how she stowed away . . ."

"However she did it, it didn't take that kind of money."

"Yeah." The commander sighed. "Structural damage?"

"*Kon-Tiki* has worked without a hitch, all the major systems—heatshields, drogue chutes, balloon, fusion pack, ramjets, life support, instrumentation, communication. . . . They crawled all over that thing before they let it separate."

"Then it's software."

"Every diagnostic has run perfectly."

"Still . . . software."

Blake nodded, reluctantly. "I think you're right. But we aren't going to find out what she did unless she tells us."

"Look, Redfield, I'm not trying to get rid of you. But the doctor in there says he's hungry. How about rounding up some slop from the mess?"

Blake started to object—why can't Vik do it? he wanted to ask. But the answer was obvious: the lieutenant had the firepower, and they might need it. Blake headed for the mess.

The commander went back into the clinic.

"Food's on the way," he said to Ullrich. "Say again what you know about this stuff she was on."

"Computer says a guanine nucleotide binding protein . . ."

"So a cop can understand it."

Ullrich flushed. "A neuropeptide—a brain chemical—associated with the visual cortex. Limited use in the treatment of some forms of reading disorder. The typical dosage is about a millionth what this woman has been taking."

"What would that do to her?"

"In rats it apparently produces hallucinations. Auditory and visual. And bizarre behaviors."

"Like schizophrenia?"

"We don't diagnose rats as schizophrenic."

"One for you, Doctor," said the commander. "Keep talking."

"The woman's left visual cortex is fragile. Redfield's blow to her jaw thrust the brain against the back of the skull. Preexisting cell-membrane permeability may account for her complaint that she can't see . . . although obviously she sees well enough in the ordinary sense of the word."

At that moment Sparta's eyes opened. Ullrich glanced at her. He felt less compassion for this patient than he should have. "In any event, her life's out of danger. Her pneumonia is under control."

"Can you talk, Linda?" the commander asked. His rough voice conveyed a curious mix of concern and command.

The doctor objected, almost by reflex. "That is not . . ."

"Can talk," she whispered. She looked away from the commander's face and frowned at the doctor. "Dangerous."

"Never mind him, he's clean," said the commander, ignoring Ullrich's puzzled, offended look. "Do you want to say what you did to *Kon-Tiki?*"

"No." Her eyes locked with the commander's. "You understand."

"You think that Howard Falcon took your place as envoy?"

"As it was intended by the *prophetae.*"

"You want to deny him that? Out of jealousy?"

"Jealousy?" She tried to smile, with ghastly effect. "Don't want Free Spirit to make first contact. You neither." Her gaze drifted to the shadowed metal ceiling. "Been busy, sir. Two years now."

"Yes."

"I know who you are. Really are."

"Howard Falcon is an innocent man," said the commander.

" 'Man' not the word," she said.

"As human as you."

"I am not a human being," she said, with force that cost her.

"You are nothing but," said the commander. He turned to the doctor. "Show her the scans."

Beyond protest, Ullrich did as he was told and brought the woman's brain scans up on the flat-screen. "The area of the hematoma," he said, pointing, "almost entirely relieved by targeted nano-organisms . . ."

"Thank you, Doctor," the commander said, silencing him. "You could see closer or farther than an ordinary human, Linda—not because of anything they did to the eyeball, but because of what they did to the visual cortex."

"Getting to like that," she said. "Gone now. Fried my brain."

"This other knot of matter is still intact," said the commander, pointing to a dense shadow in the forebrain. "And this. And this."

"Can still compute trajectory," she said.

"What did you do to *Kon-Tiki*'s computer?" he repeated.

"Can still *listen*." She closed her eyes. For a single second—it seemed to last forever—she was perfectly still. When she opened them again she said, "Maybe persuade me—if we had longer."

"What do you mean?"

"Don't waste time on me. Mission Control."

He understood. "So it's already happening."

25

It had been growing darker, but Falcon had scarcely noticed as he strained his eyes toward the living cloud. The wind that was steadily sweeping *Kon-Tiki* around the funnel of the great whirlpool had now brought him within twenty kilometers of the creature.

"If you get much closer, Howard, I want you to take evasive action," Buranaphorn said. "That thing's electric weapons are probably short-range, but we don't want you putting it to a test."

"Future explorers," Falcon said hoarsely.

"Say again please?"

"Leave that to future explorers," Falcon repeated. One part of his brain watched the unfolding events with brilliant clarity, but another seemed to have trouble forming words. "Wish them luck."

"That's a roger," came the voice of Mission Control.

It was quite dark in the capsule—strange, because sunset was still hours away. Automatically he glanced at the scanning radar as he had done every few minutes. That and his own senses confirmed that there was no other object within a hundred kilometers of him, aside from the medusa he was studying.

Suddenly, with startling power, he heard the sound that had come booming out of the Jovian night—the throbbing beat that grew more and more rapid, then stopped in midcrescendo. The whole capsule vibrated like a pea on a kettledrum.

Falcon realized two things simultaneously during the sudden, aching silence: this time the sound was not coming from thousands of kilometers away over a radio circuit. It was in the very atmosphere around him.

The second thought was more disturbing. He had quite forgotten—inexcusable, but there had been other things on his mind—that most of the sky above him was completely blanked out by *Kon-Tiki's* gas bag. Lightly silvered to conserve heat, the great balloon also made an effective shield against both radar and vision.

Not that this hadn't been considered at length and finally tolerated, as a minor design trade-off of little importance. But suddenly it seemed very important.

Falcon saw a fence of gigantic tentacles descending all around his capsule.

"Remember the Prime Directive! The Prime Directive!"

Brenner's scream filled his head with an extraordinary bright confusion—as if words alone had the power to bend his attention, subvert his very will. For a moment Falcon thought the words had welled up from his subconscious mind, so vividly did they seem to tangle with his own thoughts.

But no, it was Brenner's voice all right, again yelling over the commlink: "Don't alarm it!"

Don't *alarm* it? Before Falcon could think of an appropriate answer, that overwhelming drumbeat started again and drowned all other sounds.

The sign of a really skilled test pilot is how he reacts not to foreseeable emergencies but to ones that nobody could have anticipated—a reaction that is not conscious, not conditionable, but a capacity for decision built in at the cellular level. Before Falcon could even form a notion of what he was about to do, he had done it. He'd pulled the ripcord.

Ripcord—an archaic phrase from the earliest days of ballooning, when there was a cord rigged to literally rip open the bag. *Kon-Tiki*'s ripcord wasn't a cord but a switch, which operated a set of louvers around the upper curve of the envelope. At once the hot gas rushed out. *Kon-Tiki*, deprived of her lift, began to fall swiftly in a gravity field two and a half times as strong as Earth's.

Falcon had a momentary glimpse of great tentacles whipping upward and away. He had just time to note that they were studded with large bladders or sacs, presumably to give them buoyancy, and that they ended in multitudes of thin feelers like the roots of a plant.

He half expected a bolt of lightning. Nothing happened.

Brenner was still yelling at him. "What have you done, Falcon? You may have frightened it badly!"

"Busy here," Falcon said, squelching the transmission. His precipitous rate of descent was slackening as the atmosphere thickened and the balloon's deflated envelope acted as a parachute. When *Kon-Tiki* had dropped about three kilometers, he thought it must surely be safe to close the louvers again. By the time he had restored buoyancy and was in equilibrium once more, he had lost another two kilometers of altitude and was getting dangerously near the red line.

He peered anxiously through the overhead windows. He did not expect to see anything but the obscuring bulk of the balloon, but he had sideslipped during his descent, and part of the medusa was barely visible a couple of kilometers above—much closer than he'd expected, and still coming down, faster than he would have believed possible.

Buranaphorn was on the link from Mission Control, calling anxiously: "Howard, we show your rate of descent . . ."

"I'm all right," Falcon broke in, "but it's still coming after me. I can't go any deeper." Which was not quite true; he could go a lot deeper, at least a couple of hundred kilometers, but it would be a one-way trip, and he would miss most of the journey.

To his great relief he saw that the medusa was leveling out, a bit more than a kilometer above him. Perhaps it had decided to approach the intruder with caution, or perhaps it too had found this deeper layer uncomfortably hot. For the temperature was over fifty degrees Centigrade, and Falcon wondered how much longer *Kon-Tiki*'s life-support system could handle matters.

Brenner was back on the circuit, still worried. "Try not to frighten it! It's only being inquisitive!"

Falcon felt a stiffness about his neck and jaws as if his gorge were rising. Brenner's voice did not lack conviction, exactly—what it lacked was the sound of integrity. Falcon recalled a videocast discussion he'd caught between a lawyer and an astronaut in which, after the full implications of the Prime had been spelled out, the incredulous spacer had exclaimed, "You mean if there was no alternative I'd have to sit still and let myself be eaten?" and the lawyer had not even cracked a smile when he answered, "That's an excellent summation." As Falcon recalled, his masters—his physicians, that is—had been quite upset to find him watching that show; they thought they'd censored it. It had seemed funny at the time.

Just then Falcon saw something that upset him even more than the exobiologist's assault on his willpower. The medusa was still hovering more than a kilometer above the balloon, but one of its tentacles had become incredibly elongated—

—and was stretching down toward *Kon-Tiki*, thinning out at the same time! Remembered video scenes of tornados descending from storm clouds over the North American plains sprang to Falcon's mind, memories vividly evoked by the black, twisting snake in the sky that was groping for him now.

"See that, Mission Control?"

"Affirmative," Buranaphorn replied tautly.

"I'm out of options," Falcon said. "Either I scare it off or give it a bad stomach ache—because I don't think it will find *Kon-Tiki* very digestible, if that's what it has in mind."

Brenner's voice came back, fast and frantic: "Howard, listen to me. You must not forget that you are under the dictates of the Prime. . . ."

At that moment Falcon killed the downlink from Mission Control, cutting Brenner off in midexpostulation—a decision that came from the same place as his decision to pull the ripcord, from some deeply engrained respect for his own integrity and survival.

A cruder, more primitive man might have put it more bluntly: screw the Prime Directive.

Perhaps that cruder, more primitive man was sensitive to something that the highly evolved, highly modified, fully conscious Howard Falcon wasn't, namely that every time Brenner said the words "Prime Directive," Falcon's head seemed to fill with throbbing white light, and he felt vague saccharine urges toward—how would one put it?— the Oneness of Being. Urges overlaid with a less romantic compulsion to do any damn thing Brenner told him to do.

Where the hell that came from, he didn't know. But cutting the squishy little Brenner out of the loop seemed to relieve the immediate symptoms.

"I'm starting the ignition sequencer," Falcon said, aware that his words were for the record only, and that if he never got back to Mission Control no one would ever really know what happened.

* * *

The clinic door stood open. The commander was gone, the guard outside the door had disappeared, and the ship's doctor had made his getaway. Blake floated into the doorway, his hands full of food containers. "What happened?"

She was oblivious to him, *listening*. She expelled a long breath. "He's offline," she said. "Moonjelly must have taken him."

"The what?"

"The medusa."

"Are you sure?"

She studied him with dull eyes. "Whatever happens, he's dead. I rigged his escape sequence to fail. Wish I hadn't."

"Linda, Linda, what's become of you?" he cried. Blake wiped sudden tears across his red face and propelled himself backward into the corridor.

At last she was alone. She tugged at her wrist straps.

Falcon was twenty-seven minutes early on the countdown, but he calculated—or hoped—that he had the reserves to correct his orbit later.

He couldn't see the medusa. It was directly overhead. But the descending tentacle must be close to the balloon.

As a heater, the reactor was running fine, but it took five minutes for its microprocessors to run through the complicated checklist needed to get it to full thrust as a rocket. Two of those minutes had passed. The fuser was primed. Computer had not rejected the orbit situation as absurd, or at least not as wholly impossible. The capsule's scoops were open, ready to gulp in tonnes of the surrounding hydrogen-helium atmosphere on demand. In almost all ways conditions were optimum, and it was the moment of truth. Would the damn thing work?

There had been no way of operationally testing a nuclear ramjet in a Jupiterlike atmosphere—

without going to Jupiter. So this was the first real trial.

Something rocked *Kon-Tiki*, rather gently. Falcon tried to ignore it.

Ramjet ignition had been planned for barometric conditions equivalent to some ten kilometers higher, in an atmosphere less than a quarter of the present density and some thirty degrees cooler.

Too bad.

What was the shallowest dive he could get away with? If and when the scoops worked and the ram fired, he'd be heading in the general direction of Jupiter—down, that is—with two and a half Gs to help him get there. Could he possibly pull out in time?

A large, heavy hand patted the balloon. The whole rig bobbed up and down like one of those antique toys, yo-yos, that had recently undergone a rage revival on the playgrounds of Earth. Falcon tried harder to ignore it.

Without success. Brenner could be right, of course. It might be trying to be friendly. Maybe he should try talking to it over the radio. It received radio, didn't it? What should he say? How about ''Pretty pussy'' or maybe ''Down, Fido!''— or ''Take me to your leader.''

Computer showed tritium-deuterium ratio optimum. Time to light the hundred million-degree Roman candle.

The thin tip of the medusa's tentacle came slithering around the edge of the balloon, less than sixty meters away. It was about the size of an elephant's trunk and, judging by the delicacy of its exploration, at least as sensitive. There were little palps at its ends, like questing mouths.

Dr. Brenner would have been fascinated.

It was as good a time as any—probably better than any time more than a second or two later—so Falcon glanced swiftly at his control board, saw all green, and started the four-second count.

Four
He broke the safety seal—
Three
And flipped the ENABLE toggle—
Two
And with his left hand squeezed hard on the dead-man switch—
One
And with his right pressed the JETTISON button.
Nothing . . . until—
There was a sharp explosion and an instant loss of weight.

Half a minute after Falcon went off line, a howl of static erupted through the speakers in Mission Control, momentarily overwhelming the automatic trackers.

A hundred bright points of radio energy blazed into life in the clouds of Jupiter, forming concentric rings that were neatly centered on Falcon's last known position.

To the human ear the radio noise was just that, meaningless broadband noise, but the analyzers made something quite different of the mess: it seemed that each of the sources was transmitting the same highly directional modulated beam, thousands of watts—straight toward Mission Control!

Cries of raw emotion burst from the throats of four of the on-duty controllers as they grabbed for their harness latches to free themselves from their consoles. Buranaphorn looked up in disbelief to find himself staring into the maw of a pistol.

At the same moment, up on the flight deck, First Mate Rajagopal turned to Captain Chowdhury and announced, "You are hereby relieved of your command. Obey me and all will be well."

Three off-duty controllers flew in through Mission Control's lower hatch, shouting through the crackling roar of the speakers, "All will be well!"

A man holding a pistol intercepted the commander as he was flying up the central corridor toward Mission Control. "If you stop there, Commander, all will be well with you."

Garuda was in mutiny.

Meanwhile *Kon-Tiki* was falling freely, nose down. Overhead the discarded balloon was racing upward, taking the medusa's inquisitive tentacle with it. But Falcon had no time to see if the gas bag had ascended so fast that it actually hit the medusa, for at that moment his jets fired and he had other things to think about.

A roaring column of hot hydrohélium was pouring out of the reactor nozzle, swiftly building thrust toward the heart of Jupiter. *Not* the way he wanted to go. Unless he could regain vector control and achieve horizontal flight within the next five seconds, his vehicle would dive so deeply into the atmosphere that it would be crushed.

With agonizing slowness, five seconds that seemed like fifty, he managed to flatten out and pull the nose up. Falcon was still accelerating, in eyeballs-out position. If he'd had a merely human circulatory system, his head would have exploded. He glanced back just once and caught a glimpse of the medusa many kilometers away. The discarded gas bag had evidently escaped its grasp, for he could see no sign of the silver bubble.

A savage thrill swept through him. Once more he was master of his own fate, no longer drifting helplessly on the winds but riding a column of atomic fire back toward the stars. He was confident the ramjet was working perfectly, steadily increasing velocity and altitude until the ship would soon reach near-orbital speed at the fringes of atmosphere. There, with a brief burst of rocket power, Falcon would regain the freedom of space.

Halfway to orbit he looked south and saw, coming up over the horizon, the tremendous enigma of the Great Red Spot, that permanent hole in the clouds big enough to swallow two Earths. Falcon stared into its mysterious beauty until a bleating computer warned him that conversion to rocket thrust was only sixty seconds ahead. Reluctantly he tore his gaze from the surface of the planet.

"Some other time," he murmured. At the same moment he switched on the commlink to Mission Control.

"What's that?" the flight director demanded. "What did you say, Falcon?"

"It doesn't matter. Are you locked on?"

"That's a roger," Buranaphorn said drily. "When we do this again, we'd like your cooperation."

"Okay. Tell Dr. Brenner I'm sorry if I scared his alien. I don't think any damage was done." Mission Control was silent so long that Falcon thought he'd lost the link. "Mission Control?"

"We are going to concentrate on bringing you in," said Buranaphorn. "Please stand by for revised reacquisition coordinates."

"Roger, and did you copy my message to Brenner?"

"We copied." The flight director hesitated only briefly this time. "This will not affect your final approach, Howard, but you should be aware that this ship is presently under martial law."

26

Three minutes after the mutiny started, it was over. The crew and controllers who'd crowded into Mission Control and onto the bridge of *Garuda*, shouting "All will be well," found themselves staring into the barrels of stun guns held by their former colleagues.

Only two rubber bullets were fired, at rebels who'd drawn on the Space Board commander and his lieutenant. The lieutenant had been on the bridge, the commander down in the corridor. They'd both drawn faster.

A swift victory. Problem was—as if the radio noise howling out of the speakers weren't enough to interfere with clear thought—that there was no place on *Garuda* big enough to hold thirteen prisoners. There they all were, up against the roof of Mission Control, a baker's dozen of them wriggling like caterpillars with their wrists and ankles bound by plastic thongs, kept from floating helplessly into the way of the working controllers by a wide-mesh cargo net drawn across the entire ceiling. The controllers paid no attention to them. They still had *Kon-Tiki* to worry about.

Sparta wobbled weightlessly, drunkenly, as she moved up the central corridor toward Mission Control. The deafening radio roar from Jupiter ceased as suddenly as it had begun, just as she approached the hatchway. Blake stopped her before she could enter the room.

"Linda, you . . ." Whatever he was going to say, he changed his mind. "You shouldn't be off life-support."

"I'll survive." She peered past him into the crowded control room. She had a good view overhead of the human menagerie under the roof. "Brenner I knew about. Rajagopal, too?"

"Half the crew—which is why they thought they could take the ship without a fight. By the time it dawned on them they needed their weapons, it was too late."

She shifted her wary gaze back to him. "Who are you, Blake?"

"I'm Salamander now," he said. "Eight of us aboard. Plus the commander and Vik. Look, Linda, sorry . . . but this isn't over yet."

He reached for her, but she flinched away. "Why not put me in the net with them?"

He paled. "Why would I do that?"

"I killed Falcon," she said. On her face was the sort of hopeful defiance with which saints and witches once went to the fire. "What you guessed: software. Rewrote the ignition sequence to send him straight into Jupiter."

At that moment, over the continuing human commotion inside Mission Control, there came a sudden loud, clear rush of words from the speakers.

"What's that?" Buranaphorn yelped. "What did you say, Falcon?"

"It doesn't matter. Are you locked on?"

"That's a roger," Buranaphorn answered. "When we do this again, we'd like your cooperation."

"He's still alive!" Blake stared at Sparta. "What should we do?"

She was a pale ghost in the corridor below him. "Clock time?" she whispered.

Blake grabbed the hatch frame and pulled himself far enough into the control room to see the nearest clock. "E minus four forty," he shouted at her.

Her face was an extraordinary screen of emotions—of shock, exultation, anguish, and shame. "Falcon's safe. I didn't know what time it was." She turned away from Blake, weeping bitterly, and tried to bury her face in her arms.

Twenty-four hours later the Space Board cutter took its crew and passengers—many of them unwilling—on a short trip back to Ganymede Base. Howard Falcon said nothing to Sparta or Blake or the commander during the brief trip. Falcon had never before met any of them. He knew nothing of them.

They exited through the long tube into the security lock. Once inside the docking bay Howard Falcon let a Space Board patroller guide him to a separate chamber. Someone he knew well was waiting for him in the VIP lounge.

For Brandt Webster the long, apprehensive wait was over. "Extraordinary events, Howard. Good to see you safe." He thought Falcon was looking very well, for a man who'd just lived through what he had. "We'll get to the bottom of this soon, I assure you."

"No concern of mine," said Falcon. "No effect on the mission."

Webster swallowed that and tried a different tack. "You're a hero," he said. "In more ways than one."

"My name's been in the news before," Falcon said. "Let's get on with the debriefing."

"Howard! There's really no rush. Let an old friend congratulate you, at least."

Falcon regarded Webster with an expression that would be impassive forever after. He inclined his head. "Forgive me."

Webster tried to take encouragement from the words. "You've injected excitement into so many lives—not one in a million will ever get into space, but now the whole human race can travel to the outer giants in their imagination. That counts for something!"

"Glad I made your job a little easier."

Webster was too old a friend to take offense, yet the irony surprised him. "I'm not ashamed of my job."

"Why should you be? New knowledge, new resources—that's all very well. Necessary even." Falcon's words were more than ironic; they seemed tinged with bitterness.

"People need novelty and excitement too," Webster answered quietly. "Space travel seems routine to a lot of people, but what you've done has restored the great adventure. It will be a long, long time before we understand what happened on Jupiter."

"The medusa knew my blind spot," Falcon said.

"Whatever you say," Webster replied, resolutely cheerful.

"How do you suppose it knew my blind spot?"

"Howard, I don't have any idea."

Falcon was silent and motionless for an interminable moment. "No matter," he said at last.

Webster's relief was visible. "Have you thought about your next move? Saturn, Uranus, Neptune . . . ?"

"I've thought about Saturn." Falcon gave the phrase a ponderous weight that might have been intended to mock Webster's sanctimony. "I'm not really needed there. It's only one gravity, you know—not two and a half, like Jupiter. People can handle that."

People, thought Webster, he said "people." He's

never done that before. And when did I last hear him use the word "we"? He's changing, slipping away from us. . . . "Well," he said aloud, moving to the pressure window that looked out upon the cracked and frozen landscape of Jupiter's biggest moon, "we have to get a media conference out of the way before we can do a thorough debriefing." He eyed Falcon shyly. "No need to mention the events on *Garuda*; we've kept the lid on that."

Falcon said nothing.

"Everybody's waiting to congratulate you, Howard. You'll see a lot of your old friends."

Webster stressed that last word, but Falcon showed no response; the leather mask of his face was becoming more and more difficult to read.

He rolled away from Webster and unlocked his undercarriage, rising on his hydraulics to his full two and half meters. The psychologists had thought it a good idea to add an extra fifty centimeters as a sort of compensation for everything Falcon had lost when the *Queen* crashed, but Falcon had never acknowledged that he'd noticed.

Falcon waited until Webster had opened the door for him—useless gesture—then pivoted neatly on his balloon tires and headed forward at a smooth and silent thirty kilometers an hour. His display of speed and precision was not flaunted arrogantly; Falcon's moves had become virtually automatic.

Outside a howling newspack waited, barely restrained by the net barriers, bristling with microphones and photogram cameras that they thrust toward his masklike face.

But Howard Falcon was unperturbed. He who had once been a man—and could still pass for one over a voice-only link—felt only a calm sense of achievement . . . and, for the first time in years, something like peace of mind. He'd slept soundly aboard the cutter on his return from Jupiter, and for the first time in years his nightmares seemed to have vanished.

He woke from sweet sleep to the realization of why he had dreamed about the superchimp aboard the doomed *Queen Elizabeth*. Neither man nor beast, it was between two worlds. So was he. As a chimp is to a human, Falcon was to some as-yet-to-be-perfected machine.

He had found his role at last. He alone could travel unprotected on the surface of the Moon, or Mercury, or a dozen other worlds. The life-support system inside the titanium-aluminide cylinder that had replaced his fragile body functioned equally well in space or underwater. Gravity fields even ten times that of Earth would be an inconvenience, nothing more. And no gravity was best of all.

The human race was becoming more remote, the ties of kinship more tenuous. Perhaps these air-breathing, radiation-sensitive bundles of unstable carbon compounds had no right to live outside atmosphere. Perhaps they should stick to their natural homes—Earth, the moon, Mars.

Some day the real masters of space would be machines, not men. He was neither. Already conscious of his destiny, he took a somber pride in his unique loneliness—the first immortal, midway between two orders of creation.

The hidden, intricate sequence of directives which supposedly had been programmed into Falcon's mind and which the mere incantation of the words "Prime Directive" had been intended to activate in him had failed to work as his designers intended—not simply because of mechanical failure, and certainly not because Falcon was less than human—but because he was still, in some essential, deep crevice of his mind, too human to do what no human would do, sacrifice himself for no good reason.

Falcon himself knew nothing of this. He did not know that his instincts for self-preservation—with a little help from electrical overload—had crushed the best hopes of a millenniums-old religious conspiracy. He knew only that he had been *elected*.

He would, after all, be an ambassador—between the old and the new, between the creatures of carbon and the creatures of ceramic and metal who must one day supersede them. He was sure that both species would have need of him in the troubled centuries that lay ahead.

EPILOGUE

"Another?"

"Why yes, very good of you . . ." Professor J. Q. R. Forster positioned his glass under the neck of the Laphroaig bottle. The commander poured the dark liquid over chunks of ice. Behind them, an oak fire burned with intense heat in the fireplace of the Granite Lodge library. Outside the tall windows, the early winter sun was setting.

"The ignition sequence was keyed to mission-elapsed time," the commander said, replacing the bottle on the silver tray. "If the count had continued, Troy's rewrite of the program would have sent *Kon-Tiki* straight into Jupiter. Half an hour before that could happen, Falcon manually overrode the sequencer to escape from the medusa."

"So the medusa actually saved his life!" Forster's terrier brows leaped eagerly upon his forehead—he loved a good yarn.

"And Troy's freedom. She would have been guilty of murder."

Forster shrugged, faintly embarrassed. "In that unfortunate event, surely she could have pled temporary insanity."

"Not something she likes to talk about." The commander settled into his armchair, remembering the recent trip from Jupiter. He was not about to burden Forster with the details—details that would remain vivid in his own mind for years.

"You can't save me from a murder charge that easily," Linda had rasped at him for the hundredth time, her eyes dull with weariness. "I killed Holly Singh. And Jack Noble. And the orange man. Maybe others. When I did it, I knew what I was doing."

One of the swiftest ships in the solar system was taking three weeks to get them back to Earth. It gave her the time she needed to recover her physical health. It gave all of them more time than they needed for debate and discussion.

But Linda was an infinite puzzle to the commander. "Does your conscience require that much of you?" he had asked her.

"You are asking me if I can find *any* reason to justify the murders I committed. I tell you no, none—even though those people tried to murder *me*. And may have murdered my parents, whatever you or I want to believe."

"The ones you named were murderers, all right. And they meant to enslave humanity. Others like them survive, with goals that haven't changed."

"That doesn't justify killing them in cold blood." Her blood had not been cold, though. It had teemed.

"Well, you're determined." He sighed expressively. "Whether you knew what you were doing is not something you're going to be left to decide for yourself, I'm afraid. Psychiatric observation is all your uncorroborated confession is likely to get you."

"Uncorroborated?"

He pretended not to hear her. "And after some indeterminate sentence in a mental hospital—you know what that's like, I think, the sort of things they can do these days with programmed nano-chips and so on—after that, if there's any evidence to support your statement, maybe they'll lock you in a penitentiary for life. But if that's what you want. . . .''

"You know I'm telling the truth.''

"Maybe. No one has reported any of those people dead, or even missing.''

"But has anyone *seen* them? They were public figures, some of them. Lord Kingman. Holly Singh.''

"No, but Jack Noble had already taken a powder, as they used to say. 'Course, he had cause.'' He shrugged. "People can disappear for years at a time for no good reason, maybe because they just feel like it. *You* vanished without warning, Linda. More than once.''

She winced to hear her name from his lips.

"But let's say I believe they are dead and that you killed them—leaving out Kingman, of course. Do you want my cooperation? Want me to help you take on all the responsibility, let you pay for your mortal sins?''

"What do *you* want?'' She swallowed, anticipating the barb in the bait.

"Help us.'' Those smooth-talking Jesuit confessors, the childless uncles and cousins of his French Canadian forebears, would have been proud of him—weren't they just as at home with the sophistries of the cloister as with the lies they told the Indians they'd come to convert?—but the commander was ashamed of himself. "We've got a problem. Bigger than your little personal problem. Maybe even bigger than *Homo sapiens.*''

"Just because you try to make it sound important doesn't let me off the hook.''

"Stay on your damned hook. You hit some of the Free Spirit, but it wasn't a clean hit. Who the hell taught you to try to hit *anything* with a handgun at five hundred meters?''—he was angry, filled with professional scorn—''Yeah, we did wreck their plans on Jupiter, without *your* help, but we haven't cleaned them out. Laird, or Lequeu, or whatever he calls himself, is still loose.''

"He can't do anything. The creatures in the clouds have spoken.''

The commander's eye brightened. "Do you claim to interpret this revelation for us? For *me*, who knows the Knowledge almost as well as you?''

"You don't know what they said." Sparta grimaced. "Don't try to make a fool of me.''

"The medusas had something to say, though.''

"Something, yes.''

"What was that? Is the Pancreator coming for us now?''

"I don't know," she said, huskily, dropping her glance. "I no longer have organs to hear.''

"If they are coming for us, it could be the oldest problem of all, Linda. Down here in the slaughterhouse, could be sheep against goats." His smile was bleak. "Always thought goats were a hell of a lot more charming than sheep. Maybe that puts me on the wrong side.''

"You make me small," she whispered. "I am not small.''

He got angry then. "You make yourself small—if you will not fight for the right of free human beings to hear this so-called revelation! You can't keep it to yourself, any more than Laird and his phony prophets could keep it to themselves.''

She ducked her head—a gesture of shame she had recently acquired—before she looked up at him, still defiant. In the end, his best Jesuitical arguments had failed to move her.

But he didn't need to tell that to Forster.

The commander found himself staring into the searing embers of the crumbling oakwood fire. He looked up at the eager little professor. "End of my story, I'm afraid.''

"Ahh—and now for mine," said Forster, leaning forward in the overstuffed armchair, making the leather squeak. A look of pure glee stretched his disturbingly youthful face. "I've analyzed the material you provided."

"So you said."

The professor couldn't resist a moment of pure pedagogy. "It is worth noting that the Medusa—the Gorgon's head—is an ancient symbol of stewardship. The shield and guardian of wisdom."

"Yeah, I think I heard that somewhere before."

"The recordings of the transmissions of the ring of medusas were easily deciphered—relatively easily, after a bit of play with SETI analysis programs—and according to the linguistic system I had previously outlined for you and Mr. Redfield, I determined that the transmissions were definitely signals, and most definitely in the language of Culture X."

"Professor, if you would just . . ."

"And they signify"—Forster drew out his words, almost crooning them—"*They have arrived.*"

"They have *arrived*?"

"Yes. That's the message: 'They have arrived.' "

Was Forster playing a joke? "I don't believe it," the commander said. "Those things were beaming straight at *Kon-Tiki*'s mission control. Why would they . . . ?"

"Why tell those who had just arrived that they had arrived?" Forster chuckled. "Good question. Especially since the medusas hardly seem to be intelligent creatures in any sense that we understand the word—perhaps no more intelligent than trained parrots. Likely they were responding to some stimulus planted eons ago. Even coded in whatever serves them for genes."

"But why aim at Mission Control?"

"I think it *un*likely their message was intended for Mission Control. I believe they were aiming elsewhere."

"Forster . . ."

"Thanks to your good offices, Commander, my

survey of the moon Amalthea has already been given a firm launch date.'' Forster peered into his newly empty glass.

''Let me freshen that,'' said the commander, leaning forward. He took the heavy silver tongs and lifted ice cubes from the bucket and dropped them ringing into Forster's glass. He reached for the whiskey bottle. ''Amalthea, you say . . .''

The sun had set beyond the western cliffs, sucking the color into the matte gray forested hills across the river. Lights came on, dim yellow bulbs hidden in crevices of the low stone wall beside the river cliffs. Blake and Sparta walked beside the wall, their boots rustling the dead leaves. Cold air moved heavily against their backs, the breath of winter sliding down the valley from the high ground. Both were hunched against the cold, hands in pockets, insulated from each other.

Blake looked up at the lodge. A light had just come on behind the stained glass window of the pantry. The staff was preparing for supper. ''That's the one I smashed through, that night.''

''When will you drop the subject?'' she said irritably.

''I remember everything that happened, as clearly as anything in my life. For weeks I thought you betrayed me—but you weren't there at all.''

It had been Blake's ingenious notion to persuade Sparta that she had never murdered Singh or the others, that those were false memories planted by the commander for reasons of his own—perhaps because he was unwilling to admit that the Free Spirit had escaped his grasp again. Blake had pleaded with her: ''Why he wants you to think so, *I* don't know. Maybe *he* killed them. But you've got to admit, you were out of your head. God, the amount of Bliss you were gobbling . . .''

But she had destroyed his argument even before he'd well stated it. ''Even if they have a way to rewrite memory, they didn't use it on me. They didn't even know where I was." And in the end, Blake could not even convince himself of his implausible scheme.

Now she was mute, insulated against his concerns, as she was insulated against his warmth.

They walked in silence, but for the dead leaves. Gradually a solitary human shape coalesced from the shadows a dozen meters in front of them.

They were alert, but neither of them was alarmed. Both knew how very unlikely it was that an unauthorized visitor was on the grounds. They were prepared to pass by the figure in silence—

—but as they approached, the shadow-man whispered, "Linda."

The flesh on her arms crept; the cold had somehow slipped inside her parka on her whispered name. She faltered. "You . . . ?" She was afraid to finish the question. The shadow had the shape and sound of him, but the cold wind blew his scent away, and she could no longer see in the dark.

"Yes, darling," said the shadow. "Please forgive me."

"Ohh . . ." She moved into his solid arms, crushed herself against him, clung to him as if she were falling.

Blake looked on astonished and said the first natural thing that occurred to him, absurd as it was. "Where the hell have you *been*, Dr. Nagy?"

Jozsef Nagy looked up, over his daughter's shoulder. "Never far away, Mr. Redfield,"

"Uh . . . call me Blake, sir."

"Yes, we are far from the classroom. Call me Jozsef, Blake."

"Right," said Blake, but it would be a while before he got up the courage to address the most imposing authority figure of his childhood by his first name.

"Linda, Linda," Nagy was crooning to his

daughter, who had broken into desperate sobs. ''We treated you so badly.''

''Where is Mother? Is she . . . ?'' Her words were muffled; her face was thrust into the folds of his woolen overcoat.

''She is very well. You'll see her soon.''

''I thought you were both *dead*.''

''We were afraid . . . afraid to tell you.'' He glanced at Blake and nodded, and although Blake could not see him well, there was diffidence in the gesture. ''We owe both of you our deepest apologies.''

''Well, she *was* pretty worried,'' Blake said, instantly thinking how foolish he sounded: Nagy wasn't exactly a lost kid who'd scared his mommy. And Ellen . . . Linda had been beyond mere worry.

''Yes, I know,'' Nagy said simply. ''There were reasons that seemed very good to us at the time. We were wrong.''

Sparta's sobs had subsided. She relaxed in her father's arms. He took one arm from around her shoulders, groped in his pocket, and came up with a handkerchief. She took it gratefully. Nagy said, ''I will try to explain—with Kit's help. Perhaps we should go inside now?'' The last was a question addressed to Sparta. She nodded mutely, swiping at her nose.

The three of them started slowly up the long slope toward the lodge. Blake had had a moment to think; there was firm insistence in his voice when he spoke again, overlying a hint of anger. ''It would be good if you just gave us a simple 'why,' sir. Now . . . I mean, without the commander's kibbitzing.''

''We are in a war, Blake. For years my daughter was a hostage. Then we realized she had become our best weapon.'' Nagy hesitated as if it were an effort, but went on in a clear voice. ''It proved too hard for us to let go the habits of parenthood, of teacherhood. We tried to protect both of you by controlling you. To do that we had to stay in hiding. At first only *you* proved difficult, Blake—finally impossible—to control.''

''Your daughter is an adult, too.'' Blake saw Nagy duck his head and suddenly understood where Ellen . . . Linda . . . had acquired her gesture of shame.

Sparta pulled a few centimeters away from her father. ''I killed them,'' she said tonelessly.

''You came to Striaphan unprepared because we failed to tell you what we had learned,'' Nagy said. ''Your resistance had already been largely destroyed by our attempts to hurry your dreams.''

''The commander's attempts,'' Blake said hotly.

''By *my* orders, though. To his credit and my shame, I forced Kit to continue when he objected. I had hoped to speed your recovery, darling. Instead I . . .'' He broke off, watching his daughter with apprehension. She had drawn away from him. ''You were acting under a compulsion we knew existed but didn't understand. Everything you did, in England and in orbit around Jupiter, was in the service of that compulsion. You tried to eliminate those who stood in your way, including those who had planted the compulsion in you.''

''You can't remove the guilt.''

''I would not try. But I ask you take the next step.''

''What do you want of me?''

''To admit that you are a human being.''

She was weary and wounded, but she refused to weep again. ''That is for me to say.''

''So it is. Please just leave the question open until you have heard all *we* have to say. You too, Blake.''

The three of them walked silently toward the massive stone house with its jewel-like windows. After a few minutes they drew closer. Linda reached to take her father's hand. There was a renewed warmth of light in her eyes, coming from somewhere deeper than the reflections of the windows.

There was a knock at the library door and the commander opened it a crack. A young blond steward said, "Dinner is ready, sir. Four settings, as you specified."

"Put it on hold. Shouldn't be long."

"Sir." The steward closed the heavy paneled door behind him.

The commander gestured to the drinks tray. "Professor?"

"I've had more than enough," Forster said abruptly. "I don't mind telling you, I'd hoped Troy and her friend would be able to come with me on the trip."

"The trip to Amalthea?"

"Unusual expertise, between them. Might possibly supplement my own."

The commander regarded him with well-disguised amusement. That anyone might be able to supplement Forster's expertise was an unusual admission for the little professor.

"Where are they?" Forster demanded. "I was so looking forward to seeing them again this evening."

The commander walked to the tall windows that overlooked the dark lawn. He watched the shadowy group on the lawn. "Give them a little time. They'll make it yet."

THE MEDUSA ENCOUNTER
AN AFTERWORD BY
ARTHUR C. CLARKE

One of the advantages of living on the Equator (well, only 800 kilometers from it) is that the Moon and planets pass vertically overhead, allowing one to see them with a clarity never possible in higher latitudes. This has prompted me to acquire a succession of ever-larger telescopes during the past thirty years, beginning with the classic 3 1/2-inch Questar, then an 8-inch, and finally a 14-inch, Celestron. (Sorry about the obsolete units, but we seem stuck with them for small telescopes—even though centimeters make them sound much more impressive.)

The Moon, with its incomparable and ever-changing scenery, is my favorite subject, and I never tire of showing it to unsuspecting visitors. As the 14-inch is fitted with a binocular eyepiece, they feel they are looking through the window of a spaceship, and not peering through the restricted field of a single lens. The difference has to be experienced to be appreciated, and invariably invokes a gasp of amazement.

After the Moon, Saturn and Jupiter compete for second place as celestial attractions. Thanks to its glorious rings, Saturn is breathtaking and unique—

but there's little else to be seen, as the planet itself is virtually featureless.

The considerably larger disc of Jupiter is much more interesting; it usually displays prominent cloud belts lying parallel to the equator, and so many fugitive details that one could spend a lifetime trying to elucidate them. Indeed, men have done just this: for more than a century, Jupiter has been a happy hunting ground for armies of devoted amateur astronomers.*

Yet no view through the telescope can do justice to a planet with more than a hundred times the surface area of our world. To imagine a somewhat farfetched "thought experiment," if one skinned the Earth and pinned its pelt like a trophy on the side of Jupiter, it would look about as large as India on a terrestrial globe. *That* subcontinent is no small piece of real estate; yet Jupiter is to Earth as Earth is to India. . . .

Unfortunately for would-be colonists, even if they were prepared to tolerate the local two-and-a-half gravities, Jupiter has no solid surface—or even a liquid one. It's all weather, at least for the first few thousand kilometers down toward the distant central core. (For details of which, see *2061: Odyssey Three.* . . .)

Earth-based observers had long suspected this, as they made careful drawings of the ever-changing Jovian cloudscape. There was only one semi-permanent feature on the face of the planet, the famous Great Red Spot, and even this sometimes vanished completely. Jupiter was a world without

---

*I feel a particular sympathy for one of them, the British engineer P.B. Molesworth (1867–1908). Some years ago, I visited the relics of his observatory at Trincomalee, on the east coast of Sri Lanka. Despite his early death, Molesworth's spare-time astronomical work was so outstanding that his name has now been given to a splendid crater on Mars, 175 kilometers across.

geography—a planet for meteorologists, but not for cartographers.

As I have recounted in *Astounding Days: A Science-fictional Autobiography*, my own fascination with Jupiter began with the very first science-fiction magazine I ever saw—the November 1928 edition of Hugo Gernsback's *Amazing Stories*, which had been launched two years earlier. It featured a superb cover by Frank R. Paul, which one could plausibly cite as proof of the existence of precognition.

Half a dozen earthmen are stepping forth onto one of the Jovian satellites, emerging from a silo-shaped spaceship that looks uncomfortably small for such a long voyage. The orange-tinted globe of the giant planet dominates the sky, with two of the inner moons in transit. I am afraid that Paul has cheated shamelessly, because Jupiter is fully illuminated—though the sun is almost *behind* it!

I'm not in a position to criticize, as it's taken me more than fifty years to spot this—probably deliberate—error. If my memory is correct, the cover illustrates a story by Gawain Edwards, real name G. Edward Pendray. Ed Pendray was one of the pioneers of American rocketry and published *The Coming Age of Rocket Power* in 1947. Perhaps Pendray's most valuable work was in helping Mrs. Goddard edit the massive three volumes of her husband's notebooks: he lived to see the Voyager closeups of the Jovian system, and I wonder if he recalled Paul's illustration.

What is so astonishing—I'm sorry, amazing—about this 1928 painting is that it shows, with great accuracy, details which at the time were unknown to earth-based observers. Not until 1979, when the Voyager spaceprobes flew past Jupiter and its moons, was it possible to observe the intricate loops and curlicues created by the Jovian tradewinds. Yet half a century earlier, Paul had depicted them with uncanny precision.

Many years later, I was privileged to work with the doyen of space artists, Chesley Bonestell, on the book *Beyond Jupiter* (Little, Brown, 1972). This was a preview of the proposed Grand Tour of the outer solar system, which it was hoped might take advantage of a once-in-179-year configuration of *all* the planets between Jupiter and Pluto. As it turned out, the considerably more modest Voyager missions achieved virtually all the Grand Tour's objectives, at least out to Neptune. Looking at Chesley's illustrations with the 20:20 clarity of hindsight, I am surprised to see that Frank Paul, though technically the poorer artist, did a far better job of visualizing Jupiter as it *really* is.

Since Jupiter is so far from the sun—five times the distance of the Earth—the temperature might be expected to be a hundred or so degrees below the worst that the Antarctic winter can provide. That is true of the upper cloud layers, but for a long time astronomers have known that the planet radiates several times as much heat as it receives from the Sun. Though it is not big enough to sustain thermonuclear fusion (Jupiter has been called ''a star that failed''), it undoubtedly possesses some internal sources of heat. As a consequence, at some depth beneath the clouds, the temperature is that of a comfortable day on Earth. The pressure is another matter; but as the depths of our own oceans have proved, life can flourish even at tons to the square centimeter.

In the book and TV series *Cosmos*, Carl Sagan speculated about possible life forms that might exist in the purely gaseous (mostly hydrogen and methane) environment of the Jovian atmosphere. My ''Medusae'' owe a good deal to Carl, but I have no qualms about stealing from him, as I introduced him to my agent Scott Meredith a quarter of a century ago, with results profitable to both. . . .

For more about the Jovian aerial fauna (or flora), I refer you to *2010: Odyssey Two* and *2061: Odyssey*

Three. Whether life exists on the greatest of the planets might already have been decided by the *Galileo* spaceprobe—NASA's most ambitious project—if the *Challenger* disaster had not postponed it for almost a decade. Meanwhile, take a good look at some of the *Voyager* images. See those curious white ovals, enclosed by thin membranes? Don't they remind you of amoebae under the microscope? The fact that they are some tens of thousands of kilometers long is no problem: after all, size is relative.

Now a final bibliographic note. "A Meeting with Medusa" is one of the very few stories I ever wrote for a specific objective. (Usually I write because I can't help it, but I am slowly getting this annoying habit under control.) "Medusa" was produced because I needed enough wordage to round out my final collection of short stories *(The Wind from the Sun*, 1972). I am pleased to record that it won the Nebula Award from the Science Fiction Writers of America for the best *novella* of the year—as well as a special bonus from *Playboy* in the same category.

I happened to mention my association with this estimable magazine, which has printed so many of my more serious technical writings, when I registered a mild complaint in New Delhi not long ago. In his witty response after I had delivered the Nehru Memorial Address on 13 November 1986, Prime Minister Rajiv Gandhi concluded with these words: "Finally, let me assure Dr. Clarke that if *Playboy* is banned in this country, it is not because of anything *he* may have written in it."

Certainly there's nothing in the original "A Meeting with Medusa" to bring a blush to the most modest cheek.

I'm waiting to see what Paul Preuss can do to rectify this situation.

Arthur C. Clarke
Colombo, 7 November 1988

BIO OF A SPACE TYRANT
Piers Anthony

"Brilliant...a thoroughly original thinker and storyteller with a unique ability to posit really *alien* alien life, humanize it, and make it come out alive on the page." *The Los Angeles Times*

A COLOSSAL NEW FIVE VOLUME SPACE THRILLER—
BIO OF A SPACE TYRANT
The Epic Adventures and Galactic Conquests of Hope Hubris

VOLUME I: REFUGEE   84194-0/$3.50 US/$4.50 Can
Hubris and his family embark upon an ill-fated voyage through space, searching for sanctuary, after pirates blast them from their home on Callisto.

VOLUME II: MERCENARY   87221-8/$3.50 US/$4.50 Can
Hubris joins the Navy of Jupiter and commands a squadron loyal to the death and sworn to war against the pirate warlords of the Jupiter Ecliptic.

VOLUME III: POLITICIAN   89685-0/$3.50 US/$4.50 Can
Fueled by his own fury, Hubris rose to triumph obliterating his enemies and blazing a path of glory across the face of Jupiter. Military legend...people's champion...promising political candidate...he now awoke to find himself the prisoner of a nightmare that knew no past.

THE BEST-SELLING EPIC CONTINUES—
VOLUME IV: EXECUTIVE
89834-9/$3.50 US/$4.50 Can
Destined to become the most hated and feared man of an era, Hope would assume an alternate identify to fulfill his dreams ...and plunge headlong into madness.

VOLUME V: STATESMAN
89835-7/$3.50 US/$4.95 Can
the climactic conclusion of Hubris' epic adventures:

AVON Paperbacks

NEW BESTSELLERS
IN THE *MAGIC OF XANTH* SERIES!

PIERS ANTHONY

VALE OF THE VOLE

75287-5/$4.50 US/$5.50 Can

HEAVEN CENT

75288-3/$4.50 US/$5.50 Can

MAN FROM MUNDANIA

75289-1/$4.50 US/$5.50 Can